WHO MOURNS ELEKTRA?

MAGNOLIA BLUFF CRIME CHRONICLES
BOOK 21

C W HAWES

CWH BOOKS, KATY, TEXAS

JOIN THE TEAM!

Become a VIP Reader.

As a VIP Reader, each month you'll get curated content, news about Magnolia Bluff, and a variety of good things to keep you up to date on the many worlds of CW Hawes.

And there are lots of worlds to catch up on: Magnolia Bluff, the Justinia Wright mysteries, Pierce Mostyn and his team of monster hunters, Bill Arthur and the post-apocalyptic world of Rocheport, and so much more.

Just click, tap, or scan the QR code to begin the adventure!

Get The Ebook

In Memoriam Caleb Pirtle III
Mentor, Friend, Brother

1

WEDNESDAY, 7 FEBRUARY 6:58 AM

Harry erased the chalkboard.

"Good morning, Mr. Thurgood. Sorry I'm late."

"Not a problem, Estrelita. All is quiet, as you can see. No one's waiting to get in."

"One of these days, Mr. Thurgood."

"Hopefully."

"I was at the church. I lit a candle and said a prayer for Lila."

"That's fine. That was important."

"Thank you. I still can't believe it."

"Another shocker, that's for sure. Do you need some time off?"

"No. I'm all right. Now, I'd best make sure these tables are okay."

Harry smiled at that. She was a good worker. Never complained and showed up rain or shine.

He turned his attention back to the chalkboard and the daily specials, but found his mind drifting back to a week ago.

That was when Judge Rutherford B. Jones found the bodies of sixteen-year-old Lila Santiago and her eighteen-year-old boyfriend, DeWayne Sanford, star lineman for the Magnolia

Bluff High School football team, brutally murdered in the parking lot of his Pickle Dilly Bait and Tackle Shop.

While the judge was saddened at the deaths of the two teenagers, he was more saddened by the negative publicity, and that half of his small parking lot had been cordoned off with yellow crime scene tape.

At least that was what Harry had heard from Tommy Jager, chief of the Magnolia Bluff Police Department.

The rumor mill speculated the kids had to have been murdered by a strange monster that had risen out of the depths of Burnet Reservoir. And what the police were calling a knife attack was just a cover up for the monster's eight-inch long teeth. After all, what kid standing six-four and weighing two hundred and ten pounds could get taken out in a knife attack?

Graham Huston, owner and editor of the *Magnolia Bluff Chronicle*, had played up the monster angle. Mostly, Harry suspected, because it sold newspapers.

He shrugged his shoulders and began writing on the chalkboard.

Mac and Cheese.
Broccoli Cheddar Soup in a homemade bread bowl.
Chicken Noodle Soup.
Strawberry Shortcake.
Homemade Chocolate Strawberry frozen custard.
Coffee of the Day: Nicaragua Nuevo Segovia, medium roast.

The chalkboard complete, Harry unlocked the front door and set the bifold board outside on the sidewalk next to the door.

The Really Good Wood-Fired Coffee Shop was now open for business.

He noticed Fergus, the mostly reformed town drunk, coming across the Green, and held the door open for him.

"Mornin' Fergus."

"Mornin' Mr. Thurgood. Make sure Miguel locks up the

knives. Make sure he does. Because they're dancin' through the streets. Dance of the Butcher Knives. And it ain't by Bach."

Now what's going on? Harry asked himself. *Is he still talking about last week's murder?*

He decided he didn't want to deal with the old vet this morning and let the guy's comment drop.

"Have a seat over there, Fergus. Are fried eggs, bacon, toast, and hash browns okay?"

"Yes, sir, Mr. Thurgood. Coffee, too, if you don't mind. It's always really good." He chuckled at the joke.

"You got it, my good man."

Harry gave the order to Miguel, who was cracking eggs into paper cups for the morning breakfasts. Estrelita waved Harry off as she poured coffee into a mug and took it to the old vet.

The chime over the door rang. Harry turned and saw the love of his life and his fiancé, the Reverend Ember Cole coming into the shop.

With a big smile on her face, she said, "Good Morning, Mr. Thurgood."

"And a hearty good morning to you, Reverend Cole."

She was wearing a heavy black wool cardigan that reached down to her ankles. And covering much of her Dutch Bob was a black Saturno.

"A bit nippy out there this morning," Harry said.

"Yes, it is. A brisk walk helps to generate some heat, though."

She removed her sweater and hat and put them on one of the counter stools.

"Man, Rev, you're looking mighty attractive."

"You like it?"

Ember twirled around to show off her new dress. It was a black A-line with long sleeves and an ankle-length hemline. The dress had a clerical collar with tabs. Black stockings, black Mary Janes, and a gold pectoral cross completed the outfit.

Fergus called out, "Mighty nice, Reverend. Maybe a red scarf to add some color."

Ember laughed. "I'll keep that in mind."

"What's with the new look?" Harry asked.

"I just wanted to be more feminine."

"Well, you succeeded. And quite admirably, I might add."

"I want to be pretty. For you."

"You're more than that. You're beautiful."

"Thank you. That means the world to me."

A siren shattered the morning stillness and flashing lights added to the ugliness.

"Oh, goodness," Ember said. "I hope it's not another murder."

From the corner came Fergus's voice. "The knives. They're dancin' again."

2

WEDNESDAY, 7 FEBRUARY 7:51 AM

REECE SOVERN SHOOK HIS HEAD. THE GREEN PERFECTO ROLLED FROM the right corner of his mouth to the left.

The storm door was closed, but the main door was open. That's what got Mabel Schmidt's attention, the neighbor who lived across the street.

Officer Helen Beauregard was with the old woman, trying to keep her calm and ask questions.

The cameraman was taking pictures of the corpse.

Officer Johnston was putting up crime scene tape.

Reece was waiting for Wylie Garrison, the Justice of the Peace and Coroner, to show up and confirm what everybody already knew: that eighty-seven-year-old Vonnie Vebelsteadt had died from loss of blood. The loss due to the large gash in her throat.

Being the police investigator, Reece didn't need Wylie to tell him the old woman had bled out on her entryway floor.

"It's incredible the amount of blood in the human body," Police Chief Tommy Jager said.

Sheriff Buck Blanton, a mirthless grin on his face, who'd stopped by to see things firsthand rather than rely on the grapevine, said, "Yep. An *awful* lot of it."

"What the heck is keeping Wylie?" Tommy asked, of no one in particular.

"You do realize what time it is, don't you?" Buck replied.

"Here he is," Reece said.

The ancient black Buick Roadmaster pulled to the curb and stopped.

Wylie got out, attempted in vain to straighten his wire-frame glasses on his stub nose, crossed the lawn to the front door, ducking under the newly strung crime scene tape.

"When are you getting a new car, Wylie?" Buck asked. "Aren't we paying you enough?"

"He's just cheap," Tommy said.

"It's a good car," Wylie countered. "They don't make them like that anymore."

"She's in the entryway," Reece said.

Wylie took a look, muttered, "Jesus Christ," under his breath, kneeled down, felt her wrist for a pulse, and said, "She's dead."

"Thanks, Wylie," Reece said.

The JP shook his head. "Good thing I didn't eat breakfast. God. Good day, gentlemen."

He walked back down to the Roadmaster, got in, and drove off.

"Now it's official," Tommy said.

Reece asked the photographer if he was done, the man said he was, and Reece signaled for the ambulance crew to take the body.

"I'm guessing the ME will confirm this is the work of the same perp," Tommy said. "You agree, Reece?"

"Sure looks the same to me. Only Mrs. Vebelsteadt didn't fight back. Must've been surprised, like DeWayne."

"Still beats the heck out of me," Buck said, "how a six-four, two hundred and ten pound kid could get surprised like that."

"Must've known the perp," Reece replied.

"Must have," Buck agreed.

"Well, that probably rules out most everyone in Texas," Tommy said.

"And most everyone in the county," Buck added.

Reece simply nodded, pushed his glassed to the top of his nose, and rolled the unlit stogie to the other corner of his mouth.

He watched the ambulance crew take away Magnolia Bluff's latest murder victim for the trip to Austin and the autopsy by the Medical Examiner.

Thinking out loud, he said, "Who would know an eighteen-year-old senior in high school, a sixteen-year-old sophomore, and an eighty-seven-year-old woman? Something's just not adding up."

With a completely straight face, Tommy said, "Probably Thurgood."

And then Tommy and Buck threw their heads back and roared their laughter.

3

WEDNESDAY, 7 FEBRUARY 8:59 AM

"NOT FUNNY," REECE SAID. "YOU KNOW AS WELL AS I DO THAT there's something not right about Thurgood. He has too much money and no visible means of support, aside from the coffee shop that doesn't make any money. If you think he's a square shooter, then I hear catfish singin' out in the reservoir."

"I'm heading over to the Really Good right now," Tommy said. "Want me to check if he's missing any knives?"

The police chief and sheriff guffawed.

Buck said, "I think I'll join you. Probably has lots of knives."

The two lawmen chortled all the way to their cars.

Reece watched them drive off and then pitched his soggy stogie halfway across the street.

Some days he wanted to buy a camper and take off with his wife, Hetta, and his dog, Pickett, for parts unknown. Maybe get lost along the way.

If it took me twenty years to get unlost, I should be able to retire and not bother to come back at all.

He took a long green grand panetella out of his pocket, removed the cellophane, and stuck the crinkly wrapper back into his pocket, while the cigar went into his mouth.

The photographer was gone. Officer Beauregard had walked

Mrs. Schmidt back across the street. Officer Johnston was standing around and Reece told him to leave.

Now he was alone with the crime scene. He liked that. No chatter. He could let his eyes roam and his nose take in the smells.

He walked around to the back door. It was unlocked, and he was glad for that. He didn't want to wade through all the sticky blood in the entryway.

Probably have to clean that up. It can wait, though. Not going anywhere.

He entered the house and found himself in the utility room.

His eyes swept the walls, ceiling, and floor. "Nothing looks out of place here," he murmured. Nothing smelled out of place either. Just a faint odor of rainwater scented laundry detergent. Which was a pleasant relief from the coppery tang hanging in the air from Vonnie's blood.

Reece took his time. Walking into each room of the house. Seeing what there was to see. Smelling the smells of an old woman's home. Opening drawers and closets.

This is just too bizarre. Nothing was stolen off the kids. It appears nothing's been taken here. Money. Her medicine. Even a few antiques. All here.

"So why did somebody decide to kill you?" he said out loud.

Jager was right. He probably couldn't pin this new round of murders on Harry Thurgood. As much as he'd like to.

He left the house by the back door. Left the front door open and the storm door closed. Made a mental note to get someone out here to clean up the entryway.

Reece walked down to his car, surveyed the house, and then walked up to the neighbor's on the left and rang the doorbell.

The door opened, and Reece said, "Hi, Harold. Betty Jean." He hooked his thumb in the direction of the deceased neighbor's place. "You happen to see or hear anything out of the ordinary? Or even ordinary, for that matter?"

"Just awful," Betty Jean said.

"That it is," Reece agreed.

"No, nothing, Reece. First thing we knew something wasn't right was when we heard Mrs. Schmidt screaming."

"Well, if anything comes to mind, no matter how trivial you think it is, give me a ring."

"Will do," Harold said.

They said their goodbyes, and Reece walked over to the house on the other side. Unfortunately, old Ardis Pennyfeather was no more helpful than Harold and Betty Jean Warkowicz.

Reece thanked her, nevertheless, and walked to his car.

Given the state of the body, the freshness of the blood, and the time of the phone call, his guess was Vonnie had been dead for at most an hour when Mrs. Schmidt discovered the body.

That would put the time of death sometime around six-thirty, or seven.

He got in his car. *At that time of day, there are enough people out and about, that one more person, even though he happened to be on a mission of death, wouldn't stick out.*

He started the car, and as he pulled away from the curb, he couldn't help but wonder who would be next.

4

POLICE CHIEF TOMMY JAGER AND SHERIFF BUCK BLANTON WALKED through the door of the Really Good.

"You're late," Graham Huston said.

"Murder tends to alter one's schedule," Jager shot back.

"Why don't you boys pull up a chair and tell us all about it," Caroline McCluskey, the town librarian, said.

Jager and Blanton sat and helped themselves to coffee and turnovers.

"Not much to tell," Jager said around a mouthful of turnover. "Vonnie Vebelsteadt had her throat slashed and died. Body was discovered by Mabel Schmidt, the neighbor across the street."

Billy Bob Baskin, pastor of New Hope Presbyterian Church, said, "Two last week. Another this week."

Blanton, a grin in place as usual, said, "Yep. At this rate, no one will be left in town in one hundred and twenty-eight years."

Harry chuckled. "Not a problem any of us need worry about."

"You do," the sheriff said.

"Me?"

Jager nodded in agreement with Blanton. "Sovern thinks you just might be involved."

"You're kidding," Harry said.

Jager shook his head. "Nope. Mind if I take a look at your knives?"

"That's it," Harry said. "I'm calling Stanton."

"Gotcha, Thurgood," Jager said, and he and Blanton started laughing.

"Gallows humor," Ember said. "This isn't something we should be making light of."

"You're right, of course," Billy Bob said.

"I just don't know what's happening to our town," Magnolia Nadine Roane, Magnolia Bluff's community organizer, added.

Harry shook his head. "You guys." He put his phone away and asked, "What do two high school kids have in common with today's victim?"

"Have no idea," Jager said. "Vonnie was eighty-seven. No sign of a struggle either, so it's possible she knew her killer."

"But don't most folks in town know each other?" Billy Bob asked.

"Probably," Caroline said. "Most everyone is related in some way, or the family has been here forever. So most people probably do know each other."

"But not all," Ember added. "There are those of us who are transplants. I certainly don't know everyone."

"I don't either," Caroline said. "Although working in the library has helped. I've gotten acquainted with all the literate people in town."

"Hopefully, Reece will get to the bottom of this soon," Harry said.

"Probably arrest you," Jager said, "and declare the case closed."

"Until the next body shows up," Harry said.

Jager chuckled. "Well, there is that."

"Anything you can add, Tommy?" Huston asked.

"Check with Reece. I don't have any details."

With a smirk on his lips, Huston said, "Very well. But does he have any?"

Laughter rippled along the tables.

Sheriff Blanton drained his coffee cup, stood, and said, "Have a good day, y'all. Duty calls."

"I need to get going, too," Jager said. He stood, and the lawmen left.

"Any news, Harry?" Huston asked.

"Nothing."

"Then I better go find some."

The newspaperman stood, and so did Reverend Baskin, Caroline, and Magnolia Nadine. They said goodbye to Harry and Ember and left.

Harry poured himself another cup of coffee and held the pot out to Ember, but she was staring off into space.

"What's on your mind, my little chickadee?"

"Oh, sorry. It's just that I can't help but think the outreach and witness ministries of the church might in some way reduce the number of murders. I mean, if people redirected their focus to God, loving him, and treating neighbors and families with kindness and love, then they wouldn't want to hurt others."

"Perhaps. Trying certainly can't hurt."

"Cally's against outreach and witnessing."

"Truly? Isn't that what the church is all about?"

"She says everyone in Magnolia Bluff is 'churched.' Which means there is no one to evangelize. At least in her opinion. And because people help each other in Magnolia Bluff, we don't need an outreach program to promote social justice, support advocacy for minorities and women, or to promote ecumenism. She wants to focus on nurturing ministries. And I'm all for that. I think the other has been neglected and we need to up our game there."

"I guess I'm lost. It's all church work, isn't it?"

"It is. Actually, though, Cally thinks this is a battle she can win and in doing so get a majority of the church to back her to get me reassigned this June."

"Oh, I get it. This is actually about Mary Lou and Gunter Fight coming back to the church."

"Yes. I heard from one of our pastors in Sabinal that the bishop was asking questions."

"That doesn't sound good."

"Yes and no. Ultimately, the bishop has the final word on who moves and who stays. Until now, the church has voted each year for me to stay and I've voted to stay. The Conference Cabinet, composed of the bishop and district superintendents, has gone along with the church and me."

"But if the bishop is asking questions…"

"And feels there is too much turmoil in the church…"

"You get moved."

"Exactly."

"That's the pits. Although you could stay here and help me run the shop."

"That's not gonna happen, Mister. I love being a minister. It's my calling."

"You could have a spot in that corner and we could advertise a daily Your Time with Jesus and Coffee."

Ember rolled her eyes. "You make a joke out of everything."

"Who's joking? I think it's a great idea."

Ember stood, and Harry joined her. "I have work to do, Mister. Church council meeting tonight. I have to get my ducks in a row or we'll be moving. Unless you don't want to live with me."

"Like heck I don't. I can't wait."

Ember stood on tiptoes, kissed Harry's cheek, and said, "I do have to run."

"Very well. See you later?"

"I'll text when tonight's meeting is over."

"Ciao."

Harry watched Ember leave. *I wonder if there's something I can do to short circuit Cally Taylor?*

5

WEDNESDAY, 7 FEBRUARY 9:31 AM

Javier Herran, known as "J" or "J-Man", to friend and foe alike, sat across from the sixty-something woman. He drank the tea she'd offered to be polite.

He'd observed her in their previous meetings. *She'd make a good spy,* he thought. *Those eyes are frigid and give nothing away.*

She set the report down on the coffee table, picked up her cup and saucer, drank tea, and set it back down.

The eyes took him in.

She looks like a kindly grandmother, but she is an anaconda and a cobra all in one package.

"You're awfully fair for a Mexican," she said.

"Does that matter?"

She shrugged. "Just an observation."

One you've made before, Mrs. Fight. "My family can trace our lineage back to the first Spanish landowners."

She smiled. "Culture and breeding. It always comes through."

He shrugged. "I am fortunate."

She picked up her cup and saucer, sipped tea, and set it back down. "This report tells me nothing I don't already know. Perhaps I missed something?"

"Mr. Harry Thurgood is all he seems to be. At least according to official records. I do suspect, however, that his real name, his birth name, is not Harry Thurgood. He seems to have a source of income that is not consistent with what is reported to the IRS."

"He's living beyond his means, in other words."

"So it seems. But there is no evidence of tax fraud and the FBI has found no evidence of illegal activities. He is not known to Interpol."

"In other words, he's untouchable."

"At this point, yes. I've exhausted all legal channels of inquiry."

She smiled. "I like how you put that. Tell me again your background."

"Lieutenant Commander in the Navy. Navy Seal. Office of Naval Intelligence. I can't disclose the nature of my missions with the ONI. I've been with Armes International for the past eight years."

Mrs. Fight smiled and Javier Herran felt an arctic chill wash over him. He smiled back, barely suppressing a shiver. *Bad vibes. Lots of bad vibes with this one.*

"I think we'll set aside Mr. Thurgood for now. I may be able to achieve what I want by means of a different approach. I'd like for you to focus on the Reverend Ember Cole."

"Very well. I can do that."

"I need you to find something that will persuade the bishop to either move her or defrock her. Either one will accomplish what I want, which is to get both of them out of Magnolia Bluff. Personally, I think they need to suffer for what they've done to me. However, one doesn't always get everything one wants. Does one, Mr. Herran?"

"No, ma'am. The rain falls on both the just and the unjust, even though most would not have it do so."

"Indeed."

"The change of subject will require a new contract."

"Very well. Send it to me. I want you to start investigating Miss Cole as soon as possible."

6

WEDNESDAY, 7 FEBRUARY 10:08 AM

MARY LOU FIGHT SET THE TEACUP ON THE SAUCER. "DID YOU follow what Mr. Herron had to say?"

Oralene Reston smiled. "Yes, I did. The remote camera worked well. I saw and heard everything. And I agree with you that the Reverend Cole is the weak link."

This young woman is everything Gunter said she was. I'm glad I rescued her from working in the bank. She will make the most marvelous apprentice.

"Good. I'm glad you agree. I shouldn't have let myself get sidetracked with that lounge lizard."

"It was worth a try."

"I suppose. In any event, we're back to where we are supposed to be. On a different note, Mrs. Dutcher said you are a fast learner. She's never seen anyone respond so quickly to her elocution lessons."

Oralene smiled. "I want to speak and act properly. That is the path to success."

"It is what separates us from the masses. Mrs. Strathmore told me the same: you are a fast learner and you will complete your finishing lessons ahead of schedule."

"I want to…" Oralene paused for a moment.

"Go ahead, my dear. You can speak openly with me."

"I want to be great, ma'am. I want to be somebody people will look up to, and... and fear."

Mary Lou smiled. "You will, my dear. You will. And to that end, I have a proposal for you. If you are willing. I'd like to adopt you as my daughter. If you agree, you may start living here immediately. And you may address me as 'Mother'. What do you say?"

Mary Lou watched Oralene's eyes grow large and her mouth drop open. Then the young woman's arms were around her.

"Oh, yes! Yes. I want to be your daughter. Thank you. Thank you."

"Good. Now please disentangle yourself and sit."

Oralene retreated to her chair.

"I will have my lawyer draw up the papers. You may move in immediately. Eliška will help you."

"Thank you... Thank you, Mother. This is the best thing that has ever happened to me."

Mary Lou smiled. "And me as well, my dear. Me, as well."

———

Oralene burst through the door, yelling, "Mama, Mama!"

Jearlene Reston came out of the kitchen. "What's all the ruckus, Oralene?"

"Oh, Mama, Mrs. Fight wants to adopt me. She wants me for her daughter."

"Her husband owns the bank? She's the one who's been giving you those fancy lessons?"

"Yes. She's paying the tutors to give me lessons so I can be a proper young woman. She wants me, me, Mama, to be her daughter. I'm going to be rich and I'll be able to take care of you."

"But I'm your mama. I brought you into the world."

"I know that, Mama." Oralene hugged her mother. "And

you'll always be my mama. But don't you see? I'm going to be rich. I'm going to be somebody. I'm going to be a very important person. Don't you want that for me?"

"Yes, of course I do. It's just that she's taking you away from me."

"No, she's not, Mama. She's making me her heir. And she's making me to be someone important. She's giving me the means to take care of you."

"I want to be happy for you, but…"

"She's giving me the life I always wanted and never thought I would ever have. I don't want to be poor. And now I won't be. And neither will you, or the little ones. This is a good thing, Mama. You wait and see."

7

WEDNESDAY, 7 FEBRUARY 1:31 PM

HARRY THURGOOD LEFT HIS SHOP IN THE CAPABLE HANDS OF HIS floor manager, Jack Bonhoffer, and walked across East Main Street, the Green, and West Main to the *Chronicle* office.

At her desk was Monika Crow. Next to Graham Huston, Monika was probably the most important person on the *Chronicle* staff. She was the gossip column editor of "Monika Hears," and the advertising sales manager for the paper. Nothing keeps a paper running like gossip and money.

Harry looked at the woman sitting behind the desk. Young, mid-twenties, not married, living at home. A hometown gal who went to the Big City and decided there was no place like home.

Surprised she's not taken, Harry thought. *Any guy would be pleased to be seen with her on his arm.*

"Can I help you, Harry? Want to buy more ad space?"

"If I buy any more, I'll have to sell the building to pay for it."

"We wouldn't want that."

Harry smiled. "Are those glasses new?"

She struck a pose. "Do you like them?"

"I do. They're completely you."

"Thanks. So, if you aren't here to give us money, I suppose you want information."

"I do."

"How may I help?"

"Since you keep tabs on the social life of our town—"

"Nice pun."

"You like that?"

She nodded. "Go on."

"Since you have your finger on the pulse of what's going on and who's who, what can you tell me about Cally Taylor?"

"Let's see…" Her finger tapped her lip. "Her name's actually Caldwell Taylor, Caldwell being her mother's maiden name. She's a Sinclair. Old family. Married to Owen Hill Taylor. Another old family. Both are in their fifties. She younger, he older. They have two children. Their son, Buchanan, lives in Fort Worth. I think he's in some sort of finance. Their daughter, Sinclair Ann, who goes by Clair-Ann, lives at home. She's twenty-six and teaches elementary school. I think, though, she's now on the substitute list. Takes care of her father, who's ill."

"And Cally?"

"As you know, she's the lay leader in Ember's church. And if anyone was ever married to her job — it's Cally. And it's a volunteer position."

"And the juicy stuff?"

A sly smile appeared on her face. "Why Mr. Thurgood, you should've told me all you wanted was the gossip."

They both laughed.

"Well, let's see…"

Harry noticed her eyes drifted to some spot over the door behind him.

After a moment, she said, "Owen is ill, as I said. Congestive heart failure, I believe. Needs a lot of care. The problem is, Cally has no desire to be his nurse. And according to Tipper Duvall, who is on the board at Ember's church, Cally's openly questioned 'why the good Lord keeps him around'."

"A match made in heaven, I see."

"And people wonder why I'm single. Oh, sorry, I—"

"No offense where none is taken."

Monika smiled and continued. "Cally and Clair-Ann have had some major fights. In public. Even to the point of slapping each other."

"Interesting. Any idea why she, Cally, that is, wants to get rid of Ember?"

"That's a good question. Ember's new. She's fairly young. You've been to the church, right?"

Harry nodded.

"All old people there. And they think old. When it comes to church, they're living in the nineteen fifties. Ember wants to move them into the twenty-first century. But a lot of them don't want to make the trip."

"Thanks for your insights, Monika."

"You're welcome. Sure you don't need more ad space?"

"I don't. But I can tell you do."

"I do like my paycheck."

"If I saw some positive return for my investment, I might be persuaded."

"Can't help you with that. This town is tough on new people."

"I think all small towns are tough on the newbies."

"Probably."

"Have a good day."

"Bye, Harry."

Standing on the sidewalk outside the newspaper office, Harry took his pipe out of his jacket pocket, lit the tobacco, and puffed for a while. His eyes moved up and down West Main, then the Green, and finally East Main. The traffic was normal for this time of day. People were out on the sidewalks. Shopping, or just enjoying the sunshine.

Another gorgeous day in Magnolia Bluff. Yet the surface picture was a mirage. Behind the illusion, there was a whole lot of nastiness going on.

Harry wondered, *How long will it take before it touches Ember*

and me?
   Again.

8

WEDNESDAY, 7 FEBRUARY 7:01 PM

EMBER LOOKED AT THE MEMBERS OF THE CHURCH COUNCIL SEATED around the table. Of the twelve, only three were under forty. One of those being herself.

Could all this turmoil simply be a generational issue? She asked herself. *Possibly. If so, how do I handle it better than I have been?*

Claiborne Allen, the chairperson, called the meeting to order. "We have a full house. Good to see all of you here. The Lord's work is serious business. Glad y'all made time for it."

"Of course we made time for it," Cally Taylor said. "The church is the most important thing in our lives. And if it isn't, it should be."

"Jane, would you mind reading the minutes from our last meeting?" Claiborne asked.

Jane Jackson, the young adult representative, stood and read the minutes, then sat down.

"Is everyone okay with the minutes?" Claiborne asked. He looked around the table and finally said, "Let it be noted the minutes were excepted as read."

He cleared his throat. "The first item on our agenda is discussion of our church nurture, outreach, and witness ministries. Is there anything we need to talk about?"

Cally stood. "Yes. Just look around this table. Just take a look at our worship services. We are an aged and aging congregation. Yet, the resources of our church are continually being siphoned off to support the outreach and witness programs.

"Ever since Ms. Cole was sent to us, the nurture of this congregation has taken a backseat to all other ministries in the church."

Cally turned and focused on Ember. "Do you even visit the shut-ins, and those who can't make it to worship?"

Before Ember could speak, Marveen Smalls, who was the lay member to the annual conference, said, "Oh, for heaven's sake, Cally. You know Reverend Cole is constantly out in the community. You're just causing trouble."

Claiborne held up his hand. "Let me remind everyone: be kind. No personal attacks. Do you have more to say, Cally?"

"I do. Many of us feel the Reverend Cole would be better suited in a different congregation."

Tipper Duvall, chairperson of the pastor-parish relations committee interrupted. "And there was the unfortunate arrest of Reverend Cole last year."

Euel Pinckney, the church treasurer, said, "Donations have been down ever since."

Cally took back the floor. "Yes. Our reputation in the community was blackened. And now the concern is that Ms. Cole doesn't spend enough time doing her job."

"What do you mean?" Ruth Ann Covington, the representative from the Methodist Youth, asked.

Cally smiled. "She's in love. Engaged. And seems to have more time for that man in the coffee shop than she does for us."

"I keep track of my hours," Ember said. "Do you want me to produce them?"

"It doesn't matter, Ms. Cole," Cally shot back. "What matters is the perception. And the perception is that you are shirking your duty to the church."

Ember was about to respond, when Claiborne said, "What's your point in all of this, Cally?"

"My point is precisely this: given our needs as a congregation, given the fact that we live in a churched community, given the fact that the people of Magnolia Bluff support each other, the ministry Reverend Cole wishes to conduct doesn't fit here. *She* doesn't fit. I move that the church council recommend to the Personnel Team and the Conference Cabinet that Saint Luke's United Methodist Church be sent a new pastor."

Tipper Duvall said, "I second the motion."

"This is not how we are supposed to do business," Claiborne said. "We are supposed to reach a consensus."

Ember watched his eyes move around the table before they finally settled on her, sitting directly opposite him at the other end of the table.

"What do you have to say about all of this, Reverend Cole?"

"I love this church and I love Magnolia Bluff. I believe our Lord sent me here. Contrary to what Ms. Taylor alleges, I have not shirked my duty to you, this church, and most of all to our God. As I said, I keep a log of my activities. If you wish, I'll produce it. You will find that I am a good shepherd.

"However, I do not wish to be the cause of dissension. Because dissension is the tool of the devil. It is how he destroys churches. And I do not wish this church to be ripped apart by our advisory.

"Unfortunately, I think the damage is done. Division is here and the wounds, whether I stay or whether I go, will not heal easily.

"If you must vote, then vote. My intention, until I hear otherwise, is to shepherd this flock of sheep."

There was a slight smile on Claiborne's lips. "Does anyone else want to say anything?"

"The United Methodist Men have had no problems with our pastor," Blake Hillwood said. "She's always been there to help us carry out our ministry."

Ruth Ann said, "And I can say the same for the UM Youth. Reverend Cole really cares."

"But Euel is right," Waymon Riggins, chairperson of the finance committee, said. "Revenues are down. Part of that due to the Fights leaving."

Ember watched as everyone fell very quiet at the mention of the Fights. *What kind of hold do they have on everyone? It's like they own the town.*

After what seemed as though an eternity had passed, Claiborne said, "Since no one else has anything to say, let's proceed to the vote. I will call the roll. I think what we are about to do is of sufficient importance that the church needs to know where we stand. Jane will you read out the motion?"

Jane Jackson stood and read the motion.

"I will call names and Jane will record the vote for the minutes. I'll just go around the table. I'll start with you, Euel. How do you vote?"

"I vote yes."

There's one against me, Ember said to herself.

"Wait a minute," Tipper said. "Aren't you going to leave, Reverend Cole?"

"No. The votes are public record and I also am entitled to a vote."

"Well…" Tipper shook her head and turned to Claiborne.

He said, "Marveen, how do you vote?"

"I vote no. This is the most ridiculous thing we've done yet."

Wilma Greening and Jane Jackson both voted no.

Claiborne looked at Ember. "Pastor?"

"I pass."

Claiborne nodded. "Ruth Ann?"

"No."

Then Maness Sebren, Waymon Riggins, Tipper Duvall, and Cally Taylor all voted yes.

"Looks like we got ourselves a tie. Sorry for you, Cally, but your motion fails. And given the mood, I'm adjourning the meeting. I don't think we had any other business anyway."

Within minutes, the room was empty, save for Ember and Claiborne.

"You probably already know, Ember, the bishop is talking to folks."

"Yes. I've heard."

"Come July, you may be somewhere else and that's... Well, let me just say, you are what we need. And I pray you'll get to stay and this church pulls together behind you."

"Thank you, Claiborne."

"You have a better night."

She smiled. "Good night. Tell your wife I said hi."

"Will do."

He left and Ember sat in the room. Her eyes taking in the empty chairs and all the vibes the occupants had left.

Anger. Sorrow. Relief. Joy. Disappointment.

This isn't over, she thought. Then to the empty room, she said, "I have to face facts: I may be leaving Magnolia Bluff come July whether I want to or not. And when faced with moving, will Harry move with me?"

9

WEDNESDAY, 7 FEBRUARY 9:47 PM

HARRY PICKED UP EMBER AT THE CHURCH. SHE DIDN'T WANT TO GO anywhere, so he drove over to the park by the reservoir. They walked for a while and were now sitting on a bench, looking at the expanse of water.

He didn't press her to talk. Something hadn't gone well and she'd tell him when she was ready.

After a time, she said, "Harry, you know that in the Methodist Church a pastoral appointment is not permanent. All appointments are up for review every year."

"So you've said."

"Are you okay with moving? Because if you're not, we'd better call off the engagement. And, well, you know, not get married."

"I thought I told you I will go where you go."

"Yes, you did. But that was just talk. And now—"

"No, Em, it wasn't just talk."

"It wasn't? You'd leave your coffee shop? Magnolia Bluff? For me?"

"I said I would."

"Seriously? You love me enough to do that?"

"Yes. I take it the meeting didn't go well."

"Cally tried to get the council to support a resolution to have me sent elsewhere, and a new pastor come to Saint Luke's."

"It didn't pass, I take it."

"The vote was a tie. And means I essentially lost. Because all the ones who voted no will talk to the bishop and that will be that."

"What was her argument?"

Ember told him about the meeting.

When she was done, Harry sat for a moment thinking through the arguments and the consequences of the vote.

"How much were the Fights contributing?"

"I don't know. My position is that it's best if I don't know who gives what."

Harry nodded. "I can see that. Who's the treasurer?"

"Euel Pinckney."

"I'll talk to him."

"He might not talk to you."

"If he's the treasurer, he understands one language, and it's green."

"Harry, you're not going to bribe him."

"That's correct. I'm not. I'm going to make up the budget shortfall."

"Harry."

"He talks money. When money's not an issue, Cally may have lost a supporter. And that's what counts in the end."

"I don't like it."

"I don't either. But this is war. And war is ugly."

"Harry, Paul wrote 'If God be for us, who can be against us?' And I believe that he received the truth from Jesus. If God wants me to stay in Magnolia Bluff, then I'll stay. We'll stay, if you want to be with me."

"Emmy, don't say 'if'. I will go with you wherever you are sent."

"Thank you. You are so good to me and for me."

"I love you. That says it all."

She leaned over and kissed his cheek. "Let's leave this in God's hands, okay?"

"What can I say? He's got the whole world in his hands."

Ember shook her head, then smiled. "Yes, He does."

Harry took her hand in his. He looked out across the water of the reservoir. *But, my love, the world knows but one language: power. And money is power. And people like Euel only understand money.*

10

THURSDAY, 8 FEBRUARY 10:27 AM

HARRY RANG THE DOORBELL. THE HOUSE WAS A TWO-STORY SALTBOX design. *I wonder if this was ordered out of the Sears catalog?*

An old woman answered the door. "How may I help you?"

"Are you Mrs. Pinckney?"

"I am."

"I'm looking for your husband, Mrs. Pinckney."

"He's not here right now."

"Do you know when he'll be back? It's very important I speak with him. It's about the church."

"Saint Luke's?"

"Yes."

"I don't recognize you, Mister..."

"Thurgood. Harry Thurgood."

"Oh. You're..."

"I'm Reverend Cole's fiancé. I wish to speak with your husband about the church. It's very important."

"I see. He's at the senior center. Do you know where that is?"

"I do. Thank you."

Harry tipped his hat and walked back to his car. Once behind the wheel, he asked his phone for directions to the senior center.

When he got them, he started the car and drove the four blocks to the building, which looked to be a converted home.

Folk Victorian, if I'm not mistaken, he told himself. *Pyramidal roof. Big windows on either side of the door. And a nice, spacious porch. Very nice.*

He got out of his car and walked up the walk. The door was open, and he entered the building. An old woman sat at a small desk.

"Welcome to the Arnold Greer Senior Center. What can I do for you, young man?"

Harry smiled. "It's nice to be called 'young.' I'm looking for Euel Pinckney. His wife told me he was here."

"The exercise session just finished. He's probably in there." The woman pointed.

"Would you mind pointing him out to me? We've not been introduced."

"Follow me."

Harry followed the woman, who walked faster than most people half her age. She walked right up to a man and said, "Euel, this fellow's looking for you." And then she disappeared back the way she came.

Euel Pinckney may have been a tall man once, but now he was stoop-shouldered. Wisps of white hair dotted the age-spotted dome of his head. His eyes, though, were very bright.

In spite of how he may look, this guy's sharp as a tack, Harry told himself.

"Do I know you? I don't believe I do."

"No, you don't. I'm Harry Thurgood."

Harry held out his hand. Pinckney hesitated, decided it would be bad manners if he didn't shake hands, and grasped Harry's hand.

Good grip for an old guy.

"How may I help you, Mr. Thurgood?"

"Is there someplace we can talk?"

"We can talk here."

"About church finances."

"Oh. Do you have a car?"

"I do."

"Then let's go to the library."

"Sounds good. My car's out front."

They walked out to Harry's car and got in.

"Mighty fancy car. Must cost a pretty penny."

"It isn't a Chevy Trax."

Pinckney chuckled. "I guess not."

They drove to the library in silence. Harry parked, got an attaché from the back, and they walked into the building together.

"Hello, Mrs. McCluskey," Pinckney said. "Do you have a room available?"

"I do." She handed Pinckney a key. "Study room number two."

"Good morning, again, Caroline," Harry said. He noticed a frown on Pinckney's face.

"Don't you boys get rowdy in there."

Harry winked at her and said, "We'll keep it down to a dull roar."

Pinckney sniffed.

"See that you do."

Harry and Pinckney walked to the back of the library. Pinckney unlocked the door, and they entered the room, and Harry closed the door behind them.

"Okay, what's this all about, Mr. Thurgood? Did the Reverend send you?"

Harry sat and indicated Pinckney should, too. The man hesitated for a moment and then sat in the other chair.

"No, she didn't, Mr. Pinckney. In fact, she did her best to persuade me not to see you. Or do anything to help her cause."

"Yet, here you are. Not a good way to start married life."

"A man must protect his woman, don't you agree? Even if she wears the pants in the family."

Pinckney chuckled. "A sense of humor. You might be good for her."

"I hope I am. Let's talk business."

"Let's."

"I assume you're retired?"

"Yes, I am. I was an accountant. Had a very good business here in town. Sold it to some young fellow from Dallas. He sold it a year later to some Yankee company out of Chicago, and the office closed the year after that."

"The town's pretty harsh on outsiders."

"Can be."

"I understand you made the comment that the donations at St. Luke's have been down since the Fights left."

"Yes, I made that comment. No sense denying it, as you probably heard it from the Reverend."

"I did. Well, I'd like to make a donation."

"You're not a member."

"Not a member *yet*. I plan on joining. Soon. Before Em and I are married."

"Good. But as I understand it, your business is losing money."

"Let's say the business is having teething issues."

"But you aren't."

Harry smiled. "Very perceptive."

"Need to be to make it in business."

"Very true. May I ask how much the church is behind because the Fights left?"

"You may ask, but—"

Harry held up his hand. "Look, Mr. Pinckney. I can easily get that information."

"Knowing the Reverend as you do, I suppose you can. Very well, the church is behind a little over thirty thousand dollars."

"Sizable, I'm sure." Harry slid the attaché across the table to Pinckney. "This is for Saint Luke's. My donation. Go ahead. Open it."

Pinckney opened the attaché. "What is this?"

"I believe it's called money."

"It's one heck of a lot of money." He picked up a banded pack of one hundred dollar bills. Fanned the ends, and put the pack back.

"It's a bundle of one hundred dollar bills," Harry said.

"Ten straps to the bundle... That's one hundred thousand dollars."

"Yes, it is. Care to count it?"

"The bank can do that."

"Yes, they can."

"Now, I wasn't born last night. What's the catch?"

"There is no catch, per se. There is, however, a caveat. I'm with Ember. If Ember goes, I go. If I go..."

Pinckney smiled. "So does the money. You're bribing us to keep her."

"Aren't the Fights bribing you to get rid of her?"

Pinckney opened his mouth and then closed it.

"Of course they are, Mr. Pinckney. They left the church, but are still pulling the strings of their lackeys."

"So, are you aiming to take their place?"

"I am merely protecting the woman I love, who loves the people at Saint Luke's and loves this town. I don't want her to lose the two things she loves most just because of some spiteful, old harridan."

"Very well, Mr. Thurgood, you've made your point." Pinckney closed the attaché case and slid it back across the table. "Donate when you become a member. Then I'll know you're sincere."

Harry smiled. "I'm sincere, Mr. Pinckney. I will do *anything* to make sure Ember is not disappointed."

"And what's that supposed to mean?"

"Exactly what the English words mean. They're in the dictionary."

"Now you're a smart-ass. Never liked smart-asses."

"I never cared much for self-important sanctimonious pricks. Seems to me we're even here. Ride home?"

"No, thank you, Mr. Thurgood. I'll walk."

"The Fights aren't God. They just think they are."

"They carry an awful lot of thunderbolts in their quiver."

"And fear becomes no man."

Harry picked up the attaché case and walked to the front of the library. He didn't see Caroline, so he walked on out to his car.

He opened the door, tossed in the attaché, and got in.

"They are going to be a tough bunch of nuts to crack. Guess I just have to up the pressure."

11

THURSDAY, 8 FEBRUARY 10:27 AM

THE NIGHT BEFORE, JAVIER HERRON PLACED LISTENING DEVICES around Ember Cole's parsonage.

He now knew that she talked to her cat, sang a lot of Christian songs, and liked 70s and 80s pop music. She hadn't talked in her sleep.

J also knew Ember Cole was not the woman's birth name. Several database searches had told him that. But he hadn't been able to find out just when and where the name change had taken place. Or what her birth name had been.

This morning he was following her movements around town. He wanted to get a feel for who it was he was gathering information on. What kind of person she was.

At this point, he'd say she was a genuinely pious person. But he also knew from experience most pious people held deep dark secrets and he was sure the Reverend Ember Cole was no exception.

———

Clair-Ann Taylor set the tray on the end of her father's desk and poured tea from the small pot into the cup. She put the saucer

over the top of the cup to keep the tea warm. When busy working, as he was now, he always forgot the tea was there.

"Thank you, Sinclair."

Only fifty-eight, Owen Hill Taylor looked ready for the grave.
He was pale and gaunt. He had trouble breathing and often had
to resort to oxygen. The sight brought tears to Clair-Ann's eyes.

But at least I'm here for you, Dad. At least I'm faithful.

"Are you warm enough, Dad?"

"I'm fine. Sit." He swiveled his chair to face the sofa.
"Making a lot of progress today. I have the Taylor history
complete through Reconstruction."

"You *are* making good progress, Dad. This is a wonderful
thing you are doing for Magnolia Bluff. The Taylors are an
important family."

His smile was bittersweet. "Were an important family. Your
brother has gone off to Fort Worth. And you're not married. Our
family dies with you, Sinclair."

"Oh, Dad, I just haven't found the right guy. Besides, I'm
taking care of *you*. And that's the most important thing I can do
right now."

She got up and kneeling before him, laid her head in his lap
and put her arms around him.

"I love you, Dad. I'm never going to leave you. Never."

———

The big Land Rover moved slowly down West Main Street.
When it was across from the Really Good Wood-Fired Coffee
Shop, the vehicle stopped, and the driver maneuvered the behe-
moth into a parking space along the curb.

The driver's door opened, and out stepped Scarlett Hayden.
The tall, statuesque and shapely blonde was wearing dark gray
slacks, a white blouse, and an ankle-length rust-brown camel-
hair cardigan. A dark gray beret was on her head, and a dark
gray purse hung from her shoulder on a fine gold chain. Around

her neck was a bright red scarf of fine silk and the long ends fluttered behind her in the light breeze.

She walked across West Main, without paying attention to the traffic, crossed the Green, walked across East Main, causing a car to come to a screeching halt, and continued on into the Really Good.

Scarlett's eyes swept the empty shop and stopped when they saw Jack Bonhoffer. "Is Harry here?" she asked.

"No, ma'am. He's out at the moment."

"Do you expect him back?"

"I do."

"I'll wait."

Scarlett took a seat, crossed her legs, and looked out the window.

Hurry up, Harry. We need to talk.

12

THURSDAY, 8 FEBRUARY 11:13 AM

HARRY PARKED HIS CAR IN THE ALLEY BEHIND THE REALLY GOOD.

Now we'll see what old Euel has to say about that, he said to himself.

After his meeting with the church treasurer, Harry drove over to the Methodist church. He'd parked on the street in front of the building.

Having transferred four straps of one hundred dollar bills to his pockets, he entered the church. One advantage of living in a small Southern town was that doors were often left unlocked, especially during the day.

It gives one hope, he thought, *that there is still a shred of honesty, decency, and respect left in humanity.*

Saint Luke's had four offering boxes in the sanctuary. Two by the main doors going in and two on either side of the pulpit and choir area for people who might enter or exit from the doors there.

Harry entered and put one strap in the box to his right. He walked down the side aisle, and put a strap in the box by the door that was on stage left of the pulpit. He crossed the front of the church, dropped another into the box by the door on stage right, and then walked to the remaining box and dropped in the last strap.

He moved to the center aisle and faced the pulpit. In a soft whisper, he said, "There you go, Euel. Your short fall is gone. But I'm not done with you. Not yet."

He turned, walked out of the church, and back to his car. He made stops at New Hope Presbyterian, where he gave an envelope to Reverend Baskin and asked him to give it to the Methodist church secretary, and at First Baptist, where he asked the same of Reverend Chris Hayes, and a final stop at the law office of Stanton Lauderbach.

The lawyer gave him a questioning look when Harry handed him the envelope and told him what he wanted.

"Some people think the way to heaven is paved with gold," Harry said. "It isn't. Not really. For them, it's paved in green."

Lauderbach, a smile on his lips, had replied, "Lay up for yourselves treasures in heaven, where neither moth nor rust doth corrupt; and where thieves do not break through nor steal: for where your treasure is, there will your heart be also."

"They probably don't have that verse in their Bibles."

"Probably not. Your wish is my command, Harry. And I won't even charge you for it."

Harry entered the Really Good through the back door.

Miguel stopped singing the Spanish song he was singing, and said, "You have a visitor out front. Jack was about to text you. She's getting antsy."

"She?"

"Mrs. Hayden."

Harry made the sign of the cross, and Miguel, with a big smile on his face, said, "May all the saints, plus Jesus, Joseph, and Mary be with you."

"Thanks. Might need help from the Buddha, too."

Harry walked out to the front part of the shop. There he found Scarlett looking out the window. Estrelita was waiting on a customer. Jack nodded towards the blonde. Harry nodded a yes in reply, got himself a coffee and a slice of pie, and walked over to Scarlett's table.

"About time you got back."

"And good morning to you, as well, Scarlett. Can I get you anything?"

"Yes. Give me some time out of your *very* busy schedule."

"I'm here." He sat. "I'm all yours."

"Like hell you are. I wish you were."

"If wishes were horses…"

"Yeah, I know, beggars would ride. Yada, yada."

"Did you stop by just to say hi and chat? I do like talking with you. You're intelligent and a good conversationalist."

"Am I beautiful?"

"Yes, very. Stunningly so, in fact."

"Thank you for saying that."

"I say so because it's true."

She smiled, then looked at her hands. "I have a favor to ask."

"Okay. Ask."

She lifted her head and her sapphire eyes met Harry's. "I would like to go to the plays this weekend, but I don't want to go alone."

"Okay."

"I'm not asking you to take me. You're probably going with Ember."

"What are the plays?"

"Don't you pay attention to what's going on in town?"

"Guess not."

"The Magnolia Bluff Players are doing a complete production of O'Neill's *Mourning Becomes Electra*."

"Seriously? How did I miss that?"

With a smirk on her lips, she said, "Attending too many submarine races?"

"Nope. Chaste as a newborn babe."

"Huh. Don't know how you do it."

"Will power."

"If you say so. Anyway, Friday night, tomorrow, is *Home-coming*. Saturday, *The Hunted*. And Sunday, *The Haunted*. The Players will do another performance next weekend, and a final performance the weekend after that."

"Sounds great. So what's your favor?"

"Stanton Lauderbach is single, isn't he?"

"Yes, I believe so. He's never mentioned a wife or partner."

"Would you ask him to ask me out to see the performances?"

"You don't want to ask him yourself?"

"I'm a bit old-fashioned that way."

"Okay. Sure. I'll ask him. Would you like to make it a four-some? You know, in case the chemistry isn't right?"

"How would Ember feel about it?"

"She's much more secure now. I think she'll be okay."

"If she has no objection, I'd like that."

"Sounds good. I'll ask Stanton."

"Thanks, Harry."

She stood and Harry did as well.

She kissed him, and the kiss wasn't particularly chaste.

"I love you, Harry Thurgood. But I've decided it's best to move on. This wasn't our time."

"No, it wasn't. I'll call Stanton and plan on seeing you tomorrow."

Scarlett left, and Harry watched her go.

I would have never expected that in a million years. Stanton is going to be one lucky guy.

Harry took out his phone and told it to call the lawyer.

13

THURSDAY, 8 FEBRUARY 2:07 PM

JAVIER HERRAN ONCE AGAIN FOUND HIMSELF UNDER THE SCRUTINY of those frigid eyes.

Mary Lou Fight put down her cup and saucer. "So, you think someone has found you out."

"Yes, ma'am. I've been at this long enough to know when I've picked up a tail. And I noticed one earlier today. He was good, too. It took quite a bit to lose him. Or her, I suppose. Walked more like a man, though."

"Interesting. So what does this mean?"

"What it means is that someone is watching you, and then started watching me to see what I was doing for you."

"Aren't you assuming quite a bit here? Why do you think this person is watching me?"

"How else would they be aware I'm working for you?"

"But does this person actually know that?"

"It's possible he doesn't. But then I can't explain why he'd be following me. He'd have no interest in me apart from a job I'm working on."

"How do you know that?"

"I have no spouse or partner. I have no debt. Any of the

common things a person hires a detective for, do not apply to me."

"What about the uncommon?"

J-Man smiled. "I can assure you, Mrs. Fight, no one's hiring a detective for those either."

"So you were sloppy."

Herran counted to ten before he answered. "Someone is watching you, Mrs. Fight. Do you want me to find out who it is?"

"It's most likely someone with money. Who else could afford to pay the fees and expenses?"

Herran let a Mona Lisa smile touch his lips. "Yes, whoever hired the detective probably has money. Good detectives aren't cheap."

"Very well. Find out who is spying on me. It is best that I learn who it is. He or she will have to be dealt with."

J wondered what 'dealt with' meant for the Ice Queen, but decided not to ask. "I'll let you know as soon as I find out."

He waited to see if there was anything more from the woman.

She picked up her cup and saucer. "You aren't going to find the person sitting here."

He stood. "No, ma'am."

Mary Lou rang a bell, and in a moment a young woman appeared in the doorway. "Eliška, please show Mr. Herran out."

"Yes, ma'am."

Herran followed the young woman to the front door, and when he was standing on the porch he let his eyes slowly move up and down the street.

He could be anywhere, he thought. *But if I were him, I'd be using remote cameras, recording devices, and maybe even drones.*

His eyes swept the sunny sky. *No drones. At least today.*

He walked out to the street, turned around, and studied the house. *It's going to be a big job just to clear the place. Best get started.*

14

THURSDAY, 8 FEBRUARY 2:10 PM

HARRY POURED A CUP OF COFFEE FOR STANTON LAUDERBACH.

"So this woman, Scarlett Hayden, wants me to ask her out to see the O'Neill plays this weekend."

Harry set the cup in front of the lawyer, who was sitting on a stool at the counter. "That's correct."

Stanton took a sip of coffee. "This is very good, Harry."

"It's a peabody coffee from the Tres Picachos mountain in Jayuya, Puerto Rico. Not easy to get a hold of. The roast is medium, towards the dark side."

"Fabulous. Love the subtle sweetness and hint of spice. Have any of this I can take home?"

"It's fifty-five bucks a pound."

"You're kidding."

"Nope. Had a very difficult time getting it."

"What the heck. I'll take a pound."

Harry turned and called out to Miguel through the window. "One pound of the Tres Picachos. Whole bean."

"Si, Mr. Thurgood."

"Now, Harry, I don't know Scarlett. I mean, I know her reputation, kind of a wild thing, but, I mean…"

"Stanton, I like Scarlett. If it wasn't for Em, I'd be with Scarlett. She's educated. She's smart. She's a great conversationalist. A good cook. And wants to please her man, and be pleased by him."

"Is she high maintenance? The last woman I was with drove me crazy."

"I don't think Scarlett is high maintenance. She wants a partner. She won't be satisfied if you're just there. She wants a companion to share her life and for her to share his."

"A good conversationalist, you say?"

"Very good. She's a fascinating person. I only agreed to do this because I think you two might work."

"Huh. OK, Harry. I'll call her."

"Do you mind a foursome with Em and me?"

"Fine with me. That way, if things don't work out, the evening won't be a complete disaster."

"Super." Harry turned around, got the bag of coffee beans, and gave it to Stanton.

"Thanks, Harry. Looking forward to this. How much did you say?"

"Gratis."

"No. I can't."

"Enjoy, my friend."

"Enjoy? My foot. Now I owe you. I know how you work."

"Takes one to know one."

The two men laughed and said goodbye.

Harry watched Stanton leave. *I hope he and Scarlett work out. It will make my life a whole lot easier.*

He poured himself a cup of the Puerto Rican coffee, and took it, with a slice of pie, to his table in the corner.

I know I shouldn't jinx this, but I wonder when Reece is going to pay me a visit?

15

FRIDAY, 9 FEBRUARY 11:07 PM

Being a Friday night, O'Gara's Bar and Grill was hopping.

Harry noticed that the owner Gill Simmons was behind the bar along with his girlfriend, Fleur Beauchamp.

Must've promoted her, he thought.

Harry still didn't understand how that autumn-spring relationship worked.

If Em was twenty-five years my junior... He shook his head and let the thought drop.

Harry watched Scarlett take command of the situation.

Her outfit was a bright red jumpsuit with very wide pant legs, which made it look like a dress. The top was so open there wasn't much left for the imagination, and a whole lot left for a wardrobe malfunction. A bright red beret sat on top of the long cascade of wavy blonde hair.

Parting the sea of patrons like a red-robed Moses, she sailed straight for a table in the far corner of the bar, talked with the college kids who sat there, and in a flash they left, and she waved for her date, and Harry and Ember to join her.

When everyone was seated, Ember asked, "How did you get them to leave?"

"Oh, that's easy. The universal language."

Stanton said, "Are you talking about—"

"Yes. Money. Four twenty-dollar bills."

Chuckling, Stanton said, "You are incredible."

"Do you really think so? There are witnesses, so be careful."

"Yes, I do."

From the smile on Stanton's lips, Harry knew Scarlett had him. Hook. Line. And sinker.

A waitress appeared. "Hello. What can I get you?"

Scarlett said, "An extra dry martini with Bombay Sapphire, stirred, rocks on the side, and three olives. I'd also like an order of your German soft pretzel sticks."

Stanton ordered a gimlet with Beefeater gin and a cheeseburger.

Ember asked for onion rings and a French 75 mocktail.

Harry said, "I'd like a cheeseburger and a Bee's Knees with Beefeater."

Scarlett gave Harry a look, and said, "What the hell is a Bee's Knees?"

"Gin, lemon, and honey. An old Prohibition drink that's pretty good. It's made something of a comeback."

"Huh. I'll stick with a martini. Simple. So what did you think of the play?"

"It's bleak," Ember said.

The waitress came with their drinks. "Food will be ready in a minute. Here's a bowl of nachos." And she was off to another table.

"Isn't it based on one of those old Greek tragedies?" Stanton asked, sipping his gimlet and nodding his approval.

Scarlett set her glass down. "The Oresteia by Aeschylus. And it is bleak. It's a tragedy."

They paused while the waitress put their food on the table.

When she left, Harry said, "The myth is the basis for the Electra complex, which parallels the Oedipus complex."

"Which, if I remember correctly," Ember said, "was a Jungian and Neo-Freudian idea, and is now discredited. Along with Freud and the Neo-Freudians."

"What about Jung?" Stanton asked.

"Jung is controversial," Ember replied. "I think there is a lot of value to Jung. Although, for day-to-day counseling, probably not so much."

"So, do you think a girl can come to hate her mother so much that she would kill her?" Scarlett asked. "Like in the myth and the play?"

"I suppose," Ember said. "I mean right here in Magnolia Bluff we've seen all sorts of reasons that people have come up with to kill somebody."

Scarlett nodded. "Very true. I mean, look at you. Mary Lou would probably love to do you in, simply because you're pastoring her church. That's cause enough for her to hate you. However, I think you're an honorable person who cares about people."

"Thank you," Ember replied.

In spite of her polite response, Harry knew Em well enough to know she was at least a little bit piqued by Scarlett's comment.

He said, "I think the acting was very good. Better than your average community theater."

"I agree," Stanton said.

That shifted the conversational focus back to the play, where it stayed until the food was gone.

"This has been a wonderful evening," Scarlett said. "But I think I'd like to go home now."

Harry and Ember bid Scarlett and Stanton a good night.

When they were gone, Ember asked, "What was Scarlett's point about Mary Lou? Was it some kind of dig?"

"Don't know, Em. I thought it a bit odd myself."

"I don't know if I want to do this again."

"We did have a good time, her comment aside."

"I suppose. Take me home, Mister?"

"Sure."

Harry put some bills on the table and they left.

The drive to the parsonage was done in silence. Harry knew Em was chewing on something.

She looked spectacular tonight. Navy blue A-line dress, with the hem of the full skirt falling mid-calf. The mock turtleneck and the long sleeves provided the right contrast for the pearl necklace. Simple, yet elegant.

Harry parked in front of the parsonage and unbuckled his seat belt. He started to get out, but stopped when Ember spoke.

"Do you truly love me, Harry?"

He turned to face her. "You know I do, Emmy."

"Scarlett. I mean look at that outfit. I think Stanton needed glue to keep his eyes in his head."

"And tongue in his mouth."

The two shared a laugh.

"Well, you know I have no shape and—"

"Neither did Louise Brooks."

"Who?"

"The silent film star I'm in love with."

"Oh, great. Now I have competition from a dead woman."

"No, you don't. But just like Louise had It…" Harry made air quotes when he said, "It." "So do you. You don't think you're sensual, but you are. You just have gotten good at hiding it. But it's there. And you have oodles of personality as well. You are my goddess."

"You truly think this?"

"Yes. You are my It Girl. Why do you doubt?"

"Okay, Harry. People are already talking. And we'll be legally married soon. Will you keep me company tonight?"

16

SATURDAY, 10 FEBRUARY 8:11 AM

HARRY WOKE TO THE SMELL OF BACON FRYING. HE TURNED HIS HEAD and saw that he was alone in the bed.

His mind drifted back to a few hours ago.

We all do what we have to in order to make life work, he thought.

He and Em had stood facing each other, naked, holding hands.

She said, "I, Ember Cole, take you, Harry Thurgood, to be my husband, my lover, and my companion, from this day forward, until death parts us."

He replied, "I, Harry Thurgood, take you, Ember Cole, to be my wife, my lover, and my companion, from this day forward, until death parts us."

Together, they said, "Amen."

She turned, still holding one hand, and led him to her bed, where they made slow-burn love to each other.

Harry recalled thinking she was the most skilled practitioner of the art of love he'd ever experienced. Something he hadn't expected, but was very happy that he was the recipient of her love.

A voice came from the doorway. Her voice. "Breakfast is ready, sleepyhead."

He turned to look at her. She was wearing a see-through baby doll.

And this woman is now mine. No matter what, I am the most fortunate of men.

"Well, are you going to stare at me all day or share breakfast with me?"

"Breakfast it is. Although I could stare at you all day."

"I doubt it. Your robe is on the chair."

"My robe?"

"Unless you eat your breakfast *au natural.*"

"You sure we have to eat now?"

She giggled. "See what I mean? You wouldn't be able to stare at me all day."

"Guess you're right."

"Unfortunately, no time for play. Even though I moved your car to the church lot, the neighbors will be talking."

"But we're married."

"*De facto,* yes. *De jure,* no. And I'm sure in this hamlet, only *de jure* counts."

"We could fib."

"Yes, we could. And we might have to. Now get up, Mister. Bacon's getting cold."

"Yes, ma'am."

Ember turned, flaunted her butt at him, and disappeared towards the kitchen.

God, if only I could hold this moment in my hands forever, you would make a believer out of me.

———

Harry left by the back door and cut over to the church when a glint caught his eye. He stopped, backed up, and there it was again. There on the tree trunk.

He walked over to the tree and saw a tiny camera stuck to the bark.

Well, I'll be…

He turned around to determine the camera's line of sight and noticed that it was focused on Ember's back door.

If someone is watching Ember, then I'm willing to wager that someone is watching me as well. I guess this confirms what Scarlett said last year. Kind of difficult to argue with hard proof.

He tried removing it, but no doing. Out came his pocketknife, and he succeeded in prying the device off the tree. He slipped it into his pocket and continued onto his car.

After parking behind the Really Good, he gave his car an examination. Attached to the fuel tank was the tracking device he was looking for.

More proof. Looks like the Hat Queen is pulling out all the stops.

He pried it off with his pocketknife, entered the back door, greeted Miguel, and climbed the stairs to his apartment.

Once inside, he turned the little tracker over in his hand. It was an advanced model that would send his location in real time to whoever was monitoring him.

With device in hand, he walked to the bathroom and dropped it into the toilet.

"Enjoy the swim," he said as he pushed the lever to flush.

Back in the kitchen, he took the camera out of his pocket, looked at it, eye to eye, so to speak, and said, "Now you know I know. Your move."

He dropped the camera to the tile floor, crushed it under his heel, swept up the debris, and dumped it in the trash can.

Stopping only a moment to give the situation some thought, he took out his phone, typed, and sent the text.

Elmore will know what to do.

17

SUNDAY, 11 FEBRUARY 7:58 AM

EVEN THOUGH THE MORNING AIR WAS COOL, THE SUN FELT GOOD ON the skin. The weatherman promised a high near seventy, which would make for a truly perfect day.

An hour ago, Harry had walked to the Green and sat on a bench facing the Really Good. There was no traffic on either East or West Main. The silence sounded good in his ears.

He was smoking an old pipe that had been his grandfather's: a Jobey Shellmoor Prince. He'd filled it with Holiday mixture. One of his favorite blends. A sippy cup of that expensive Puerto Rican coffee was in his hand.

Ember's decision to consummate their marriage early was quite a surprise, and he still found it difficult to believe she'd been willing to do so.

Probably half the town knew he'd spent the night, even with her moving his car. But if Em was okay with her decision, he was, too.

On a whim, he'd called Stanton yesterday and asked if Texas had common law marriage. The lawyer told him the state did indeed recognize common law marriage. All he and Ember had to do was live together and hold themselves out to the community as married, and they were married. What's more, Texas law recognized them as married immediately. No waiting period.

Harry'd called Em and told her what Stanton had said. She was all in favor of going the common law route to squelch any possible blowback from their night together.

She thought an announcement today at church and a notice in the *Chronicle* should take care of the provision that they had to hold themselves out to the community as married.

His mind drifted back to their lovemaking. Her skill surprised him and convinced him she was no virgin. Not that it mattered. He'd have been surprised if she was. Her being accomplished in the art of love was like icing on the cake.

He smiled. To Ember, everything was sacred. And their commitment ceremony simply reinforced that.

As far as she was concerned, they were married. State license or no.

She's a true child of God. I just hope my lack of faith doesn't cause problems down the road.

Although when it came to faith, Em's Christianity wasn't exactly orthodox. In fact, it was pretty weird. At least according to what he'd been taught in Sunday school.

Good thing she keeps her beliefs to herself.

"No sense in me adding to my problems," she once told him. And he thought that was a smart move.

His pipe smoked out, he put it in his pocket, finished his coffee, and walked back to the Really Good. He entered his shop, locked the door, and made sure the sign said "Closed."

Honoring Sunday as a day of rest and keeping the Really Good closed was about as religious as he got.

Nevertheless, he'd be at Em's eleven o'clock service. After all, it's what the pastor's husband should do.

He climbed the stairs to his apartment above the shop to get dressed for church.

For whatever reason, his mind drifted to the Old Testament stories. Adam and Eve had never had an official wedding. Isaac simply took Rebekah into his tent. And Jacob, after a feast, went into his tent and took Leah.

Harry chuckled. *I guess I can say I had my feast at O'Gara's and then went in unto her. About as Biblical as you can get."*

———

After the service, Harry drove the two of them to Austin.

"Where are you taking me?" Ember asked.

"Julie's Noodles. Best Chinese noodle restaurant east of Kazakhstan."

"Isn't Kazakhstan west of China?"

"It is."

"Hm. Must be pretty good then."

"It is. So what did you make of the congregation's reaction to our announcement?"

"About what I expected. Those who like me were happy for me, and those who don't said nothing and will somehow make this another strike against me."

Harry smiled. "You're right about the naysayers. But in the big picture, they and this whole situation are insignificant."

"I suppose so. After all, we're all going to die; and at some point, even the earth is going to cease to exist. So, yes, this is insignificant in the big picture. In the small picture, though, it's all a pain in the butt."

"It is. But we have enough money you could start your own church if you wanted. Let Mary Lou and her minions keep that dead dinosaur."

Ember was quiet for a moment before saying, "I could. But I don't want to be a church splitter."

"You wouldn't be splitting any church. You'd be starting a new one. A place more conducive to your beliefs."

"Well, it's a thought. I'll think about it. On a different note, when should we put the notice in the paper?"

"Let's see Monika tomorrow. You going to keep your name?"

"Will you be angry if I do?"

"Not in the least. If we have kids, they'll be Cole-Thurgoods. How's that?"

Ember giggled. "I love you, Harry Thurgood. And I'm perfectly fine with a common law marriage. Because as far as I'm concerned, we were actually married Friday night."

"And that was the most beautiful wedding I ever attended."

"I bet. Was it because we were naked?"

"Adam and Eve were."

"You would come up with that. It was beautiful, though, wasn't it? So simple."

"It was. Truly. So where do you want to go for your honeymoon? Can you get time off?"

"I'll ask the church council. They'll have to get someone to cover. As for where, surprise me."

"Surprise you, I will."

"This is so good. I hope it lasts forever."

18

MONDAY, 12 FEBRUARY 9:07 AM

"You two did what?" Caroline McCluskey said.

"We got married," Harry said.

Ember's face was beaming. "We committed ourselves to each other, and then, well, you know."

Billy Bob Baskin asked, "Who presided?"

"Ember did," Harry said.

"In other words, you two took the common law route," Magnolia Nadine said.

"Righto," Harry replied.

Graham Huston was scribbling in his notebook.

"You don't need to take notes," Ember said. "I asked Monika this morning to put it in her society column."

"Might want to add something," Graham replied. "Where are you two going to live? Or are you using a tent, like Isaac and Rebekah?"

Harry chuckled. "Haven't decided. Friday night it was the parsonage. Saturday, we were separate."

"Uh-oh," Graham said. "Trouble in paradise already."

"No," Ember said. "I wanted to make sure I focused on my sermon for Sunday."

"And last night, we were here," Harry said.

"I'm a little surprised," Caroline said. "Don't you want a real wedding?"

Ember thought a moment before answering. "What is a wedding? It's a ritual to formally announce a marriage. What's a marriage? It's an agreement between two people to live together, have sex, and create a family. Jacob was given a feast, and then entered his tent and had sex with Leah. The light must've been pretty bad that he didn't recognize the switch until morning. But that was it. A meal and sex."

She laughed. "Well, Friday night we did a Jacob. Ate and had sex. And we're married."

"Congratulations," Graham said. "I'm happy for you. And if Texas makes it all that simple, why complicate things? We make simple things complicated all the time. It's where ninety percent of our problems come from."

"Thanks, Graham," Harry said. "And I agree with you. We make life too doggone complicated. Tomorrow, to go with the announcement in the paper, I'm offering free coffee and food. All day."

Graham laughed. "Two-thirds of the town will show up."

"And then you'll probably never see them again," Billy Bob added.

Harry looked over at Chief Tommy Jager. "You haven't said a word. Cat got your tongue?"

"I'm stunned. I never expected you two to do something like this. You've been dancing for so long… Well, I'm shocked. Happy for you. If this is what you want. Never would have guessed it was coming in a million years. Be prepared for the gossip, though. It will probably be vicious."

"You're right, there, Tommy," Magnolia Nadine said. "Ember, they'll have you pregnant. That's for sure. They'll see it as confirmation you've been in carnal relations. And don't be surprised if your church uses this against you."

"It's always the woman who suffers," Caroline said.

"That's for sure," Magnolia Nadine agreed.

"I've thought about this for a long time," Ember said. "And you're absolutely right, Magnolia Nadine. This will probably be used against me. But the ones who don't want me at Saint Luke's use everything against me anyway. What's important is serving God and to enjoy. The more we enjoy, the happier we are. And if we're happy, we serve God and our neighbors with joyful hearts. And that's all that matters to me. It doesn't matter where I serve or how I serve. With Harry by my side, I will be the best of servants. Period."

"Well said, Ember," Billy Bob said.

"You're a spitfire, that's for sure," Tommy added. "Congrats, and good luck." He stood. "Had enough coffee and chat. Now I'd best go do some serving myself. And a little protecting, too. Have a good day, y'all."

Tommy left, and the table grew quiet. After a few moments had passed, Graham said, "I've seen a lot of senseless death. I've seen a lot of senseless pain and suffering, and I've seen people in the grip of fear become shriveled up, dried out prunes.

"There are a lot of people who are breathing, but they aren't living. At the very least, they aren't happy and content. Miserable is more like it."

"Harry and Ember, I wish long and happy lives for you. I think you two are already miles down the road to achieving happiness and contentment."

Graham stood. "You all have a good day."

He left, and Billy Bob, Caroline, and Magnolia Nadine quickly followed.

A customer came in and Estrelita took her order.

"Well, Mister, by the time the paper comes out our being married will be old news."

"Very true. I wonder how this will alter Mary Lou's campaign against us?"

"Probably not much. Although, what we've done has given her one target, instead of two."

19

MONDAY, 12 FEBRUARY 2:27 PM

MARY LOU ENDED THE CALL FROM GOODY PREMINGER AND RANG for her maid.

In a moment, the young woman appeared. "Yes, Mrs. Fight?"

"Tea, please, Eliška. And I'm in the mood for Thé Russe, if you don't mind."

"No, ma'am." She curtsied and left.

"So the strumpet put a veneer of legality to her behavior," she said out loud, although she was talking to herself.

Mary Lou picked up her cell phone, the one she used for conducting business, and sent a text to Javier Herran informing him of the fresh development.

A moment later she received a text back: a thumb up emoticon.

"Don't people know how to write anymore?" she murmured. "We're descending to the level of the ancient Egyptians and the Chinese."

She slowly walked to the glass wall that gave her a view of the reservoir. And she did so without the help of her walker.

Will power. Determination. That's what's lacking in society today. People are self-absorbed and gutless hedonists. That makes them easy prey, though.

A sailboat was tacking into the wind.

Will power and determination. I will walk again. I will be in my church again. And the strumpet and her lothario will vanish from my world.

———

Cally Taylor was stunned. She'd been out of town, lobbying District Superintendents to move Ember Cole to a different church and hadn't heard the news.

"She did what?" she said.

The voice on the other end of the call said, "She got married. Married Harry Thurgood. You know, the guy who owns the coffee shop and lives off of a big inheritance."

"Where did you hear this, Liana?"

"From my cousin, who was talking with her friend who works at the Silver Spoon."

"You sure she heard right?"

"Go ask her yourself. Or better yet, ask the Reverend."

"I intend to. Thanks, Liana."

"Just thought you'd like to know."

"Thanks. Appreciate it. Bye." Cally put the phone down.

"That's, well, it's… I don't believe it," she muttered, while getting up from behind her desk and walking to the door of her office.

She opened the door, poked her head out, and said to Larrilyn Hammer, the receptionist and secretary, "Is Reverend Cole in?"

"No, ma'am, she's not. She should be at the hospital, and then she'll be visiting Mrs. Cloudele Weaver."

"Have you heard that Ms. Cole got married?"

"Yes. She announced it in church yesterday."

"I can't believe it."

"I know. She sure got herself a looker. How someone that frumpy could get Harry Thurgood…"

Cally shook her head. "Where are they living?"

"I don't know. He's been seen at the parsonage, so maybe there."

"And you're sure they are married?"

Larrilyn shrugged. "I didn't see the certificate. I was at church and Reverend Cole announced it. Her dreamboat was there too. That's all I know."

"Thanks, Larrilyn." Cally retreated into her office and closed the door.

Something's odd about this. But it doesn't matter. Now she has a no-good husband. And that just makes my job easier.

20

MONDAY, 12 FEBRUARY 7:32 PM

HARRY THURGOOD SAT AT EMBER'S KITCHEN TABLE. SHE WAS AT THE microwave heating the apple pie for their dessert.

"It will probably be easier if I just move in here with you. What do you think, Em? Won't disrupt Wilbur's routine overly much."

"Thank you for thinking of him." The microwave dinged. She took the pie out and brought the two slices to the table. "Do you want frozen custard? You brought enough of it."

"How about plain old vanilla?"

"Good idea." She got the carton from the freezer, put a scoop on each of the slices, and returned the carton to the freezer.

"Homemade frozen custard is a good idea," she said.

"I have the Reston boy, Elisha, to thank for that."

"Are you going to hire him when it's summer?"

"I think I will. Although, I've been thinking of selling the Really Good to Goody."

"Goody Preminger?"

Harry nodded.

"What on earth for?"

"Well, what would I do with the place if we have to move?"

"You could let Miguel manage it for you."

"You're right. I could do that." He ate pie. "That's an excellent idea, actually. Thanks, Emmy."

She smiled, ate pie, then said, "Anything to help my man."

"I like the sound of that, Missus."

"I'm glad you do, Mister."

"So, what did you think of the play?"

"Three nights of tragedy is a bit much. It was all very depressing."

"It made me think of the Reston family."

"Oralene orchestrated the murders, the boys carried them out, and no one gets punished. It's not right."

"The Restons aren't from here, and neither was Tully. What does Magnolia Bluff care about strangers killing strangers? Nothing. If they'd killed someone from Magnolia Bluff, the town might not have waited for a trial."

"But in the play, the perpetrators became what they killed. A bit of eternal recurrence there, don't you think?"

"I suppose you're right. We can't escape what we are. And what we are isn't shaped by us. It's what clings to us from our ancestral past."

"That's too depressing for me. If I can't escape my past, then I want to end it. An endlessly repeating tragedy is not my cup of tea."

"But that's what eternal recurrence is: a big circle. A big circle that never ends. What is, is. And to quote Pope, whatever is, is right. For all eternity."

"Not my metaphysics."

"Yet, you believe Paul. Don't you?"

"Oh, man. Don't go there."

Harry chuckled. "Okay, my love, I won't. I guess I saw in the plays that there may not be divine justice, but there will be justice for our crimes. We will bring it upon ourselves."

"We become our own divine justice."

"Yes."

"Scary thought, that. We are our own executioners."

"Good thing we got married. I'd hate to have to brand myself with a great big F on my chest."

"You make everything a joke."

"Not everything."

"Glad to hear it. Now, will you make love to me? We're not young and I want to collect as many rosebuds while I can."

"Kiss me with the kisses of your mouth — for your love, my Emmy, is better than wine."

"I will kiss you, my love, with the kisses of my mouth, for you are handsome and pleasant to behold. Lay your head between my breasts for you are to me the scent of magnolia blossoms."

"My desire is for you. Come, let us away to paradise."

"I love you, Harry. I pray this lasts forever."

21

TUESDAY, 13 FEBRUARY 7:01 AM

THE LINE WAS OUT THE DOOR AND HALFWAY DOWN THE BLOCK. THE big pasteboard sign in the window of the Really Good proclaimed the open house to celebrate Harry and Ember's marriage.

Jack Bonhoffer, Miguel, Estrelita, and a very pregnant Joetta Reston were serving coffee; strawberry pie; doughnuts; poppy-seed rolls; Czech kolaches; Harry's special basil and sun-dried tomato bread, with aromatic cheese and brown olive relish; and his cashew butter, bacon, and banana turnovers.

The coffees were very special: a Tanzanian Peaberry light roast, a Sumatran Mandheling medium roast; and a Brasil Nossa Senhora de Fatima dark roast. Also available were MTW Irish Breakfast and Cheericup Ceylon teas for non-coffee drinkers.

Harry and Ember stood off to the side. Harry was wearing dark chocolate slacks; a white shirt with a golden yellow ascot, covered in rust-brown pin dots; a rust-brown camel hair sport coat; and dark brown loafers.

Ember was wearing an ankle-length navy blue A-line dress with long sleeves, navy blue Mary Janes, a white clerical collar, and a gold pectoral cross.

Harry was doing a lot of smiling, handshaking, and making

small talk with people he vaguely knew or didn't know at all. Ember, on the other hand, seemed to know most of the people and appeared to be enjoying herself.

What I know for sure, he told himself, *is that I'll be glad when this day is over.*

———

The white Cadillac CT6 glided to a stop on West Main Street across from the Really Good.

"James, would you get me a tea from that coffee shop? I'd also like you to get me a head count of how many people are there."

"We're double parked here, Mrs. Fight. Should I find a spot along the curb?"

"No, you should not. There's plenty of room to drive around my car. Now get going, and don't dawdle."

"Yes, ma'am."

James got out of the car, made his way across West Main, the Green, and East Main, elbowed his way to the front of the line, and said, "I'd like a tea to go, please."

Estrelita poured tea into a to-go cup, put it into a bag with creamer and sugar packets, and handed the bag to James.

"Would you like a pastry to go with that?" she asked.

"Uh, sure. Pick one."

Estrelita put a strawberry kolache in a bag and gave it to him.

"Thanks."

He stepped aside, ate the kolache in three big bites, stuffed the bag in the waste bin, and hurried out the door.

Back across the divided main street and Green, he trotted to Mrs. Fight's Cadillac. He opened the door, gave her the bag with her tea, got in behind the wheel, and asked where she'd like to go.

"Home, James. How many were in that wretched shop?"

Oh, crap, he thought, realizing he'd forgotten to take a head count. "Forty-three, ma'am," he lied.

"Really? The strumpet and her lothario are more popular than I'd imagined. I may have to re-assess my plans. Home, James, and don't make me tell you again."

The chauffeur put the car in drive, his foot on the gas, and drove off down West Main.

Mary Lou sampled the tea and smiled. *The lounge lizard does know how to make an excellent tea. I need to tell Goody to up her offer. I will get them to leave my town one way or the other. After all, he isn't the only one who can make good tea.*

22

TUESDAY, 13 FEBRUARY 9:18 AM

"Where's your lovely bride, Harry?" Graham Huston asked, balancing a cup of coffee, a doughnut, and a slice of poppyseed roll.

"Yes, where is she?" Magnolia Nadine chimed in.

"She had to take a break. She should be back momentarily."

"Are you two going to have a formal wedding at some point?" Caroline McCluskey asked.

"We might."

"If you don't mind my asking," Reverend Billy Bob Baskin said, "why the common law marriage all of a sudden?"

Chief Tommy Jager laughed. "Are you serious, Reverend? I think it's obvious. These two reached a point where they couldn't keep their hands off each other and decide common law was better than burning in hell."

Graham could see Billy Bob was a bit surprised at the police chief's comment, and decided to come to the preacher's rescue. "You know, Jager, you're like sixty grit sandpaper on a baby's bottom."

"Okay, Huston, what's your explanation?"

"I don't need one. That's up to Harry."

The chief turned to Harry. "All right, Thurgood, am I right or am I right?"

Harry laughed. "I don't believe in hell. Don't recall if Em does or not. But look at it this way: a couple wants to live together as husband and wife. In most states, they can't. They have to live in 'sin', so to speak. Unless, of course, they get a piece of paper that entitles them to say they're married because they paid a fee to the state.

"Now living together doesn't matter to me. But it does to Em. Texas let's us live together in a common law marriage. Which, by the way, is very biblical. It is how marriage was done back there in ancient times.

"So Em and I made our own little ceremony to swear our fidelity to each other and then consummated our commitment. No state involvement. No church involvement. Just us. The parties involved. It's a beautiful thing, really. I think more people should consider going the common law route. Get the state *and* the church out of the bedroom."

"You mind if I quote you on that, Harry?" Graham asked.

"Which part?"

"About keeping the state and church out of our bedrooms."

"Go ahead, if you want. In for a penny, in for a pound."

Graham chuckled. "Might quote you on that, too."

"Look!" someone shouted.

Graham turned around, and there on the sidewalk were Ember and Cally Taylor in a shouting match. Since he was closest to the door, he dashed out to break up the argument.

"Okay, ladies, take a break."

"Leave me alone, Cally," Ember shouted.

"You're nothing but a bitch in heat. Some pastor you are. You're done, Ms. Cole."

"I want your resignation on my desk today," Ember shouted back.

"Fat chance of that happening."

"If it isn't there, you're finished, Cally Taylor. Finished."

"Come on, Em." Graham had his arm around her and pulled her towards the Green.

Cally charged, and before Graham could stop her, she slapped Ember, causing blood to start from her nose.

Her voice deep with menace, Ember said, "You're dead, Caldwell Taylor. You are so dead."

23

TUESDAY, 13 FEBRUARY 10:03 AM

GRAHAM STOOD WHEN HARRY ARRIVED TO ALLOW HIM TO SIT NEXT to Ember. Clustered around the bench on the Green were Tommy Jager, Caroline McCluskey, Magnolia Nadine, and Billy Bob Baskin. Caroline was sitting next to Ember opposite Harry.

"You want to press charges?" Tommy asked. "I saw her slap you."

Ember, holding a tissue to her nose, shook her head.

"So what was the dust up about?" Tommy asked.

"I don't think I've ever seen you yell at anyone," Caroline added.

Ember nodded. "Doesn't happen often. Cally must've caught me at a weak moment. She has a knack for knowing your buttons and when to press them, and she pressed the right one today. I need to apologize to her."

"Might want to let some time pass," Tommy advised.

Ember shook her head. "Don't let the sun set on your wrath."

"That is Biblical," Billy Bob said, "but it might not do any good so soon."

"Doesn't matter," Ember said. "I'm not responsible for her acceptance or rejection."

"Sounds like it should be the reverse to me," Tommy said.

"Cally's undoubtedly the instigator," Graham said, "but it never hurts to take the high road."

"Maybe we should cancel the rest of the open house," Harry said.

Ember shook her head. "No. Everything's fine now. I'm just a bit embarrassed about losing my cool. This is not the worse thing that's ever happened to me."

A big smile appeared on her face. "Besides, the show must go on."

Graham couldn't help but think that Ember was a real gem. She was human to the point where she could get into shouting matches with her parishioners, and yet saintly enough to admit wrong and want to mend fences.

Ember Cole, you almost persuade me, he thought.

————

Ember and Harry led the group back to the Really Good.

Once inside, Ember apologized. "If any of you saw the disagreement between Mrs. Taylor and myself, I'm sorry you had to see that, and I hope it didn't spoil your day."

Ember heard a few *soto voce* comments about a minister's conduct. The ones making those comments took their coffee and food and quickly left. No word of congratulations on their lips.

More, however, were of the opinion that Cally Taylor needed to be taken down a peg or two, "like a number of others in this town," who those were, Ember noticed, remained unnamed.

I'll be very glad to have this day over. Especially after apologizing to Cally. In the meantime, I smile and shake hands; knowing the whole town will have heard about my shouting match within the hour.

To the woman in front of her, Ember said, "Thank you, Mrs. Hancock, for your well-wishes. I'm looking forward to many wonderful years with this man."

And they may be spent as co-manager of this coffee shop.

24

TUESDAY, 13 FEBRUARY 8:04 PM

HARRY LOOKED AT HIS BRIDE SITTING ACROSS THE TABLE FROM HIM.

She was pushing Miguel's homemade ravioli around her plate.

I wonder, he asked himself, *if I could advertise this as Tex-Mex Italian?*

A sniffle brought him back to his quiet dinner with Em.

He said, "You're not eating. Don't you like it?"

"It's wonderful. Very nice of Miguel to make this for us."

Harry took a sip of the Nebbiolo, set the glass down, and said, "She slammed the door in your face and didn't give you a chance to apologize. This is Cally we're talking about here. Did you expect the tigress to change her stripes?"

"This is really bad, Harry. I'm the pastor. I can't lose my cool."

"But you did. Why? Because you're a human being. Not some saint who is beyond sin. You tried to apologize and she refused to even give you the chance. I think the onus is on her."

"I sure hope the church council sees it that way. *And* the bishop. Otherwise, I am out of here."

She put half of a ravioli in her mouth, and while chewing, said, "This is really good."

"Tex-Mex Italian."

Ember giggled. "He might be onto something there."

"Don't worry about Cally."

"You don't understand church politics. I have to worry. This is *big*."

"I don't know church politics. You're right there. But I do know about politics and power plays. Cally is an agent, as it were, of Mary Lou. We really need to focus on Mary Lou."

"How do we do that?"

"I'm working on it."

"If you don't have her dealt with in the next couple of months, we'll either be in a new place come July or I'll be behind the counter at the Really Good."

"The hostess with the mostest."

"Very funny, Mister. This is serious."

"I know it is, Em. Let me remind you of two things from *your* Bible. First, there is a season for everything. A season comes and then it goes. And a new season takes its place. Nothing is static. All is change. And second, all things—"

"Work together for the good to those who love God, even to those who are called according to his purpose."

Harry smiled and continued. "So, ultimately, this situation will change. It's not here to stay. And the end result, whatever it is, will be good."

"Maybe you'd like to fill in for me this Sunday."

"Nope. You can run, but you can't hide. So gird up your loins and prepare for battle."

She reached across the table and took his hands in hers. "Thank you. You are my best friend. And now you are my husband and lover. You are the best thing has ever happened to me."

"You, my darling, are the best thing that has ever happened to me. I am so very happy to have you as my companion in this life."

"Thank you." She took a deep breath and exhaled it as a sigh.

"God will make the rough places plain, and the crooked straight. We just need to be patient."

"Amen. Preach it, sister."

Ember laughed. She cocked her head towards the bedroom. "Want to help me work up an appetite to finish this?"

"Thought you'd never ask."

———

When she heard the door slam, Clair-Ann walked out to the entryway to see what was going on.

"Who was at the door, Mother?"

Cally turned around. "That bitch-slut who desecrates the pulpit every Sunday."

"What do you have against her? She's sweet, dedicated, and a good speaker. She cares about everyone."

"She said she's going to kill me. How's that for your sweet little pulpit whore?"

"I don't believe that, Mother. I can't imagine Pastor Em even swatting a mosquito."

"Well, she'll be gone once the bishop hears about this."

"Why don't you admit it, Mother? You want a man in the pulpit so you can fantasize about riding his crotch rocket."

Clair-Ann was unprepared for the slap that sent her staggering against the wall.

"Don't you ever accuse me of lusting after the minister. I have the hardest job in the church." She thumped her chest. "I'm the one who keeps that church going. But all I ever get is grief."

"Maybe you should quit that job and take care of Dad."

"There is nothing wrong with your father. He's been a goddamn hypochondriac ever since I've known him. Wish to God I never married the loser."

"Dad is a great man. Better than you."

"You're pathetic. Just like him. I should've said no once your brother was born. You're a disgrace."

Cally grabbed her jacket off the peg by the front door.

"Where are you going? To church, so you can get your jollies flicking Fiona while lying on the communion table?"

"You just cut yourself out of the will. Now pack and get out. You're done living here. Done. You hear me?"

Cally put on her jacket and Clair-Ann watched her leave. She closed the door and walked to the den where her father was sitting in his rocker-recliner listening to old country-western songs.

At that moment, one of her favorites was playing: Patsy Cline singing "Walkin' After Midnight."

"Were you fighting again with your mother? I wish you two would at least declare a truce if you can't sign a peace treaty."

"Don't worry, Dad. We'll work it out. The most important thing is you. I'm going to take care of you. Mother's never here for you. But I am. I'm here for you, and I will always be here for you."

25

"THE ALARM WENT OFF TEN MINUTES AGO, SLEEPYHEAD," EMBER said, while giving Harry a playful shove.

He turned over and held out a box to her. "Happy Valentine's day."

Ember turned and grabbed a box off her nightstand. "And happy Valentine's day to you. Open it. Open it."

Harry tore off the wrapping paper and opened the box. "Oh, my goodness. A Vauen pipe of the year. I don't own a Vauen, so this is a treat. Doubly so. Thank you, my love. Like you, it's beautiful."

"I love you, Harry Thurgood."

"And I love you, Emmy Cole. Now open yours."

She tore off the wrapping and opened the box. "My goodness, Mr. Thurgood, but you are spoiling me rotten."

"Put it on."

"What? Like this?"

"Sure. Skin is good. Especially your skin."

Ember put the necklace on. It was a large green malachite egg, with white swirls, on a gold chain that was studded with tiny rubies.

"And you can wear it with your pectoral cross, if you like, as the chain is shorter and won't interfere with the cross."

"The sacred and the profane?"

"Hadn't thought of that. I do like the profane part. How about we do something profane right now?"

"You know, I look like a little girl. Some men like that, I've heard. I could dress—"

"Nope. I like a woman. Especially a woman who's only wearing a necklace."

Ember laughed. "Then take me. I'm yours."

———

Miguel entered the Really Good and turned on the lights. He sang words to an improvised tune: "Looks like I'm alone, again. All by myself, again. And Harry will be late, again."

He laughed, and added, "That lucky devil."

———

Larrilyn Hammer had a lot of typing to catch up on and decided to get to the church office early. She parked her car, got out, and walked up to the back door of Saint Luke's.

Why's the door open? Who'd be here at this hour? She chuckled. *Cally, of course. She's here all the time. Probably thinks she's the Bride of Christ. Although it's not like her to not latch the door.*

Larrilyn hesitated a moment, then shrugged her shoulders and walked in. The lights were on in the office area. The pastor's door was closed. Cally's door was open and her light was on.

She sang out, "Good morning, Cally. Happy Valentine's Day."

A frown descended when she heard no answer. She walked to the open door to see if Cally was in her office. What she saw made her scream, then cry out, "Oh, my God. Not Cally. Not here."

Larrilyn turned, ran to her desk, dialed 911, and then threw up.

26

REECE SOVERN LOOKED AT THE BODY. *THREE IN THREE WEEKS*, HE thought. *What in the devil's name ties these murders together?*

Police Chief Tommy Jager and Sheriff Buck Blanton joined him.

Tommy said, "Jesus H. Christ. This one was personal."

There was no mirth in Buck's grin. "Must've beat the crap out of her with that cross, then cut her belly so it could be shoved up her vagina. You're right, Tommy. There's a whole lot of anger and some kind of message here. And it ain't a happy Valentine's Day message."

Reece pushed his glasses up and shifted the cigar to the other side of his mouth. "The secretary says this is Cally Taylor, but the condition of her head… Probably have to check dental records."

"Any stab wounds?" Tommy asked.

"Can't tell," Reece said. "Too much blood."

"If it's the same perp," Buck said, "there'll be a knife wound somewhere."

"Wylie been here yet?" Tommy asked. "Not that we need him."

Reece shook his head.

"Don't mean to do your job for you, Reece," Buck said, "but

looking at the blood spray patterns, whoever did this was really giving it some muscle."

"Yeah, I noticed," Reece replied. "Made sure the photographer got it. Poor devil lost his breakfast."

"Can't blame him," Tommy added. "Well, I've seen enough."

"Yeah, me too," Buck said.

"Who do you want to interview, Reece?" Tommy asked. "I'll start rounding them up."

"Family. Friends." He shook his head. "The whole damn church. God. What a mess."

"Yep. It is," Tommy agreed, then left.

Buck followed, and over his shoulder said, "Good luck, Reece."

After they were gone, the police investigator walked out of the room and crossed over to the secretary's desk, where Officer Hans Winkler was watching the forensics people at work.

He greeted Hans, watched for a moment, and then walked out the back door.

The cigar shifted to the other side of his mouth as he turned around to examine the door.

No sign of forced entry. His eyes took in the back wall. *Security light, but no camera.*

Hands on hips, cigar jutting from his mouth, he let his mind roam over the three other murders.

DeWayne Sanford. Throat slashed. Must've rolled down the window to talk to the attacker, not knowing he was going to become a victim.

Lila Santiago. She was on the passenger side of the car. Perp entered the car from the driver's side after pulling out Sanford. Would take some strength to do that. Then once inside the car, slashed at Lila until he got in the stab to the throat and the killing cut that severed the carotid.

Vonnie Vebelsteadt. Apparently answers the door. Perp slashes her throat and leaves her to bleed out in her entryway. The old woman didn't try to defend herself.

Now, Cally Taylor. Was she attacked by the knife-wielding perp? Or was she just bludgeoned to death? If the latter, then this could be a new perp they were dealing with.

Because perps rarely change their method of killing. They find what works and stick to it. Reece shook his head. *God help us if we have two killers on the loose.*

He pushed his glasses back up to the bridge of his nose, took the cigar out of his mouth, pitched it into the grass, and took the cellophane off of a new one. Once it was in the corner of his mouth and his teeth had hold of it, his mind ran to who and why.

Because in the end, it didn't matter if the perp was the same one or not.

Somebody committed this murder for some reason, and it's my job to find out who.

A determined look descended on his face. "First up are the husband and daughter. The second is Ember Cole."

27

EMBER WAS OUT OF THE PARSONAGE FIRST WHEN SHE SAW THE flashing lights. She ran the forty feet from the back door to the church.

"What's going on?" she asked Officer Winkler, who was keeping gawkers away.

"Looks like you have one less parishioner, Reverend."

"What do you mean?"

"Someone killed Mrs. Caldwell Taylor. At least we're guessing it's Mrs. Taylor. Coroner figures a couple hours ago at the most. But he's not a doctor."

"What do you mean by 'guessing it's Mrs. Taylor'?"

"Well, Reverend, someone used your altar cross to bash her head into a bloody pulp. Mr. Sovern thinks we'll have to go the dental record route for a positive ID. Although, your receptionist recognized the clothing as Mrs. Taylor's."

"Bashed her head to a bloody pulp? Oh, my God."

"Whoever it was had a lot of anger. At least that's what all the head honchos think."

"I need to go see Owen and Clair-Ann."

"Mr. Sovern is probably there by now. You might want to wait half an hour or so."

Ember saw Hans's attention shift. She turned and saw Harry coming down the walk to the church.

"This can't be good," he said.

"No, it's not," Ember confirmed.

"Who is it?"

"Cally Taylor."

"No, this is not good. Not good at all."

———

Ten minutes later, Harry and Ember were in Harry's car and pulled up in front of the Taylor home.

"That's Reece's car," Harry said. "I think we'll wait until he leaves."

"Probably a good idea. Although he'll be talking to us eventually."

"Very true." Harry took out his phone and sent a text to Stanton Lauderbach, letting him know about the murder and that he and Ember might be needing his services.

A few minutes later, a text came back: a thumb up emoticon.

"Who did you text?"

"Stanton. I hope we don't need him. But if wishes were horses…"

"Very true. This is a big mess in the making. I just know it."

"Let's not jinx things with negative thinking, okay?"

"Okay. I'm so glad you're with me."

"Me, too."

They watched Reece Sovern exit the house and head for his car. But when he looked in their direction, he changed course and headed straight for Harry's car.

Harry rolled down the window, and when the police investigator arrived, he bid him a good morning.

"Morning, Thurgood." He ducked down to better see into the vehicle. "Morning, Reverend. Are you Reverend Thurgood now?"

"No. Still Cole."

"I see. Should've known. So, what are you doing here?"

"Ember's going to talk to her parishioners."

"Father and daughter are pretty broken up. Especially Owen. Poor guy is gutted. Hope you can give them some comfort. We'll be talking soon. Very soon."

Sovern stood up and strode off to his car. When he'd gotten in and driven off, Harry and Ember got out of the Alfa Romeo.

"What do you say to someone in this situation?" Harry asked.

"I mostly let them talk. Because there's nothing you can say in a situation like this. Although sometimes they want you to talk."

"Makes sense."

They walked up to the door and rang the doorbell. Clair-Ann answered, and let them in.

"I'm so sorry," Ember said.

Clair-Ann nodded, and said, "Dad's in the den. He's really broken up."

"Perfectly understandable," Ember said.

They followed Clair-Ann to the den.

"Hello, Reverend. Mr. Thurgood, isn't it?"

"Yes, it is," Harry said, and shook hands with Owen Taylor.

Good grip, Harry thought.

"Please sit," Clair-Ann said.

Ember said, "I won't take up too much of your time. I'm so sorry about this, Mr. Taylor."

He nodded.

Ember continued. "I want you to know I'm here for you. Whenever you need an ear, just let me know."

"Thanks, Reverend. I'm not much of a churchman."

"Mr. Taylor, I'd be lying if I didn't say otherwise. Sure, I'd like to see you in church every Sunday. But I'm not here to judge. I'm here to minister. You're a member of Saint Luke's. You're one of my parishioners. This is your time of need. I'm here for you. But I'm also here for you every other day of the week."

"Thank you, Reverend. I want to know why. Why would a loving God take away my wife?"

"I don't have an answer for you, Mr. Taylor."

"Why not? You're the minister."

"I am. But God doesn't tell me His secret plans. And if I told you right now that all things, including this, work for the good, you probably wouldn't believe me."

"You're right. Because this isn't good. Not good at all. In fact, I hate God for it. Does that make me a sinner?"

"Mr. Taylor, I've said the same thing myself."

"You have?"

"Yes, I have. I've challenged God to tell me how the bad can be good."

"Did he answer you?"

"No. Not directly."

"Coward."

Ember smiled. "Seems like it, doesn't it?"

"You don't think he's a coward? You don't think he's evil?"

"No, I don't. I do know I don't understand everything. And if God is Who I believe He is, then He is way beyond my understanding. That's why He sent Jesus. So I and you can understand something of what God is like."

"Would Jesus have killed my wife?"

"He wouldn't kill your wife directly, no."

"So, is the devil stronger than God?"

"No. God has a mission that is beyond our knowledge. This is seen in the book of Job. It's a story, an explanation of why bad things happen to good people."

"And why do they?"

"Ultimately, they display God's grace, love, and mercy. Ultimately. Which means when we are in the midst of despair, we probably won't see God at work. We might. But even Job ended up stumbling in the story. And that's because we usually want to justify ourselves instead of God."

"That's not a lot of comfort, Reverend."

"No, it's not. Not right now, anyway. And maybe not for a long time to come. For myself, I was bitter for a very long time before I finally came to see and understand I don't know everything. Even everything about myself."

Owen Taylor wiped his eyes.

"We'll go now. But if you want an audience when you curse God, I'm here. I'll listen."

"The language might be colorful."

"Mr. Taylor, I may look young and naïve, but I assure you I have seen, heard, and done things that would curl your hair."

"I don't believe it."

"I am not lying. I am ashamed of my past. But Jesus told the Apostle Paul that we are new beings in Christ Jesus, and in that truth I take comfort and put my trust."

Ember stood. "May the Lord bless you, Mr. Taylor. May He make His face to shine upon you, and may He give you peace in this your hour of need."

"Goodbye, Reverend. Mr. Thurgood. I believe you were being honest. Maybe we'll talk again sometime."

"I hope so, Mr. Taylor. God be with you."

When they were in the entryway, Clair-Ann thanked them for coming.

Ember asked, "How are you holding up?"

"I'll be fine. It's Father I'm worried about. In spite of how Mother treated him, it seems he truly loved her. I guess it's something I never considered."

"If you need to talk, or just want some company, don't hesitate to call me. Please. I'm here for you."

"I know you are. It's Father. He has me worried. He needs help more than I do."

"I'll be back."

"Thanks, Rev. I appreciate that. You're a good minister. Maybe the best we've ever had. Thank you."

Ember hugged Clair-Ann, and then she and Harry left.

Walking to the car, Harry noticed Reece Sovern's car parked across the street.

"Look who's back, Em. Our good friend, Reece. I have a feeling a trial's coming our way to work some patience."

The driver's window on the black car rolled down and Sovern said, "Why don't you two head down to the station? Time we had a little chat."

28

WEDNESDAY, 14 FEBRUARY 9:01 AM

THE ROOM WAS PAINTED OD GREEN. MILITARY. WORLD WAR II. Olive Drab Green. It smelled of Pine Sol.

Who on earth okayed painting this room this color? Harry Thurgood wondered. *This is downright hideous.*

A police officer he didn't recognize stood by the door.

Insurance, I suppose, that I don't kill myself now that I've been caught.

He checked his watch. *Eighteen minutes and counting.*

When Reece had driven off, Harry texted Stanton asking him to meet Ember at the police station as soon as possible.

"What about you?" she'd asked.

"I'll be all right. Reece will be going after you, because you are the one who has history with Cally. Say nothing. Let Stanton do the talking."

As soon as they got to the police station, they were separated. Ember taken to one interrogation room, Harry to the other.

The door opened and in walked two women. They sat on the opposite side of the table from him.

Both women were about average height. The one had blonde hair that was severely pulled back into a bun on the back of her head. She wore a charcoal gray pants suit with a white blouse. No jewelry.

The other woman was obviously a police officer. The uniform being the dead giveaway. She had brown hair cut in what would be considered a man's short hair style. It was combed over to the side. And Harry guessed she didn't use any hair styling product.

The blonde spoke. "I'm Assistant District Attorney Amanda Horton and this is Officer Georgia Jean Riggins. And just to let you know, we're recording this interview. It's cheaper than having a stenographer present and alleviates taking notes, which are invariably incomplete."

"How convenient for you," Harry said.

"And you," the blonde retorted. "This way we don't have to drag your sorry ass back in here to clear things up. Capiche?"

"I'm truly puzzled why women today seem to feel the need to be vulgarly aggressive," Harry said, and then folded his arms across his chest, leaned back in the chair, and favored the Assistant DA with a smile.

Horton started to say something, stopped, took a deep breath, exhaled, and then asked, "Did you know the deceased, Mr. Thurgood?"

"Which deceased is that? There are so many."

"Caldwell Taylor. Usually went by the diminutive 'Cally'," Riggins answered.

"A positive ID has been made?"

"Yes. Dental records. From right here in town."

"I see. Uh, no, I didn't know her. Just a face I recognized and said hello to on occasion."

"Your wife never mentioned her?" Horton asked.

"You didn't ask me that. You asked if *I* knew her and the answer is no, I did not."

"You a lawyer, Mr. Thurgood?" Horton asked.

"I'm not licensed to practice law in the state of Texas."

Horton closed her eyes and Harry imagined she was counting to ten.

"Do you smoke?" Riggins asked.

"Why do you want to know?"

"Do you own a coffee shop known as the Really Good Wood-Fired Coffee Shop?" Horton asked.

"That's common knowledge and the answer is yes."

"Did your wife ever mention Mrs. Taylor to you?" Horton asked.

"Now *that*, Ms. Horton, is a very interesting question. I'll have to hold off answering until my attorney is present. And maybe I won't answer it at all. I mean let's be honest here: anything I say can and will be used against me. Isn't that so, Ms. Horton?"

"Do you want to be arrested for obstructing justice, Mr. Thurgood?"

"How am I obstructing? I haven't lied to you. I haven't tried to bribe you, or threaten you. I haven't destroyed evidence. I haven't interfered with your investigation. In fact, you're fishing. You don't even know if I have any evidence."

"You're not answering my questions."

"And that's because I have the right to remain silent. And anything I say can be used against me in a court of law. So why in God's name do I want to give you ammunition to use against me or my wife? *And* my attorney is not present. I assume he's currently with my wife."

"So you aren't going to answer my questions?" Horton asked.

"It all depends on the questions. Let's be honest here. My track record with you folks has not been good. I have nothing against Reece Sovern. Nevertheless, for some reason, he has an issue with me. I seem to be his go-to guilty party. Now, as it turns out, I could sue you all for harassment."

"Why don't you?" Riggins asked.

"Because you all have a job to do and I'm more than willing to help if I can."

"Like getting that lawyer of yours to get that Reston kid off the hook when everybody knows he's a killer. Killed his father and the business manager of that religious freak show the family put on."

Horton put her hand on Riggin's arm.

"The kid was entitled to an attorney, Officer. Or didn't they teach you that in school? I don't have to talk to you. At all. If you have enough evidence compiled to arrest me for a crime, then arrest me. If you don't, then go fish elsewhere. This fish ain't biting."

Assistant DA Horton stood. "Very well, Mr. Thurgood, you're free to leave." She shut off the recorder. "But be forewarned, we have two excellent investigators in our office. And you have just moved to the top of my list."

"Now who is threatening whom? Is it any wonder why a majority of citizens in this fair land have no respect for the government, the courts, or law enforcement? You people are out of control."

Harry turned to the door, the officer opened it for him, and he strode from the room.

He found a place to sit while waiting for Em. He wasn't worried about her. Lauderbach was the best. He could argue circles around these jokers.

What concerns me is the ongoing harassment. These guys are good at it. And I'm afraid it's coming.

29

WEDNESDAY, 14 FEBRUARY 9:01 AM

THE REVEREND EMBER COLE SAT AT THE BATTLESHIP GRAY TABLE IN the battleship gray interrogation room. Her head was bowed, her hands folded, her lips faintly moving in prayer.

Standing by the door was Officer Hans Winkler.

There was a knock at the door, and Hans opened it.

In strode Stanton Mirabeau Lauderbach. He turned to face Hans. "If you don't mind, I'd like a few minutes with my client."

Hans nodded and left.

Stanton sat in the empty chair next to Ember. She lifted her head and turned to look at her attorney.

"Hello, Stanton. How bad is it this time?"

"Why don't you tell me?"

"Cally and I had a fight outside the Really Good."

"Physical?"

"She slapped me and I told her she was dead."

"Anyone hear that?"

"Graham Huston."

"Anyone see the slap?"

"Chief Jager. He wanted to know if I wanted to press charges. I said no."

"The slap is in your favor."

Ember continued. "But there's a history of political opposition at church between us. Sometimes quite heated."

"The DA might make something of that. We won't volunteer it. Let them find it out themselves. Anything else?"

"No. I didn't kill her."

"That's nice to know. But my job is to defend you. Guilt or innocence is up to judge and jury."

"You don't care if I'm innocent or guilty?"

"Not really. I will do my best to defend you. Haven't lost a case in twenty-five years. If you are in fact innocent, that just makes my job easier."

"So what do I do?"

"They'll ask questions. At this point, they're fishing. I'll tell you which ones not to answer. The rest are up to you. Unless there's one I think you should answer in case you're inclined not to."

The door opened and in walked a man that Ember immediately remembered. Assistant District Attorney Chuck Dillon.

She'd watched him interview Jearlene Reston for the murder of her husband, and Ember thought at the time he'd be running for office someday. She still held the same opinion.

His dark hair was perfectly coiffed. The charcoal gray three–piece suit he was wearing was exquisitely tailored. His shirt was white, collar crisply starched, and around his neck he wore a light gray and red repp tie.

Following him into the room was Reece Sovern. He was wearing his rumpled navy blue two-piece suit. White shirt, with the top button unbuttoned, and his tie hanging loose around his neck.

They sat on the opposite side of the table from Ember and Stanton.

"I'm Chuck Dillon, an Assistant District Attorney with the DA's office."

"I know who you are, Mr. Dillon. Have you decided to run for office yet?"

Ember enjoyed the look of surprise on his face.

"Uh, I'm not running for office."

"I see."

Dillon cleared his throat. "It seems, Ms. Cole, that you and your boyfriend—"

"Husband. Harry Thurgood is my husband."

"Ah, yes. Very clever of you to take the common law route."

"We took the common law route not because it was clever, but because we didn't wish to pay the government to do something that is none of their business."

"I see. It's no wonder you and your *husband* are always at cross purposes with the law. You two sound like a couple of anarchists."

"Now, Chuck," Stanton began, but Ember's hand on his arm stopped him.

"Mr. Dillon, I'm a Christian. And if you were taught any history in school, you will know that Christians were unfairly persecuted for being atheists and anarchists. We are neither. I am neither. And the same for Mr. Thurgood. Yet, it does seem that we are unfairly persecuted..." Ember cast a glance towards Sovern, before continuing. "And continue to be unfairly persecuted. Now, I believe you have a few questions to ask."

Dillon cleared his throat. "We're recording this interview because it's better than taking notes and provides more information than a stenographer's transcription.

"Now, Ms. Cole, did you know the deceased, Caldwell Taylor?"

"Yes."

"In what capacity?"

"She was my lay leader at Saint Luke's Methodist Church. The church I pastor."

"Will you describe your relationship with the late Mrs. Taylor?"

"This isn't a courtroom, Chuck," Stanton said. "What do you want to know?"

Dillon shot Stanton a perturbed look before refocusing on Ember. "Where were you from midnight to six this morning?"

"I was in bed with my husband."

"He'll verify this?"

Stanton chuckled. "Now, you know as well as I do that you can't make spouses testify against each other. What's your next question?"

Ember watched Dillon look at Reece Sovern, who shrugged, pushed his glasses up, and rolled the green corona to the other side of his mouth.

Dillon then focused on her. "There are witnesses to the fact that you had an argument yesterday with the deceased in front of the Really Good. You were shouting at her and then she slapped you, causing a nosebleed. Did you kill her in retaliation?"

"No. I didn't kill her."

"You're going to stick with that?"

"Yes."

Reece Sovern said, "There are a lot of witnesses that you and Mrs. Taylor had an acrimonious relationship. Do you stand by your answer? I mean, maybe the fight yesterday was the proverbial straw."

Stanton stood. "You gentlemen are fishing. There are no fish to be caught here."

Dillon said, "Sit down, Stanton, I'd like to get the Reverend's opinion."

"Very well." Stanton sat back down.

"If you didn't kill Mrs. Taylor, do you have any idea who might have done so?"

"No."

"None at all?"

"No. Like anyone else, she had people who liked her and people who didn't. I did not travel in her circle. I do not know everyone she knew. Of the people we both knew, I cannot imagine any of them would kill her. Shun her maybe. But not kill her."

"Did you hate her?" Sovern asked.

"I don't hate anyone, Mr. Sovern. There are people I don't particularly like. But hate? No. I try to love everyone as Jesus would."

"Who has keys to your church building?" Dillon asked.

"I don't know. You'll have to ask Fred Hampton. He's the building manager and sits on the board of trustees."

"That will be all for now," Dillon said.

"Let us know if you take any trips," Sovern added.

Ember and Stanton left. Harry, who'd been waiting for a few minutes, joined them.

"How did it go?" he asked.

"Early days," Stanton said. "Cut short a fishing expedition. But they'll be back."

"That's what I'm afraid of," Harry said. "Reece is still angry about the Reston kid."

"The kid needed an attorney," Stanton countered. "You did nothing wrong."

"No, I didn't," Harry agreed. "But Reece sees it as a betrayal of trust. Em and I have bullseyes on our foreheads, as far as he's concerned. This isn't going to be pretty."

30

WEDNESDAY, 14 FEBRUARY 10:14 AM

HARRY DROPPED EMBER OFF AT THE CHURCH AND CONTINUED ON TO the Really Good.

He parked in the alley behind the shop, searched his car, found a tracking device, smashed it, and walked into his place of business.

Miguel flipped an egg on the flattop grill. "They didn't arrest you. That is good, Mr. Thurgood. Very good. We have had a steady stream of customers all morning."

"Interesting," Harry replied. "Seems murder is good for business."

"I have a cousin," Miguel began, then laughed, and said, "Not really."

Harry chuckled. "Some days I'd be tempted to hire this cousin."

"No worries today. It is a good day."

"That it is." Harry straightened his tie, ran his fingers through his hair, and walked out to the front of his shop.

Jack Bonhoffer was at the counter taking an order. There were three other people sitting at the counter eating breakfast.

Estrelita was waiting at a table of four women. Single women occupied two other tables, and a single man occupied a third.

The man drew Harry's attention. He was dressed in blue jeans and a flannel shirt in some sort of tartan pattern that was heavy on the blues and greens. The sleeves were rolled up to mid-forearm.

He was drinking coffee and eating a doughnut. His eyes gave the shop the once over every minute or so. Not overly obvious, but obvious enough if you were paying attention.

I wonder who he's working for? Harry asked himself. *Maybe he's Mary Lou's new guy. And the one putting tracking devices on my car.*

Harry's phone chimed. He took it out of his pocket and looked at the screen. The text message read:

The fat lady's on stage.

He smiled while slipping his phone back into his pocket.

At least I can still spot them, he said to himself. *And now I know who to keep an eye on.*

He let his eyes take in the activity in the shop. Everything seemed under control. He poured himself a cup of coffee, asked Miguel to make him a bacon sandwich, and made his way to his table in the corner.

The coffee was excellent. Miguel had gotten the roast perfect.

Maybe I should give the shop to Miguel. That would allow me to follow Em and let me help her in the church if she needed me.

Estrelita brought his sandwich. He smiled and told her thanks.

She winked at him and left.

He was just about to take a bite when the bells above the door chimed and in walked Goody Preminger.

Harry watched her make straight for his table.

Her long hair fell in a dark chocolate cascade about her shoulders. She was tall. Harry guessed her age to be in the upper forties. Nevertheless, she took very good care of herself and was still very shapely and appealing to the eye.

Her exceedingly fair skin made a stark contrast with her dark hair. But she knew how to work the contrast and looked stunning in the bottle green dress she was wearing.

"May I sit?" she asked. Her voice was mellow, with a hint of seduction.

Harry stood. "Sure. How are you?"

He pulled a chair out for her, and she sat. "Doing well. Thank you."

"Coffee? Tea? Something to eat?"

"A cup of coffee would be nice."

"I have a wonderful Tanzanian Peaberry."

"Sounds fine. Cream. No sugar."

Harry smiled and got up from the table. *Cream, but no sugar. A little indulgence, but wants to watch her weight.*

He filled the cup, put it on a small tray with a pitcher of cream and a spoon, and returned to the table. He set the tray before her and took his seat.

"Thank you." She added cream, stirred, and took a sip. "Rather luxurious. Not something you'd find at the Piggly-Wiggly."

"Or the Spoon, or the Flower, or anywhere else in town, for that matter."

"So why didn't you respond to my offer? Was it too low? Or is there another reason?"

Harry took a bite of his sandwich, chewed, and swallowed. Goody drank coffee.

"I did think about it. In some ways, I'm still thinking about it."

"Is it money?"

"No, it's not money. It's more along the lines of why."

"Why? Why what?"

"Why do you want to become my business partner?"

"I thought I explained. I'd like something to do. I'm an empty nester. I have my roses. I fence. I sail our boat on the reservoir. I swim. But I still have time on my hands."

"You forgot the Hats."

She smiled.

"You see, I can't help but think Mary Lou is behind this. And I definitely don't want to do business with Mary Lou."

Goody drank coffee.

Harry took a bite of his sandwich.

She looked at him.

He looked at her.

"Yes, you're right. At least partially. This was Mary Lou's idea. I didn't want to. At first. But I've been watching you. And well, I got thinking that if we were business partners that maybe we might become just partners. You're a very handsome man, and, well…"

"Thank you for the compliment. But I'm married."

"*Newly* married. What if I said that doesn't matter? I'm married. Being married takes the pressure off. It's just for fun. No concern about either of us getting serious."

"Unfortunately, it matters to me. You are stunningly attractive. In any other universe, I'd say yes. But not this one. In this one, I'm committed to Ember."

"I see." She sighed. "You can't blame a girl for trying, can you?"

"It never hurts to ask."

"Although the answer may hurt."

"Yes. The answer may hurt. Sometimes a lot."

Goody finished her coffee. "Well, goodbye then. Can we at least be friendly?"

"Very much so."

She stood, and Harry did as well.

"It's a small town. I'll see you around sometime."

"I hope so."

Harry watched her leave.

He sat. *That was weird. Scarlett. Goody. Who's next?*

———

Goody walked over to the Green and sat on a bench. She got out her phone and typed a message.

> Mission failure. Can't buy him out. Can't seduce him.

A moment later there was a reply:

> Cally's murder will give us everything we need to get rid of them. Be at tonight's meeting.

Goody put the phone back in her handbag. *Now things are going to get very nasty.*

31

WEDNESDAY, 14 FEBRUARY 10:15 AM

EMBER COLE WALKED INTO SAINT LUKE'S METHODIST CHURCH through the main doors off Church Street.

She stood in the narthex. The light was soft and dim. The doors to the worship area stood open and the area beyond where she was standing was bathed in a rainbow of light.

She stepped into the worship area. The juxtaposition of the incredible beauty of the biblical scenes in the stained glass and the incredible sadness in her heart formed an incongruity she could not resolve.

"Why, Lord, why?" she called out.

No answer came forth. None from the large cross on the wall at the back of the church. None from the stained glass windows. And no message from the heavens broke through the very solid roof.

She dropped to her knees, and the sobs shook her slender frame. They filled the empty church with the pain of her soul. She lifted her head, extended her arms and hands to heaven, and cried, "*Mea culpa! Mea culpa! Mea culpa!*"

For a moment she held the pose: hands and eyes reaching out to heaven. Then she fell forward and lay on the floor. And in gut-wrenching sobs, cried, "My fault. My fault. It's all my fault."

From the front of the worship area, a voice broke through Ember's grief. She realized the voice was asking a question.

She lifted her head and saw a man and a woman standing in front of the altar.

The woman repeated her question: "What's your fault?"

Ember noticed the woman was wearing a police uniform. The man standing next to her was wearing a navy blue suit.

A fine time for the police to show up, Ember said to herself.

She slowly got to her feet, ran her hands down the front of her dress, and asked, "Who are you?"

"I'm Officer Riggins with the Magnolia Bluff police department," the woman said. "And this is David Scott, an investigator with the district attorney's office."

Ember put a smile on her face. "I'm Ember Cole, the pastor of Saint Luke's, and I'm afraid you interrupted my time of prayer. You might say I was in the confessional of my God."

"Very clever, Ms. Cole," Riggins said. She turned to the DA investigator. "This one and her husband, the coffee shop owner, Harry Thurgood." She left the sentence a fragment.

"Since you are in my church, may I ask what you are doing here?"

"Your church?" Riggins said. "I thought it was the people's church."

"It is. I am the chief operations officer, you might say. I am the shepherd who is responsible for the welfare of the sheep. God is the founder, owner, and CEO. I'm the COO of this particular branch of His company. Does that clarify things for you?"

"Yes, it does," Riggins answered. "Thoroughly."

The man said, "Officer Riggins was just showing me the crime scene when we heard you. We didn't mean to intrude." To Riggins, he said, "Let's go and leave the pastor to her prayers."

When they were gone, Ember looked around the sanctuary, and then laughed. "No sanctuary here," she said out loud.

She turned around, walked out the front door, crossed the lawn to the parsonage, got her car, and drove out to the west side of the reservoir. And there, in the seclusion of her car and nature, poured her heart out to God.

———

When they were in the office area, looking at the crime scene tape across the office door, Georgia Jean Riggins said to David Scott, "You can count on it. She and her common-law husband are up to their necks in this. Guilty as sin."

"Where's the proof?"

"That's our job to get it. And we will. Just like I learned in Sunday school. Pick up the manna and you don't go hungry. The evidence is here, David. We just need to pick it up."

32

WEDNESDAY, 14 FEBRUARY 1:29 PM

HARRY THURGOOD UNLOCKED THE FRONT DOOR OF THE PARSONAGE and entered. He called out Ember's name, and when he received no response, he walked to the kitchen and set the bag he was carrying on the table.

Returning to the living room, he saw Wilbur, and said, "Hey buddy, where's your mistress?"

Wilbur looked at him, yawned, and put his head back down.

"Yeah, there are days when I feel exactly like that."

He took out his phone, typed, and sent the text.

A minute later, he read,

On my way home. See you soon.

He looked at the cat. "Your mistress will be home soon."

Wilbur moved so that his head was upside down.

Harry shrugged and returned to the kitchen. He took the food out of the bag, set the table, and waited for her in the living room.

He was stretched out in one of the wingbacks by the fireplace, hands behind his head, thinking about nothing in particular, when he heard the key in the door lock.

When he saw Ember, he did a double take. She was wearing a dark blue dress with a pattern of flowers in red, green, and yellow. The sleeves were long, the neckline rounded, and the hem was mid-calf. On her feet were white socks, with fold-down lacy tops, and dark blue Mary Janes.

"I have to say, you look nice."

She smiled. "Thank you. Bought it at Lily's. I think the necklace goes well with it."

"It does. You were out shopping all morning?"

"No. Spent a lot of time in prayer. Did you bring lunch? Or should I make something?"

"I had Miguel make us lunch. It's on the table."

"Let's eat. I'm hungry."

"Sure."

"What do we have?"

"Hamburgers, cheeseburgers actually, fries, and coleslaw. Is that all right?"

"Yep."

"What do you want to drink?"

"Did you bring anything?"

"No, but we have in the refrigerator Bass Pale Ale and Sam Adams Cream Stout. In the wine rack there's Texas Zinfandel and Black Spanish, plus California Merlot. We also have iced tea."

"I'll have a Sammy. I'm starved."

She sat, and Harry opened the bottle of beer for her and poured it into a glass. He poured himself a glass of Zinfandel and sat opposite her at the small table.

He waited for her to say grace. Instead, he watched her drink beer, lick her lips, and pick up the cheeseburger.

"Are you okay, Em?"

"I am, my love." She took a bite of the burger. Mouth full, she managed to get out, "Oh my God, this is so good."

"Miguel gets the best beef."

She poured ketchup, dunked a fry, and popped it into her

mouth.

"Care to let me in on what's going on?"

"I'm resigning. In fact, I'm leaving the ministry. I'm going to be your wife. The hostess with the mostest at the shop. And hopefully have your baby."

Harry set the wineglass down. "What brought this on?"

"I was in the church praying and an Officer Riggins interrupted me. A DA investigator was with her. She was nasty. The cop, that is."

"She interrogated me. And yes, she is."

"Since I couldn't pray in peace at the church, I drove over to the west side of the reservoir and prayed there."

"Did God appear out of the water and tell you to quit?"

Ember popped a French fry into her mouth. "Very funny, Mister. No, He didn't. But I got thinking."

"That's dangerous."

"Watch it, Buster." Em smiled and continued. "For three years, I've struggled at the church. Age. Being a woman. Mary Lou. Being a Yankee."

"I remember. We talked about all that."

She nodded. "Then it wasn't long after that writer group came here for a retreat that the troubles really began. Louisa's murder. Me being arrested. Effie's death. Then learning it was Rebekah who'd committed all those murders. One every May. After that, we discovered, thanks to Bliss, that Merrick didn't die of natural causes but was murdered.

"Add to all of that Mary Lou's continued attempts to get me in trouble. And now this. A murder right here in Saint Luke's.

"Harry, I just want it all to end. I want to be a simple housewife. That's all I want. Please, can I just be your wife?"

Harry watched her face scrunch up and the tears roll down her cheeks.

He got up, kneeled beside her, and held her.

"Whatever you want, Emmy. I'm okay with whatever you want."

33

WEDNESDAY, 14 FEBRUARY 3:00 PM

POLICE CHIEF TOMMY JAGER HEARD THE KNOCK ON HIS DOOR AND looked up. "Oh, Reece, come on in. Have a seat."

Police Investigator Reece Sovern entered and took a seat on the other side of the desk from the Chief.

"What do you want to see me about?" Sovern asked.

"Got good news for you."

"I could use some."

"I've decided to promote you to Sergeant Investigator."

Sovern pushed his glasses so they sat on the bridge of his nose. The green stogie rolled to the other side of his mouth. "Seriously?"

Jager laughed. "Seriously. The mayor informed me that the city counsel approved my budget request. You get a promotion *and* we're hiring an investigator for your old position."

"Oh, that's fabulous. The wife is going to be so happy. Thanks, Tommy."

"Don't mention it. You've earned it. Any suggestions for your investigator?"

Sovern thought for a moment. "Georgia Jean is a real bulldog. Sharp mind. Helped me on a couple minor cases and was a real asset."

"She is good. Well, then, why don't you let her know she has herself a new job. If she wants it."

"Be glad to."

Jager stood and so did Sovern. They shook hands, and Tommy watched his new sergeant leave.

Now catch us a killer, Reece.

———

Reece was walking on air. Hetta was going to be so happy. And with GJ helping him on a permanent basis, he felt confident they'd solve these murders in no time.

I wonder if they'll put me in a new office. He looked around. *I think I'll stick with this one. I'm used to it.*

There was a knock at the door. Reece looked up and saw Georgia Jean and David Scott.

"Come in. Grab a chair. Got some good news for you, GJ. Well, hopefully good news."

"What's that?"

"I've been promoted to Sergeant Investigator. And if you want it, the Investigator position is yours."

Reece watched her eyes grow big with excitement.

"Oh, yes! Yes! I want it. When do I start?"

"Tommy didn't say. But I see no reason why you can't start right away. After all, we have a murderer to catch. Isn't that right, David?"

"It is, indeed, Sarge."

"Hey, I like that. Sarge Sovern."

They all laughed.

David Scott said, "GJ was showing me the latest crime scene. The one at the church?"

Reece nodded.

"Well, we had a strange experience there." He explained the interaction with the Reverend Ember Cole.

When Scott was done, Reece said, "That is strange. Very strange."

"Sounds to me like the behavior of someone who's guilty," GJ said.

Reece nodded. "Doesn't sound normal. In fact, I'd say we have probable cause to arrest her. We have a murder in her church and she's saying she's guilty."

"But what if she was confessing to something else?" Scott said.

"Possible," Reece replied.

"But we know those two are up to something. And this is the second time murder has occurred because of that church." GJ had a smug look on her face.

Reece nodded. "True."

His index finger repositioned his glasses, and the cigar made its way to the other side of his mouth. "Let's see if Judge Jones will give us an arrest warrant."

34

WEDNESDAY, 14 FEBRUARY 5:51 PM

HARRY SAT IN THE ROCKER-RECLINER WATCHING HIS WIFE SLEEP. IT was obvious she'd reached her limit.

From his childhood, a verse floated to the surface of his mind.

Somewhere it says God won't tempt us beyond what we can bear.

He paused, then said, "Okay, God, if you're out there, Emmy has reached the wall. Now is the time to back off and leave her alone. I hope you're listening. For whatever reason, she loves the church. Don't take that away from her. I know what she said, but she really wants to be a minister. Don't hurt her. Please don't hurt her. There's nothing I can do to you. If you're actually out there somewhere. So I'm simply asking. Be merciful to her. All I want is her happiness."

"Are you talking to me?" Ember asked.

"Hey, sleepyhead. No. I was talking to the man upstairs."

"Is this one of the days you believe in Him?"

"I don't know. I'm just concerned about you."

"Thanks, Harry, love. I guess I had a bit of a breakdown."

"Are you all right?"

She sat up. "Do you like this dress?"

"Very much."

She smiled. "I think I'm better now. Oh, who's at the coffee shop?"

"Jack assured me he could handle things. I assume he closed up at five."

"You've been here the whole time?"

"You bet. I was here looking after the one person who means the most to me in all the world?"

"Truly?"

"Truly."

"Will you make love to me? And afterwards take me out to get something to eat?"

"I like that plan. Are you really going to quit the ministry?"

"Would it be okay if I changed my mind?"

"Fine with me."

"Good. I'll hold off resigning."

"Glad to hear it."

"Come to me?"

The doorbell rang and there was pounding on the door.

"Who the heck is that?" Harry asked.

"Sounds important."

"That it does. Stay here."

Harry went to the door. "Who is it?"

"Police. Open up."

Harry opened the door. "Hello, Reece. What do you want?"

"You and the Reverend Ember Cole."

"What's this about?" Ember asked, standing next to Harry.

Sovern said, "Ember Cole, I have a warrant for your arrest for the murder of Caldwell Taylor. You have the right…"

Everything faded to a sea of red in Harry's vision. The only thing in Harry's mind was the thought, *No more Mr. Nice Guy. Now I fight fire with fire.*

———

Stanton Mirabeau Lauderbach thought, not for the first time, that the city desperately needed to repaint the interview rooms at the police station.

This is shockingly depressing. No wonder the cops get so nasty. After a pause, he continued his thought. *Probably why they painted the rooms these ghastly colors to begin with.*

The door opened, and a police officer entered escorting Ember Cole. The officer then handcuffed her to the table.

"Is that necessary?" Lauderbach asked.

"Just following orders," the officer said.

"This is ridiculous," the lawyer muttered.

The officer left and Stanton studied his client. "How are you holding up?"

"I'm okay." A smile lifted her lips. "They might be getting tired of hearing me sing."

"Good for you. Pulling a Jerri Reston."

Ember laughed. "She sure had them completely helpless when they arrested her. She and her kids not saying a word. Just singing."

"It was a novel twist on not saying anything to incriminate yourself."

"So what's next?"

"Tomorrow, Judge Jones will set bail. The assistant DA is going to push for a high amount because of your arrest a year ago."

"But I was cleared."

"Precisely. I will remind the judge of that. In addition, I'll insinuate the incompetence of the police and DA's office, emphasize you aren't a flight risk, and that you are an asset to the community."

"What about Harry?"

"Wylie will set bail for Harry, as well as the court date. The trial, if we have one, will be before Judge Jones. Wylie's just helping Jones clear his calendar so the judge can get down to his bait shop."

"Wylie can do that?"

"He's a justice of the peace. He can do that."

"Okay."

"No need to be nervous. I have this in the bag. Just sorry you have to spend the night in jail."

"I guess I'll be doing a lot of singing."

"That's the spirit."

Stanton got up, went to the door, opened it, and told the officer he was finished.

He watched Ember leave in handcuffs. *Whoever is responsible for this, their boss is going to get an earful.*

35

WEDNESDAY, 14 FEBRUARY 10:08 PM

REECE SOVERN LOOKED AT THE MAN SITTING ACROSS FROM HIM. Harry Thurgood. Next to Thurgood sat that smarmy lawyer.

He truly did not like Stanton Lauderbach. Too many criminals were walking the streets because of him.

As for Thurgood, Reece didn't not like the man. But he didn't trust him. There was something about the coffee shop owner that just didn't add up.

Reece cast a sidelong glance at the man sitting next to him. Another lawyer he didn't like. Assistant DA Chuck Dillon.

A pompous ass if I ever saw one.

"Look, Thurgood," Dillon began, "we are searching the parsonage, your apartment, and the coffee shop for the knife that killed those people. Why don't you help us and yourself out here?"

Thurgood replied, "And throw my wife under the bus while slitting my own throat? Are you nuts?"

"So, Chuck," Lauderbach began, "you're saying it was a knife that did in Mrs. Taylor?"

"Yes. She was stabbed in the right kidney from the back, then stabbed in the stomach from the front, with a four-inch slash down and to the left. The ME said she might have been alive when her attacker hit her with the cross. Probably dying from the repeated bludgeoning, unless she died from blood loss first. Although the ME thinks it was the bludgeoning that probably killed her."

The Assistant DA turned back to Thurgood. "So, why the kids?"

"The kids? I'm sure I don't know what you're talking about."

Reece said, "DeWayne Sanford and Lila Santiago."

"Tragic. Those kids. So young."

Reece caught Lauderbach's hand going to his mouth to cover a smile and gritted his teeth until he bit off the cigar. He took the soggy wad out of his mouth and picked up the piece that had fallen into his lap and put them in his pocket.

He noticed Thurgood had a Mona Lisa smile on his face.

Dillon began, "What about—"

But Thurgood cut him off. "Look, Mr. Dillon, Reece, I've killed no one and I've not helped anyone to kill anyone. You're wasting your time, my time, and cheating the taxpayers out of their money by collecting a salary while wasting my time and your time.

"In addition, you're also depriving me of a bit of connubial bliss with my wife. Neither of us committed these horrendous murders. My suggestion to both of you is this: go out and find the real killer. And as a warning, when this is over, at least Ember's and my part in it, Stanton will be suing your sorry asses for false arrest. Now, I've said my peace. I will not talk to you from here on out."

"Unless, of course, I encourage him to do so," Lauderbach said.

Dillon shook his head, and the look on his face was venomous. "Interview terminated at ten twenty-seven pm."

To Officer Dick Schreiber, Reece said, "Get him out of here."

Schreiber escorted Thurgood out, with Lauderbach following.

When they were gone, Reece turned to Dillon. "Do you think they'll get low bail?"

"All depends on how fast Jones wants to get down to the bait shop. And these days, he wants to get down there on the double."

Reece nodded. "They'll be walkin' down Main Street by noon, having forked over a buck fifty."

"I hate to say it, but you're probably right. Some days, I wonder if I wouldn't be better off defending these scumbags."

Reece took the cellophane off of a green perfecto and stuck the stogie in his mouth. "Yep. Might be time to rub some dirt on the ol' white hat."

36

THURSDAY, 15 FEBRUARY 10:38 AM

HARRY SAT ON THE BENCH ACROSS FROM THE STONE STEPS AND THE great doors by which one entered and exited the Burnet County Courthouse. He didn't have his pipe with him. He would've enjoyed a smoke.

Justice of the Peace Wylie Garrison had taken ten minutes to listen to the charge against Harry, think about the free coffee he periodically got down at the Really Good — and it was really good — and released Harry on his own recognizance, with the promise that he would show up whenever the police, DA, or the court wanted to see him; especially on the date of his trial.

Harry agreed. Signed the form that said he agreed. And walked out a more or less free man.

He sat on the bench and waited for Ember.

To his mind, the courthouse was one of the most easily forgettable pieces of architecture he had ever seen. The building was just one big rectangular cuboid, clad in beige stone, punctuated with a symmetrical pattern of windows on either side of the central doors.

Whoever the architect was, Harry thought, *he was uniquely devoid of imagination.*

Fergus sat on the opposite end of the bench. "Mornin' Mr. Thurgood."

"Morning Fergus."

"Waitin' for the Missus?"

"I am. Although, I wonder if she is a missus since she kept her name."

"She's a missus. Even if she kept her name, she's still Mistress Thurgood of the House of Thurgood. She's your mistress." He chuckled. "Your legal mistress."

Harry smiled. "My only mistress. Can't handle one woman, let alone more than one."

Fergus pointed with his chin at the building in front of them.

"Built in the Depression with WPA money. The style is Moderne, and it was designed by Lewis Milton Wirtz of Columbus, Texas."

"Interesting. One of the most forgettable buildings I've ever seen."

"Unless you were convicted of murder."

"I suppose. That might make me remember the place."

"There's Mistress Thurgood now. A good day, Master Thurgood."

"Bye Fergus."

Harry didn't watch Fergus leave. His eyes were on Ember.

She and Stanton Lauderbach walked down the steps, across the small plaza, and joined Harry.

"Looks like Judge Jones let you out," he said.

Ember sat next to Harry. Stanton stood in front of them.

"He did," Ember said. "Stanton was wonderful, as usual."

The lawyer laughed. "It's all in the timing. The most important thing to Rutherford B. Jones is holding court in the Pickle Dilly Bait and Tackle Shop. And he's probably on his way there right now."

"Did your freedom cost us anything?" Harry asked.

Stanton answered. "Jones was going to let her go on her own recognizance, but Dillon put up such a big fuss about her prior arrest, which I said was unwarranted, and that Ember and the deceased had been 'enemies', his words, that Jones, to shut him up, set bail at a dollar. Which I think made Dillon even madder."

The lawyer chuckled.

"Stanton paid it for me since they took me away without my purse."

Harry reached for his wallet, but Stanton shook his head.

"I'll get it from you in coffee. How's that?"

"Fine with me."

"Were you serious about suing for false arrest?"

"Yes."

"All right. I'll get the ball rolling so that when they drop the charges, we file."

"Sounds good to me. I'm sick of the harassment."

Stanton had a big grin on his face, and in an exaggerated Texas drawl, said, "You need to git yourself cowboy boots, a ten-gallon hat, and start talkin' like this."

"If I do, shoot me. Please."

Stanton laughed. "Don't say that too loudly, Harry. Someone just might be listening and honor your request. Can I give you two a lift?"

Harry looked at Ember. She shook her head.

"Looks like we're walking. Thanks, Stanton."

"My pleasure."

Ember said, "Before you go, on a different subject, have you seen any more of Scarlett?"

"I've seen a lot more of Scarlett, and beyond that, a gentleman keeps quiet. Thanks for the phone call, Harry."

"My pleasure."

"Take care you too. I'll see you soon."

Stanton walked off to get his car, and Harry and Ember, hand-in-hand, started walking to the Really Good.

"Good to see you, Mister."

"Good to see you, Rev."

"I don't know why Reece doesn't like us."

"Beats the heck out of me. Then again, I think he doesn't not like us either."

There was a pause in the conversation, and then she said, "This is a strange world here."

"Small town Texas?"

Ember nodded.

"Kind of is. I've decided to start a new business in addition to the coffee shop."

"You have? What is it?"

"I'm going to become a hard money lender."

"What is that?"

"A hard money lender is someone with money who loans it out to people. A private lender."

"A loan shark."

Harry smiled. "That's the dark side. A hard money lender is an above board loan business. He loans money to people without a lot of red tape, usually for short time periods. I'll loan money to people who want to flip houses, or renovate rental property, things like that."

"Do you have money to do this?"

"Yes, I do."

"You're quite rich, aren't you?"

"I have enough. *We* have enough."

"That's good to know. I guess. I've never been rich."

"A new experience for you, then."

"It doesn't hurt, does it?"

Harry noticed the smirk on her face and said, "Only when you spend it."

"Oh, great. I'm going from no money to spend to having money I can't spend. Thanks a lot, Mister."

"How much do you want?"

"What do you mean?"

"How much do you want a month?"

"You mean like an allowance?"

"Sure. An allowance."

"For just me?"

"For just you."

"Five hundred?"

"Five hundred thousand is a bit much, don't you think?"

"Like, duh."

They both laughed.

"I don't know, Harry. I've always had to work hard to get money. I'm a good saver. Now, anyway. Wasn't always. Used to spend it as fast as I made it. Or faster. Like most people, I guess. But I learned to be frugal and to save. And I do get a salary from the church that's quite adequate for my needs. So how about this: if I need or want something and can't afford it, I ask you?"

"Works for me."

"So when is Harry the Loan Shark going into business?"

"Immediately. Only I am calling the business Really Good Loans."

"That's original."

"Isn't it, though?"

"I still don't get why."

"I'm going on the warpath, Em. I've had enough of being a target. I'm striking back. My loan business will compete with Fight and hopefully hurt his bank. Even if just a little. I'm going to apply to be on the police department's citizen advisory board. I'm going to start donating to the campaign funds of the mayor, the sheriff, the judges, the JP, and maybe even the dogcatcher. The world runs on money, sad to say, and I'm going to grease the rails — so *our* world runs a whole heck of a lot smoother."

37

WHEN HARRY AND EMBER REACHED THE REALLY GOOD, HE KISSED her goodbye, and she went on to the parsonage to check out what manner of disaster the police had left them.

Harry entered the coffee shop. Estrelita was waiting on a customer and gave him a smile. He greeted Jack Bonhoffer, who was sitting at the cash register.

"Morning, Boss. The police made a right mess of things. But everything is shipshape now."

"Thanks, Jack."

Harry went on back to the kitchen.

"Good morning, Mr. Thurgood."

"Morning, Miguel. Jack said the police made a mess of things."

Miguel spat out an expletive in Spanish. "Yes, they did. But we got everything put back in order. My Tio Diego got us a new door and installed it. We were only an hour and a half late in opening."

"My thanks to your uncle. Do you know how much I owe him?"

"Nothing. Tio had a bad experience with the police three or four years ago. He was glad to help."

"Tell him thanks, but I'd still like to pay him. He can give the money to charity, if he wishes."

"He won't take money."

"Food?"

"Maybe."

"Well, give him a couple pounds of our best coffee and cook him and his family a special meal."

"I'll do that."

"Thanks, Miguel. Now to see what mess they left for me in my apartment."

Harry mounted the stairs to his apartment above the shop. When he saw the bashed-in door, he was royally pissed. Entering his former home did nothing to improve his opinion of the police.

"What a mess," he muttered. "I'll deal with this later. Maybe Tio Diego can fix my door. In the meantime…"

He negotiated the mess and entered his bedroom. The room was in the same shambles as the rest of his place. Luckily, they had not found the loose baseboard behind his dresser.

"Now to begin my campaign."

He grabbed a hip pack and put it on his belt, and from the space behind the baseboard, withdrew several stacks of cash, and put the money in the hip pack.

His pipes were scattered all over the place, and after collecting them and putting them back on his dresser, he chose a beautiful old GBD Prince-shape briar and filled it with Briggs Mixture. *When a feller needs a friend.*

After he got the pipe going, he left the apartment, asked Miguel if his tio could fix the apartment door, and headed off to the *Chronicle* office.

Monika Crow was at her desk when Harry entered.

"Graham's not here, Harry, you'll have to put up with me. And there's no smoking in here."

Harry put his pipe in his pocket. "Truth be told, I'd rather put up with you."

"Now you shouldn't have said that. It just might find its way into my column.'

"If it does, I'll cut Graham off from my coffee and take my business to Marble Falls."

"You must be in a bad mood to go nuclear."

"I am. But, to show that I'm committed to peace, love, and harmony, I want to buy a full-page ad."

Harry watched Monika's mouth drop. "Say what?"

"A full-page ad. Page two ought to be fine. In fact, let's make it two full-page ads. One on two and one on four."

"Well, sit yourself right down. Sorry, all I have is this tacky plastic chair."

"That was a fast recovery."

Monika laughed. "Yeah. Money does that."

Harry chuckled. "That it does."

"So you want two full-page ads for the coffee shop?"

"No."

"No?"

"No. The page two ad is to announce my new business. Really Good Loans."

"Are you serious?"

"Yes, I am." Harry went on to explain what the business was and what he wanted in the ad, while Monika took notes.

"No one in town is doing this," Monika said. "As a legitimate business, that is."

"Now someone is."

"May I ask why?"

"You may ask, but I'm not saying. At least for now."

Monika winked. "Keeping a girl in suspense, eh?"

Harry laughed. "For now."

"Your page four ad?"

"The launching of Really Good Frozen Custard. Just like ice cream — only better."

"I like that. Well, Mr. Got Bucks, I've never known anyone to take out one, let alone two, full-page ads. That's going to set you back thirty-five hundred dollars."

Harry opened his hip pack, counted out the money in twenty, fifty, and hundred dollar bills, and set it on Monika's desk.

"And no one's ever given me this much cash before. What did you do, break the piggy bank?"

"Something like that."

"You sure are the man of mystery, Harry."

He smiled. "Good. I like it that way."

Monika laughed. "Must be nice to get what you want."

"At least some of the time."

"So, do you care to give me a scoop?"

"About what?"

"Why you're out walking around, instead of over there doing an imitation of a caged bird?"

Harry thought for a moment. "Will the article show Em and me in a favorable light?"

"You just bought yourself some favorable press with those ads. Graham will be very happy about them, and that means I'll get another paycheck. So sing to me, Harry, and I'll make sure it's a sweet song."

Harry sang.

38

THURSDAY, 15 FEBRUARY 12:01 PM

HARRY WAS SITTING ON A BENCH ON THE GREEN FACING THE REALLY Good. He was smoking his pipe.

The frozen custard launch was Saturday. A phone call to Elisha Reston confirmed the young man would be there for the launch.

After all, if it wasn't for Elisha, I probably wouldn't be doing this.

As for the loan business, Harry had quickly made a sign announcing the new enterprise and put it in the window of the Really Good. An official-looking sign would arrive in three weeks.

I've tried to live a quiet and unassuming life to no avail. These people want to play hardball. Okay. Game on.

Step one. Improve financial standing in town. Now in progress.

Step two. Em and I have to solve the murder of Cally Taylor. Because Reece and company keep barking up the wrong tree. So how do we go about doing that?

He watched Scarlett Hayden get out of her enormous Land Rover, cross the street, and the Green, and sit next to him on the bench. So much next to him a butter knife would have had difficulty separating them.

"Hello, Scarlett."

"Hello, Harry."

"Welcome to my bench."

She laughed a deep, throaty laugh. "I want to thank you for making that call for me."

"You're welcome. My pleasure. I like to help my friends."

"I love you, Harry, but Stanton is a worthy substitute. He's charming, engaging, interesting, listens, and has good manners. He's a bit stuck on himself, but it is just a bit. And he knows how to make a girl very happy in bed."

"Probably too much information. However, I'm happy that you're happy."

"So, what's with this new business?"

Harry told her.

"Very interesting. Well, I will do my best to steer business your way."

"Thank you."

There was a brief lull in the conversation and then Scarlett asked, "What are you going to do about the Taylor murder?"

"Try to solve it."

"That's a given. How?"

"Find someone with a motive who also had the means and opportunity."

"Everyone has access to a knife. And access to the altar cross was easy enough as well. So that leaves motive and opportunity."

Harry nodded. "True. Cally was a termagant—"

"A what?"

"A termagant. A female curmudgeon."

"Learn something new every day."

"Indeed. Cally was a mean-spirited, angry woman. She was power hungry. Obsessed with controlling her church. And she did indeed see it as her church."

"Like Mary Lou."

"Exactly. How those two got along is beyond me."

Scarlett smiled. "Marriage of convenience. Divide control of the church. Each, of course, vying for ultimate control one day."

"Which means Mary Lou should be a suspect. With Cally gone, she can return and take over the entire enchilada."

"It's a thought. Although, still mending from her injury, I can't see her killing Cally."

"No. She'd hire somebody, or convince somebody, to do it."

"Yes. That's much more her style. So, Harry, you have one suspect. Who else?"

"What's the standard line? Those nearest and dearest are the most likely suspects?"

"That's what they say. But the police seem to have dismissed the family. Do you know why?"

"No, I don't. And that's a good point. I'll have to find out."

"I'll nose around and see if I can uncover anything."

"Thanks, Scarlett."

"Don't mention it. It's what we do for those we love."

———

Eliška poured tea for Mary Lou Fight and Tipper Duvall.

"Thank you, Eliška. You may go."

The maid left and Mary Lou turned her attention to her guest.

"I must say, Tipper, the situation at Saint Luke's could not be better for us now that Cally is out of the way."

"Very true, my Queen."

"You've done a marvelous job keeping your true relationship to me a secret. I knew I was doing the right thing making you a secret Crimson Hat member."

"Thank you, my Queen."

"Now with Cally gone, you can focus your full attention on Ms. Cole. You will continue making sure the members of your committee do not support Ms. Cole as pastor of the church."

"Yes, my Queen. The committee is solidly behind you."

"Good. I, of course, have ways to discover if they are not."

"You can trust me fully, my Queen."

"I should hope so. I doubt your husband would be sympathetic if he learned of your little indiscretion."

Tipper bowed her head. "Please, my Queen. I'm loyal."

"I know you are. We shall see how this plays out. We may have to do nothing. Cally's murder and Ms. Cole's arrest may accomplish all that we desire."

"Yes, my Queen."

Mary Lou rang a bell. "Eliška will show you out."

———

Ember was busy putting the parsonage back together after the police search, when she heard the doorbell ring.

She opened the door and saw Claiborne Allen, the chairperson of the church council, standing on the other side of the threshold.

"Hello, Claiborne, please come in."

"Hello, Reverend. I hate to trouble you, but I think this is important."

Ember stood aside to let the older man enter, then led him to the chairs by the fireplace where they sat.

"Euel Pinckney has more or less forced me to call a meeting of the council," Claiborne said. "Tonight. Eight o'clock."

"Well, this can't be good."

"No, it's not. The bishop's also going to be at the meeting."

"Definitely not good. Do you know what the meeting's about? Although I can probably guess."

"Discussion on putting you on a leave of absence until this arrest is no longer an issue, and to decide on a new lay leader."

"Who do they want as the new lay leader?"

"Don't know. Euel wouldn't say a word."

"Okay. Thanks for the warning. I'll be there."

"I don't like it that the bishop will be there."

"Do you know whose idea it was?"

"No, I don't. My guess is that he was invited by Euel, or someone on that side."

"Reasonable."

"I'll do what I can to make sure everyone is there."

"Thanks, Claiborne. I appreciate your support."

"You're God's servant to us. And you've been a mighty fine pastor. Thanks for puttin' up with us."

Ember walked him to the door, where they said goodbye. When he was gone, she sat on the sofa and prayed.

39

THURSDAY, 15 FEBRUARY 8:04 PM

EMBER COLE, SEATED AT THE FOOT OF THE TABLE, WATCHED THE LAST minute arrivals file into the conference room and take their seats.

At the head of the table was Claiborne Allen. To his right sat Bishop Harold Oscar Cobb. Ember knew the bishop was near retirement age. And according to the gossip, he was counting the days. The last thing he wanted was hassle.

To Claiborne's left sat Euel Pinckney. He was a humorless man, at least in Ember's estimation. Numbers were all that mattered. And since he was the church treasurer, Ember supposed he didn't need humor. But it would be nice if he smiled once in a while.

Everyone was present, save for Cally. And she would never be present again.

Sitting in a corner behind her was Harry, and in the opposite corner was Berneice Sharpless.

Ember assumed Berneice was the candidate the other side was putting up for lay leader to replace Cally.

"We're all here," Claiborne said, "so let's get this meeting started. Bishop, would you mind saying a prayer?"

"Certainly not," Bishop Cobb replied. "Heavenly Father, the work of your church…"

Ember tuned out. The bishop would be at it for at least two minutes. Her mind turned to Berneice. She was a lifelong member. Not overly active in the church, but not an absentee member either. If she was willing to be talked into trying for the lay leader position, she was at least nominally in the Fight-Taylor-Pinckney camp.

The real question, as Ember saw it, was how much did Berneice truly want the position of lay leader, which was often a thankless job.

Claiborne's voice broke into Ember's thoughts. "Our first order of business is deciding on a lay leader."

Maness Sebren, Chair of the Board of Trustees, blurted out, "What's Harry Thurgood doing here?"

Claiborne said, "Reverend?"

"Harry is now your pastor's husband. He will be joining our church and being my spouse he'll be taking an active part in the life of our church. I asked him to join me so he could see how our church is run."

Sebren said, "I don't like it. It's highly irregular."

Wilma Greening, President of the United Methodist Women, said, "What's the problem, Maness? Our meetings aren't closed."

"No, they aren't," Sebren replied, "but he's not a member."

Ruth Ann Covington, the seventeen-year-old representative from the United Methodist Youth, said, "Can we just get on with this? I have homework to do."

"Is Mr. Thurgood's presence a problem?" Claiborne asked.

Ember watched his eyes take in everyone at the table.

"Okay. Not a problem. By the way, welcome, Mr. Thurgood."

"Thank you," Harry replied.

"All right," Claiborne said. "Let's talk about the lay leader position."

Tipper Duvall, Chairperson of the Pastor-Parish Relations Committee, said, "I move that we elect Berneice Sharpless Lay Leader of Saint Luke's Methodist Church to fill out the term of Caldwell Taylor."

"Second," Euel Pinckney called out.

Ember could see the frustration on Claiborne's face.

"Tipper, Euel, this is not how we're supposed to do things," Claiborne said. "You know that."

Jane Jackson, the Young Adult representative, said, "Aren't we supposed to come to an agreement? Voting just causes problems."

Claiborne looked at the bishop, who gave him a slight nod of his head, then turned back to the people sitting around the table. "The Book of Discipline recommends consensus and discernment for making decisions."

Sebren said, "The key word there is *recommends*. Consensus is not mandatory. There's a motion on the floor. I say we proceed."

"Very well," Claiborne said, "Do you want to speak in favor of the motion, Tipper?"

"I do. Berneice is a lifelong member of our church. She's grown up here. She knows our church and what our church needs. Her service on numerous committees speaks to her dedication. I think she'll make a wonderful lay leader."

"Does anyone wish to speak against the motion?" Claiborne asked.

Jane Jackson said, "I have a question for Ms. Sharpless."

"Okay, ask," Claiborne said.

"Ms. Sharpless, what do you think is the most important ministry of the church? I know they're all important, but which one should be our primary focus?"

Berneice Sharpless got to her feet. "Well, uh, yes, they are all important and I'll do my best to see to it that no ministry area is neglected."

She started to sit down, but Jane stopped her. "You didn't answer my question."

Berneice stood up straight. "I didn't?"

"No. We only have so much money. What ministry would you advocate for and recommend that the most money and volunteers be committed to? Because, when we draw up a budget, we are setting priorities. So, what would be your top priority?"

"I think we should focus on the ministries that provide for the nurture of our aging congregation. Everyone in Magnolia Bluff is churched. And we aren't growing. So it only makes sense to take care of our own."

"What about spreading the gospel as John Wesley did?" Blake Hillwood, President of the United Methodist Men, asked.

"We shouldn't ignore evangelism. But who would we share it with? Everyone is churched. We shouldn't steal the members of other churches. That's why focusing on our own seems the best course."

Marveen Smalls, the lay member to the annual conference, said, "You make it sound like we're on our deathbeds, Berneice. Reverend Cole has repeatedly mentioned that there is a college on our doorstep filled with the unchurched. Spring, summer, and fall, the unchurched visit us, many staying at Hayden's Resort. On any given Sunday, nearly half of Magnolia Bluff doesn't go to church. Seems to me we have a lot of work to do and we aren't doing it. We're letting the Baptists do it."

"Mr. Chairman?"

"Yes, Reverend?"

"Unless someone else wishes to speak, I think we've heard what we need to in order to make a decision. Perhaps we can pray and then take the vote."

"Any objection to praying and then voting?" There was a pause. "Seeing no objections, let us pray over this decision we are about to make. Pray silently and in about thirty seconds or so, we'll vote."

Ember bowed her head and prayed for a decision that wouldn't cause further acrimony.

"All right folks," Claiborne began, "the Lord has heard our prayers. Berneice, do you want to stay or would you prefer to leave and I can call you with the results later?"

"Um, uh, I think I'll go. You can call me."

"Will do."

Ember watched the older woman leave. *I wonder if she truly wants the position or was railroaded into it?*

"Okay. All those in favor of the motion to elect Berneice to the lay leader job, raise your hand."

Ember watched Claiborne count.

When he finished, he said, "All opposed, raise your hand."

Claiborne counted. "Well, as you can see, we have ourselves a tie. The motion fails. I suggest we all do some more prayin' and come up with a new candidate everyone can accept. Now to the next order of business. It seems some are of the opinion that Reverend Cole should take a leave of absence until there is an outcome on the arrest warrant. The bishop is here. Y'all speak your minds. And no motions."

"We have to think of the reputation of our church," Tipper Duvall said. "How does it look to the community if we have a minister who's under suspicion of murder? And suspicion of killing one of her own parishioners. One with whom she had an acrimonious relationship."

"How did it look when Christians were thrown to the lions on trumped-up charges?" Ruth Ann Covington said.

"That's hardly the same thing," Euel Pinckney responded.

"I don't know," Jane Jackson said. "Lazy ass authorities looking for easy scapegoats are lazy ass authorities looking for easy scapegoats. Doesn't matter the country or the century."

Ember tuned out the discussion. It was the same stuff her detractors repeatedly brought up. She looked at Harry. He winked and smiled at her. She smiled back.

What would I do without that man? He's my rock and shield. My staunchest defender.

She turned around just as the bishop was finishing asking a question. "I'm sorry Bishop, would you repeat that please?"

"What is your opinion on this?"

"If I should take a leave of absence?"

"Yes."

"I do think often about this question, because it seems we discuss it often."

There were several sniggers.

Ember continued. "William Cowper wrote a wonderful hymn. We know it as 'O for a closer walk with God.' It's a prayer, actually. Pray it with me." She sang:

> *O! for a closer walk with God,*
> *A calm and heavenly frame;*
> *A light to shine upon the road*
> *That leads me to the Lamb!*

> *Where is the blessedness I knew*
> *When first I saw the Lord?*
> *Where is the soul-refreshing view*
> *Of Jesus, and his word?*

> *What peaceful hours I once enjoyed!*
> *How sweet their memory still!*
> *But they have left an aching void,*
> *The world can never fill.*

> *Return, O holy Dove, return,*
> *Sweet messenger of rest;*
> *I hate the sins that made thee mourn,*
> *And drove thee from my breast.*

> *The dearest idol I have known,*
> *Whate'er that idol be;*
> *Help me to tear it from thy throne,*
> *And worship only thee.*

> *So shall my walk be close with God,*
> *Calm and serene my frame;*
> *So purer light shall mark the road*

That leads me to the Lamb.

After a few moments passed, Tipper Duvall said, "That's a nice prayer, Reverend, but how does that answer the question of whether or not it would be best if you took a leave of absence?"

"Did you pray the prayer with me?"

"I did."

"Then you confessed with me that we are sinners lured away from God. Those of you who want me to leave look for anything to urge me, or the congregation, or this board, or the bishop to get me to move on. My duty is to minister to sinners and show them the grace of God. Your actions compel me to stay. There are sinners here who need to see and feel and experience the love of Jesus. I did not kill Cally. You either believe me or you don't. But by law, I am innocent until I am proven to be guilty. I will not shirk my duty to you all."

"Any need to pursue this?" Claiborne asked.

Bishop Cobb cleared his throat. "That was well said, Reverend Cole. The problem, as I see it, is negative publicity."

"I know I'm not a member, yet," Harry said, "and excuse me for interrupting, but I am your pastor's husband and by virtue of that fact am in the soup with her. I haven't been in Magnolia Bluff long, but my time here has taught me that this town loves gossip. Which I believe is a sin. Am I right, Bishop?"

Bishop Cobb's eyes opened wide. "Uh, yes, yes it is."

Harry continued. "I will wager that come Sunday, Saint Luke's will be packed. Standing room only. Perhaps you could be here, Bishop, and help Em minister to the gossipmongers. It would also show that you believe a person is innocent until proven guilty. Something to think about. There are a whole lot of you staring at the fly on the painting, and not seeing the painting."

Claiborne said, "Seeing that I'm the chairperson of this council, and knowing we aren't going to reach a consensus tonight, I'm tabling this discussion until our next meeting."

"Can you do that?" Euel Pinckney asked, with more than a bit of venom in his voice.

"I just did. Now, if you want to challenge me, Euel, which isn't how the Book of Discipline urges us to do things, then go right ahead."

Euel stood and walked out of the meeting.

Claiborne stood. "Reverend, please dismiss us with prayer."

"Send us home with your blessing, O Lord, and with your peace. Amen."

Everyone filed out of the room until only Claiborne, Harry, Ember, and the Bishop remained.

Bishop Cobb said, "I'd like a few words with Ember, if you gentlemen don't mind."

40

THURSDAY, 15 FEBRUARY 9:41 PM

BISHOP COBB RESUMED HIS SEAT, AND EMBER TOOK A SEAT NEXT to him.

Cobb spoke. "Ember, I like your zeal, your compassion, and I admire your piety."

Ember smiled. "I feel like a 'but' is coming."

Cobb chuckled. "But Saint Luke's is becoming an administrative nightmare."

"I'm sorry, Bishop, I–"

Cobb held up his hand. "I'm well aware of the politics going on here. One would have to be blind and deaf not to be. And I'm not convinced a new pastor would change anything. Male or female. However, you have a powerful advocate on your side."

"I do?"

"Yes. That husband of yours is a shrewd politician."

"He is? He always says he doesn't like politics."

"He might not like politics, but he knows how to play the game. He sent me a letter."

"He did? He didn't tell me."

"*You* would have told him not to send it. But Harry knows how things work."

"What did the letter say?"

"He told me you two were married. That his intention is to join the church, and that he has deep pockets. Very deep pockets. Now before you get angry, Harry is shrewd. He knows the one thing all churches need is money. And quite frankly, Saint Luke's is not a wealthy congregation. There are a few, yes. And right now it's holding its own. However, the future won't be so bright unless some young blood joins and is active.

"And that's the main reason why I keep you here. You're good for these old fuddy-duddies. And if anyone can bring in new blood it's you."

"But we do have to do something about my unwanted notoriety."

"Yes. And the sooner the better."

"I didn't kill Cally. We didn't see eye-to-eye, but I didn't kill her."

"And I believe you. I'll do what I can to smooth ruffled feathers."

"Harry and I will do the rest. We'll get the police pointed in the right direction."

"Good. You're not ready now, but I hope someday you're sitting where I am."

"Thank you, Bishop, for the vote of confidence."

"This is the trial of your faith. It will not only teach you patience, it will also teach you how to negotiate the dirty world of church politics. Which is essential if you are to survive in the church."

––––––––

Claiborne had gone home by the time Ember and the bishop emerged from the meeting room.

Harry shook hands with the bishop, and then Cobb said goodnight and left.

"Well, Rev, you did okay in there." He put his arms around

her and gave her a hug. "I feel good about your prospects of staying."

She tilted her head up, looking him in the eyes. "I'd say so, Mister, when you bribe the bishop."

Harry laughed. "That, too. Although, I was referring to the council dynamics. With Cally's death, you just might have a leg up on things. Especially with Claiborne stalling the move to fill the lay leader position. The bishop's behind you, isn't he?"

"He is. But he wants to see results in order to justify his support. A few new members would help. Or at least an increase in attendance."

"They'll come, Em. They'll come."

"I hope so. In the meantime, we have to find out who killed Cally."

"That we do. Someone hated her. And hated her to the point she had to die."

Ember nodded. "Bludgeoning to that degree usually indicates hate; or at the very least, extreme anger. Do you think that her death on Valentine's Day was also part of the message?"

"Could be. Hadn't thought of that. But given the brutality, Cally's murder on Valentine's Day could be saying just how much her killer hated her. Hate is stronger than love."

"Wow. You might've nailed it."

"Now we need to find the hater to know for sure. And we possess one advantage Reece doesn't."

"What's that?"

"The gossip hotline."

"Why doesn't Reece?"

"He's a cop. People don't usually volunteer things to cops. It might come back to haunt them. After all, the first word in police state is police."

41

FRIDAY, 16 FEBRUARY 6:02 AM

JAVIER HERRAN, J OR J-MAN, AS PEOPLE USUALLY CALLED HIM, HAD monitored both the Reverend Ember Cole and Harry Thurgood.

He knew Thurgood knew someone was watching them. The man had found and destroyed virtually all the cameras and listening devices J had planted. And J was also pretty sure that whoever was watching him and Mrs. Fight was employed by Harry Thurgood.

This situation was clearly a case of spy versus spy. And they'd made each other. Even so, Mrs. Fight was insistent that he continue working on the case. And money was money.

The one advantage both sides had was that in this modern technological era, surveillance was a whole lot easier. Easier for both government and civilians alike.

So even though Harry Thurgood had destroyed over a thousand dollars in equipment, he hadn't destroyed everything. A drone hovering by the bedroom window told J-Man volumes. Or the information bought and sold on the Dark Web, often worthless, but occasionally priceless.

The morning air was cool. The heater in his car alleviated the chilliness. Soon he'd be at the Dallas-Ft. Worth Airport. J knew where to start looking into the Reverend's past. And it wasn't in Magnolia Bluff, Texas.

In five hours, he'd be on a plane heading for Las Vegas, Nevada. The information Mrs. Fight wanted was there.

He had plenty of pictures. Sure, she'd probably had some plastic surgery done. Most likely, though, there was enough of the original person remaining that her former associates would be able to recognize her. All he had to do was show the right picture to the right person and it would be open sesame.

———

The phone dinged and Harry stirred awake. He cast a glance to the other side of the bed and noticed that Ember was not there.

Must be up saying her morning prayers. Maybe making breakfast.

He picked up the phone and looked at the text.

> Target is on the move. Heading north out of town. Following.

"That doesn't sound good," Harry muttered.

He texted back:

> Stay with him.

In a moment there came back a thumb up emoticon.

"Hey, Mister, breakfast is ready. And which beguiling lady of the night is texting you now?"

Harry looked up from his phone to see his wife in that red babydoll and red high heels.

"You're the only beguiling lady of the night in my life. In fact, you're the only beguiling lady of the night, morning, afternoon, and evening that's in my life."

She sashayed towards him, the fabric hiding nothing, and sat on the edge of the bed.

"You going to get up and share breakfast with me, Mister, or stay here playing whatever on your phone?"

"I'd rather have breakfast in bed."

She touched the tip of his nose. "After breakfast. Right now, this girl is hungry for eggs and bacon."

She stood, sashayed to the door, did a half-turn, and said, "Now get yourself up. Food's getting cold."

I've died and gone to heaven, Harry told himself as he got out of bed. He slipped on his robe and chuckled. "Death, where is thy sting? Oh, grave, where is thy victory?"

————

Reece Sovern sat in his car watching the Methodist parsonage. He'd reached a brick wall. After talking with dozens of extended family members, friends, and acquaintances of the late Cally Taylor, he, GJ, and David Scott had found no one with a motive. Nor was he able to push the animosity between the Reverend and the Taylor woman further than what he had. And that wasn't far enough.

He had no proof the Reverend was in the church at the same time as Mrs. Taylor, which didn't help his case either. Besides, the alibis for both Thurgood and the Reverend were pretty unshakable. Ironclad, in fact.

Sure, they only alibied each other — but as long as they stuck to their guns, he was dead in the water.

And if truth be told, the animosity had almost totally been on the side of the Taylor woman. Ember Cole was looking like a saint in all of this. Other than her little shouting match with the victim, she'd never said an unkind word about Caldwell Taylor. At least according to everyone he'd talked to.

He shook his head. *Have no idea how she does it. Maybe she is a saint.*

But saint or no, Reece knew he couldn't pin the murders on Thurgood or the Reverend. He was going to have to drop the charges and start over. And once again eat one hell of a lot of crow.

42

FRIDAY, 16 FEBRUARY 7:18 AM

"Ah, Mr. Thurgood, you're here early this morning. Did you have a fight with the Reverend?"

Harry laughed. "Very funny, Miguel. No, no fight with the Reverend. We're still enjoying our honeymoon, so to speak."

"That is good. A good woman brings joy to a man's heart. And she makes him a good man."

"Very true, Miguel. Very true. Ember is a wonderful woman. She'll make me a steadfast companion as we journey through life, and I hope I make the same for her."

"You will. You love her. You will take good care of her. Do you want breakfast?"

"Em made breakfast. But I would like a coffee and a cream cheese kolache. Or two."

Harry walked out to the front part of the shop. Jack Bonhoffer, sitting by the cash register, gave him a lazy salute, and said, "Good morning, Boss."

"Morning, Jack."

Estrelita was behind the counter talking to a customer and gave him a little wave.

Harry looked over the tables. A man and a woman he didn't

recognize sat at one, and a couple he did recognize sat at another. He walked over to Brandon and Joyce's table.

"Kind of early for you two, isn't it?"

"Morning, Harry," Joyce said.

Harry and Brandon shook hands.

"Joyce has a busy day," Brandon said, "so we thought we'd get breakfast early."

"Glad you're here. Anything I can get you?"

"Estrelita took our orders," Joyce said.

"Very good. Thanks for coming in. Hope you have a great day."

"You too," they said in unison.

Harry ambled over to the other table with the couple he didn't recognize. They were snowbirds from Wisconsin and had their motorhome over at Hayden's resort.

Two other tables were occupied by a single woman each. One was a snowbird from Minnesota. The other was a local woman.

"I figured it was about time I tried your coffee," the local woman said. "You've been here long enough that it looks like you might stick around."

Harry smiled. "That's the plan."

"Well, the coffee's really good." She tittered. "Couldn't resist that."

"I'm glad it is. Hope your day is wonderful."

"Oh, it will be. I'm retired. Every day's like a holiday."

Harry got his cup of coffee, a couple cream cheese kolaches, and grabbed his tablet from under the counter.

He was going over the cash flow for the week when he heard the bells over the door ring. He looked up and saw Graham Huston heading towards his table.

"Harry, have I got good news for you. Although the news itself isn't good."

"Have a seat, and spill it."

"Another murder and the same MO."

"When?"

"Wylie took a guess based on experience and thought sometime after midnight."

"When was the body discovered?"

"About a half-hour ago. Otis Onsgaard was walking his dog. Found the body lying against the curb over on Cinnamon Loop."

"Never heard of that street. Where is it?"

"Small housing development about a half-mile outside the city limits to the east."

"Who was the victim?"

"Zelmo Reed."

"Don't know him."

"Top player for the college basketball team."

"That's gonna hurt."

"Definitely. Hurt him even more. Stabbed in the esophagus and then a slash that severed the kid's jugular vein and carotid arteries. Wiley guessed he was maybe stabbed in a vehicle and then dumped out. Based on the lack of blood on the street."

"Yeah. Not good for him."

"Looks as though Reece will be withdrawing the charges. Same MO in all five murders, and I assume you and Ember weren't out driving around Cinnamon Loop in the wee hours of the morning."

"Never heard of the street for one; and, for two, Em and I were in bed. Sleeping."

Graham chuckled. "Glad you added that."

Harry laughed, then said, "The MO, though, isn't completely identical."

"You're thinking of Cally Taylor."

"Right. She was stabbed and then brutally bludgeoned. The others were just stabbed. And Cally's brutal death happened on Valentine's. Might be something to that."

"Very observant, Mr. Amateur Detective."

"I'm sure you made the same observation."

"In fact, I did. And I'm thinking what you're probably think-ing: the Taylor woman is the actual target victim here."

Harry nodded. "And all the others are decoys."

43

FRIDAY, 16 FEBRUARY 9:08 AM

THE NINERS WERE ALL ON TIME. AROUND THE TWO TABLES THAT had been pushed together were Caroline McCluskey, the town librarian; her friend Magnolia Nadine Roane; Police Chief Tommy Jager; Billy Bob Baskin, pastor of the Presbyterian church; Graham Huston, owner and editor of the *Magnolia Bluff Chronicle*; LouEllen Mueller, owner of LouEllen's Lounge; and Ember Cole, who, Harry noted, was wearing a knee-length black pleated skirt, light gray blouse, with clerical collar, black jacket, and black shoes. She was also wearing her saturno hat, a large pectoral cross, the Valentine's necklace, and her engagement ring.

His mind drifted back to the morning, and he found it difficult to reconcile the image of Ember in the red see-through baby doll and red high heels with the black and gray public persona.

Not for the first time, he found himself wondering who Ember had been before Magnolia Bluff. Before seminary. Because it was obvious she was no stranger to the ways of the world and the flesh.

"Hey, Thurgood, you going to stand there all day holding that plate of pastries?" Tommy asked.

"Oh, leave him alone," LouEllen said. "He's probably day

dreamin' about how they used that hat of Ember's this morning."

The table exploded in raucous laughter. Harry felt the heat rise to his face. He cleared his throat, set the plate of pastries on the table, and took his seat next to Ember.

He whispered to Em, "Thank God no one else is here."

"Amen to that," she whispered back.

When the laughter died down, Tommy looked at Harry and Ember and asked, "Has Reece talked to you two?"

They shook their heads.

"Probably afraid to face you. Well, we're withdrawing the arrest warrants. After today's murder, I think you two are clearly off the hook. And the DA is of the same opinion. I'll make sure the arrest is taken off the record."

"Thank you, Tommy," Ember said.

"Appreciate it," Harry added.

"In addition," Tommy began, "I give you the department's heartfelt and deepest apology."

"Apology accepted," Ember said.

"You should publish it in the newspaper," LouEllen said.

Graham smiled. "Oh, I'm sure Monika heard. And if she didn't, she will."

"Where does that girl get all of that stuff?" Magnolia Nadine asked.

"I wouldn't be surprised if Mary Lou asks her to become a Hat," Caroline said.

Graham shook his head. "Doubt she'd join. Probably gets half her information from them to begin with."

Billy Bob nodded. "Have yet to see a gossip who can keep quiet."

Harry asked, "So, Tommy, if Em and I are off the hook, who is Reece looking at?"

"You know I can't tell you that," Tommy began, and then was cut off by Graham.

"I'll tell you who." Graham had a knowing look on his face. "Nobody. Our chief investigator doesn't have a clue."

"Now Graham," Tommy chided, "that's unfair. Reece is working the case with the help of the DA's investigator. I'm very confident he'll have this wrapped up soon."

"Glad you're confident," LouEllen said. "The rest of us ain't so sure."

Tommy stood. "With five murders, I can't sit here on my prat all day. Thanks for the charming conversation. Catch y'all later." And he was out the door.

Within a few minutes, the other members of the coffee klatch were also out the door to get on with their day.

Estrelita arrived to clear off the tables. Ember helped her, while Harry moved the tables back to their original positions.

He and Ember walked outside, crossed the street, and sat on a bench on the Green facing the Really Good.

Harry took a pipe out of his pocket, filled it with Holiday Pipe Mixture, and put a match to it. When he had the pipe going, he said, "It's a good feeling knowing that we are no longer suspects."

"Yes, it is. Maybe now the anti-Ember faction at church will give it a rest."

"That would be nice. But it's not you they are against. It's a power struggle. You represent change and you're new. The old guard is trying to hang on. Trying to cling to what they've always known."

"Yes, I know. They're afraid they are going to lose their church. But as long as I wear the robe and stand in the pulpit, I'm the one with the bullseye on my forehead."

"You'll deal with their fear and survive. I have a feeling you've been a survivor for a long time — and that's in your favor. On a different subject, when do I become a member?"

"The Membership Committee approved your request. So this Sunday I will present you to the church as our newest member and you will publicly agree to follow the Book of Discipline and agree to faithfully support the church."

"Sounds simple enough."

"There hasn't been a new non-Methodist adult member in ten years."

"Really?"

"Just transfers and births. Which aren't keeping pace with those who are passing on."

"That doesn't sound good."

"It isn't. But it's a situation all the mainline denominations are facing. The church doesn't know how to reach people anymore. Its message isn't taken seriously, and no one in the church knows how to make it relevant."

"Sounds to me like it's a marketing issue. You can't sell the sin angle. No one believes in sin. Which means they don't believe in hell. What they might believe in is some kind of after-life that everyone is going to. And because everyone is going to the big light at the end of the tunnel, who needs the church?"

"I think that's a large part of it. But Christianity is more than just heaven or hell. It's a worldview designed to give us purpose and meaning in life."

"That may be, but the church isn't doing a very good job getting the message out. You have the heaven and hell group. There's the existentialist group. And the social justice group. None of those groups are speaking to the mainstream of the western world. The church has made itself irrelevant."

"How do we make ourselves relevant?" Ember asked.

"Wesley could create a great revival because the Christian worldview was one even the worst of sinners ultimately bought into. The early church succeeded because everyone in the ancient world believed in gods and goddesses.

"Today, most people don't believe in deities of any sort, and they definitely don't believe in a Christian worldview as it has been traditionally presented.

"Look at where people are going today. Buddhism. Taoism.

Stoicism. Epicureanism. Paganism. The Tarot. Spiritualism. Why? Because there's no judgmental God. No sin. Just a focus on living a good life. And that's where the majority of us are in the western world. We want to know how to live so that we can enjoy life and be happy.

"Quite honestly, Emmy, my love, I don't see the church showing us how to enjoy life and be happy. Being a social justice warrior doesn't cut it because that only makes us unhappy. Hugging trees doesn't cut it either, nor does praying for peace. People really don't care about any of that. At least not until they're happy and enjoying life."

"But I think Jesus does want us to enjoy life and be happy."

"If he does, then that's what you need to tell people — and you need to show them *how* Christianity helps them to achieve a happy state of mind so they can enjoy life."

Ember took a deep breath. "That's a lot to think about. But thanks."

"You're welcome."

A familiar car pulled to the curb. The door opened, and Reece Sovern got out.

44

FRIDAY, 16 FEBRUARY 10:42 AM

It was a bitter pill to swallow, but Reece had to swallow it. *One serving of humble pie loaded, please,* he said to himself.

He shook his head, pushed his glasses back up to the bridge of his nose, and stuffed a fresh stogie in his mouth. A bright green perfecto.

It's now or never and never is not an option.

He got out of the car and crossed the grass to where Thurgood and the Reverend were sitting.

"Mornin' Reverend. Harry."

They both replied good morning in unison.

That's a start. A good start, he thought. *They didn't tell me to take a flying leap.*

"I've come to apologize. I'm sorry for jumping to conclusions without enough evidence to warrant the jump."

He saw a smile appear on Harry's lips. "A lot of jumping there. Too bad this isn't Calaveras County."

What on earth is he talking about? "You lost me there, Harry."

"Mark Twain's 'The Celebrated Jumping Frog of Calaveras County'."

"Never read it."

"Don't feel bad, Reece, I never read it either," Ember said.

He smiled. *Kind of her to side with me.* "In any event, I'm sorry. We're withdrawing the warrants. This episode has taught me to be more careful."

"It's over and done with, Reece," Harry said.

"You're not, uh, going to sue, are you?"

"No, I'm not."

"Thank you, Harry, I'm grateful. Believe me." He paused a moment and then continued speaking. "A real shame about Zelmo. He was a super basketball player. Would have probably made it to the pros."

"I don't follow basketball," Harry said, "but it is a shame a life was cut short so young."

"I don't follow basketball, either," Ember said, "but he seemed to be a fine young man. Active with Holy Crusaders for Christ, wasn't he?"

Reece checked his notebook. "Yes, he was. He, um, he also liked white girls. You think there's any racial motive in this?"

Harry shrugged. "Difficult to say. But it's possible. It seems to me there are some interesting aspects about the case."

"Care to share?" Reece asked.

"There's a possible racial aspect with DeWayne and Zelmo. DeWayne dating a Hispanic girl and Zelmo liking white co-eds. But the old woman—"

"Vonnie Vebelsteadt."

"Yes, Vonnie," Harry said, "she and Cally don't fit that."

Reese nodded. "True. True."

"Everyone was stabbed."

Reece nodded.

"Throat slashed."

Reece nodded again.

"But," Harry held up two fingers, "two of the victims were excessively injured. The young girl, Lila, and Cally Caldwell. Now Lila was quite savagely cut up. But that may have been due to her attempting to fight off the attacker in the confines of the car."

"Probably," Reece said.

"But maybe not. It's possible the attacker was making a statement."

Reece nodded. "I suppose."

"It seems to me you have to rule that out for sure. As for Cally, her bludgeoning seems excessive — especially with the cross being used. Seems to me that's a statement, but maybe one made unintentionally by the killer."

"I'm not so sure, my love," Ember said. "Don't forget that Cally was killed on Valentine's Day. A day celebrating love. There may be a message in there as well."

Harry nodded. A thoughtful look on his face.

"Huh," Reece said. "Hadn't thought of that."

Ember continued. "And the cross, another symbol of love, being used to kill her, may tie into a possible statement being made by the killer."

Reece took his glasses off and pinched the bridge of his nose. Pinch completed, he put his glasses back on and said, "So you aren't buying the racial aspect?"

Harry shrugged. "It might be secondary. Might be coincidental. It's possible the use of the cross was mere convenience. Cally's bludgeoning seems to me to be excessive and the use of the cross symbolic, as well as the day of death." Harry smiled at Ember. "The *modus operandi* in these killings is made to look like the work of a serial killer, but it doesn't quite fit with how serial killers work."

Reece thought, *This makes a lot of sense. That's some excellent reasoning on Thurgood's part.* Out loud he said, "Thanks, Harry. And you too, Ember. Appreciate your perspectives. Well, best get at it. Have a killer to catch."

"For what it's worth, Reece, unless this person has discovered he truly enjoys killing people, this will probably be the last murder."

"I hope so." Reece paused, then asked, "Why do you think that?"

"Just my view," Harry said, "But I think because this doesn't really fit the profile of a serial killer, one of those victims was the intended target. The others are decoys."

Reece nodded, walked back to his car, and got in.

"Too bad Thurgood isn't a cop. On the other hand, he is insufferably vain and patronizing. He's the kind of guy my uncle said they'd frag in Vietnam."

He started the car, put it in drive, and headed back to the station.

Time to go over the list of family and friends for each one of the victims and see if someone shows up on all five lists.

45

FRIDAY, 16 FEBRUARY 11:37 AM

Sergeant Investigator Reece Sovern took a last look at the large board that listed the victims and the key people in their lives. He turned around and took in the people in the conference room. They were a diverse group.

Police Investigator Georgia Jean Riggins was a no-nonsense cop, with a penchant for being too aggressive. At five-ten, and with muscles a man would envy, she could be a formidable opponent. Her brown hair was cut very short. Her strong features would probably earn her being called handsome over pretty.

DA Investigator David Scott had a good analytical mind. He was tall. A couple inches over six feet. Lanky in build. His brown hair was cut in a 1950s Ivy League style.

Police Evidence Technician Teo Ruiz had a good eye for detail and his mind was sharply analytical. He was the shortest one in the room, wore his jet black hair in a comb over, and looked comfortable in a flannel shirt and jeans.

"I think we need to look at this case from a different angle," Reece said.

"How so?" Georgia Jean asked.

"The pattern doesn't fit your normal serial killer."

"I agree," David Scott said.

"Thanks, David. Nevertheless, my thought is that we are still looking for one person who committed these murders."

Georgia Jean had a frown on her face. "If one person killed all these people, what's the motive if they aren't a serial killer?"

Reece repositioned his glasses on the bridge of his nose and rolled the green stogie to the other side of his mouth. "Don't know. There's a certain racial feel with the first two and the fifth murders, but Vonnie and Cally don't seem to fit, unless there's something that we haven't discovered yet."

"Vonnie and Cally could have been decoys," Georgia Jean volunteered.

"Good point, GJ," Reece said.

"Although Cally's death stands out from the others," David said.

"You're talking about the bludgeoning," GJ said.

"Right," David replied. "And the desecration of her body."

"Could be racial *and* anti-Christian," GJ suggested.

"And don't forget that Cally was killed on Saint Valentine's Day. The brutality of the murder on a day celebrating love might mean something," Reece said.

He saw thoughtful looks descend on their faces.

Continuing, he said, "That's why I think we need to look through the friends and contacts to see if there are any who are connected to all five of the victims."

GJ and David nodded their heads in agreement.

Reece looked at Teo. "You've been quiet. Anything to add?"

"From the standpoint of evidence, we don't have much. We think the knife used was a kitchen knife. Probably a slicing knife. Seven, seven and a half inches long. And maybe an inch and a quarter at the base of the blade."

"That's a good-sized knife," GJ said.

"It is," Teo agreed. "It would probably be somewhat unwieldy inside a car. Which may account for the attacker's difficulty in killing the Santiago girl. Other than that, there are no fingerprints."

"Thanks, Teo," Reece said. "I think it safe to say the victims knew their killer. Only Lila put up a fight. But that's probably because DeWayne was killed first and Lila was then fighting for her life. A battle which she unfortunately lost."

"So we are going to go through the lists of family, relatives, friends, acquaintances, and recent contacts to see if we can find a person, or persons, who show up on all five victim's lists. Because that will be the person who knew all five and, therefore, is most likely our killer.

"Any questions? No? Then let's hop to it, folks. We have a killer to catch."

46

FRIDAY, 16 FEBRUARY 6:47 PM

HARRY WAS ON THE COUCH IN THE LIVING ROOM. HE WAS SMOKING a bowl of Edward G. Robinson's blend in an old Jobey Shellmoor Prince.

In the kitchen, Ember was humming some Christian song while making salad and garlic toast to go with the lasagna Miguel had made for their supper.

He puffed on his pipe and looked at the message Elmore had sent him. The private detective was lucky and got the last seat on the same flight as Mary Lou's man.

Both detectives were now in Las Vegas. Elmore was able to get a room at the same hotel as the other detective, but not on the same floor.

Elmore planned on tailing the other detective to see if he could find out why he was in Vegas.

Harry texted back, letting his PI know money was available if he needed it.

He puffed on his pipe. *Las Vegas. Why would Mary Lou's PI go to Las Vegas?*

He had no answer. He'd only been to Vegas once. But maybe the PI wasn't digging into his past. Had Ember ever lived in Vegas?

He'd ask her, but they'd agreed to leave the past in the past. Consequently, asking was out of the question. As much as he'd like to do so.

His curiosity, though, nagged him.

Next to that PI in Minneapolis, Elmore's the best there is. He'll find out what's going on.

"Everything's ready, Harry."

He set his pipe on the end table and got up from the sofa. "I find it difficult to grasp this transformation you go through."

"And what transformation is that?"

He joined her in the doorway and walked with her to the table in the kitchen and sat.

"The black and white preacher lady metamorphoses into a normal person wearing sweatpants and a sweatshirt."

"Don't forget the necklace."

"Right. Sweats and a very expensive necklace."

She giggled. "I am normal, you know. Not some stylite saint or something."

"Yeah. You are normal."

"Don't you like normal?"

"I love normal. And I love you."

"Harry, I've waited so long for this. I find it difficult to believe that God blessed me with such a wonderful man to be my husband."

"Quite honestly, I'm ecstatic I have such a wonderful woman for my wife. Such a wonderful *sexy* woman for my wife."

"Do you want to make love to me now, or eat first?"

"Man does not live by bread alone."

———

It was Ember's idea. Eating their supper by candlelight, wearing only their birthday suits.

Harry was surprised by how bashful he felt about doing so, while Ember seemed completely at ease.

"This lasagna is really good," she said.

"Did you say that on purpose?"

"Maybe."

"Thought so. It is, though, truly superb. Miguel outdid himself."

"So what are we going to do about Cally's murder?" Ember asked before putting the forkful of lasagna in her mouth.

"Do we need to do something about it?"

"Does Reece truly have a clue?"

"I wonder sometimes if the entire Magnolia Bluff and Burnet County constabulary are up to the task of handling our murder epidemic."

"Harry, you and I both know they aren't. If some husband, drunker than the proverbial skunk, kills his wife, yeah, they can handle that. But something complex? Not on your life. Rebecca was killing one person every May for nine years and it took Graham Huston to figure that one out. We figured out it was Effie and possibly her son who killed Louisa and ran down Mary Lou. Mike Kurelek stopped that serial killer, not Reece. And Bliss, a complete stranger in town, figured out Merrick was murdered."

"You've made your point, my love."

"I still find it difficult to believe God gave me a truly magnificent man to love me and be my companion for life."

"Well, he did."

"Yes, He did. And I'm forever grateful."

"And I find it difficult to believe my otherwise reserved and prudish wife would be the one who wanted us to eat lasagna in the raw."

"You don't like being naked?"

"Well, it has its place."

"I like it. It's freeing. Nothing can be hidden. Naked is honest. I haven't always believed this. But God did make Adam and Eve naked. And I came to realize naked is normal. It's clothes that are abnormal. But we have such a weird view of naked as a society. We can't be naked, but we can be almost naked, and that's good. We're obsessed with the naked look, but not okay with naked. Which, to my mind, is stupid. And I've not been a prude since I was twelve, Mister."

"I'll take your word for it." Harry paused before continuing. "So, before we were married, did you go around here in the nude?"

"Sometimes. I'd lower the blinds and pull the curtains. It's freeing. Naked before God. He sees everything. Being naked in prayer reminds us we can't hide from God."

"What did the church council say about prayer in the buff?"

Ember giggled. "Too avant-garde for them."

"I can imagine."

Ember, suddenly serious, said, "Back to Cally's killer. How do we find him? Or her?"

"I like what the Hairless Mexican told Ashenden."

"Is this from a book?"

"It is. By Somerset Maugham."

"Okay."

"Ashenden was a handler for British spies back in the first world war. The Hairless Mexican was hired by the Brits to assassinate someone in Italy and Ashenden was to accompany him, posing as a writer.

"On the train trip, Ashenden tells the Mexican that he'd written the perfect murder and couldn't solve it. The Mexican tells him that's nonsense. 'What's the killer's motive?' the Mexican asks. He tells Ashenden that he must get inside the killer's head and see why the killer had to kill the person. Once Ashenden identified the why, the motive, then all of the facts regarding the murder will fall into place.

"Which is why the Mexican said Jack the Ripper was bound not to be found. No motive could be established to make sense of the murders."

Ember nodded. "So we need to come up with why those five people had to die, according to the killer."

"Yes."

"That's a pretty tall order."

"Yes, it is. The easiest is probably Lila Santiago."

"Because she witnessed DeWayne's death."

Harry smiled. "Exactly. Of course, it's possible Lila was the intended victim. But if she was, all the killer had to do was approach the passenger side of the car instead of the driver's side."

"Unless the killer wanted to take out the guy first."

"Possible. But a big guy like DeWayne, his first reaction is to get the perp. Not dial nine-one-one. So if Lila's the target, stab and run."

"Okay. But what if, as you speculated, they were just decoys?"

"Then order doesn't matter. But if I was the killer, I'd take out the big guy first. Then go after the smaller person."

"That makes sense. So Vonnie was also a decoy?"

"I think so. Very simple execution. Stab and slash to the throat. Once done, the killer walks away and leaves her to die. Same *modus operandi*."

"I'm with you," Ember said. "Makes sense. Nothing stolen. Just the killing. Unless the person loves killing."

"Possible. And if it weren't for Cally, I'd say it was a strong possibility. Although one would have to ask, why start now?"

"You're right. Cally's murder doesn't fit. The killer went the extra mile to make sure she was dead. And then desecrated the body. I wonder if the murder taking place on Valentine's Day was just as much a message as using the cross?"

"Could be. A saint. Love. The church. All elements of some statement the killer was making that was fitting for Cally and not the others."

"Might be something there."

Harry nodded. "Might be. So the question is: who hated Cally enough to kill her, and kill her in such a horrible way? And then cover it up by killing four other people?"

47

FRIDAY, 16 FEBRUARY 7:04 PM

"HERE YOU GO, SARGE," GEORGIA JEAN SAID. SHE SET BEFORE Reece several to-go containers of food.

"Thanks. Did you eat?"

She held up another bag. "Got mine right here."

Reece opened the containers. The aromas of chicken-fried chicken, biscuits and gravy, mashed potatoes, corn, okra, and apple cobbler tantalized his nose.

"This is a feast for a king," he said. "How much do I owe you?"

"My treat. For your promotion and choosing me for this job. Thank you."

"You're welcome. And thank you."

"For what?"

"Accepting."

She smiled at her boss and sat down at the table. "Today didn't go so well."

Reece looked at the large operations board. "No, it didn't. None of Zelmo's friends or relatives showed up on any of the other victims's list of friends or relatives. Lila and DeWayne had quite a few mutual friends and acquaintances. No one on Vonnie

Vebelsteadt's list showed up on any of the others. And the same goes for Cally Taylor."

"Maybe we have two killers, Sarge."

"Possible. But is it likely both would be at work at the same time?"

"Why not? Someone kills the Sanford and Santiago kids because they're against race mixing. That same person kills the basketball player because he liked white girls. Race mixing."

"Okay. So why does person two kill the two women?"

"I don't know. Maybe because they were both into the church."

"We know Cally was. But did Vonnie even go to church?"

"I don't know. That's something we'll have to find out. But the guy who kills the women is using the other murders as cover. So two killers kind of using each other for cover."

"I don't know, GJ. It's all a bit too complex for me. The reasons for crime are usually pretty simple. Money or ego."

GJ slowly nodded her head, absorbing the information, and focused her attention on chicken-fried chicken.

Reece turned his attention back to the board while he mixed corn into his potatoes.

His eyes swept over the photos of the victims and the absence of suspects, and that troubled him. They hadn't been able to pin down a motive. Their best bet had been Reverend Cole and her sidekick. But the DA had told them they had a better chance of catching halibut out of Burnet Reservoir than getting the grand jury to let that case go to trial.

So they'd withdrawn the arrest warrants for the Reverend and Thurgood. And gave them the department's heartfelt apologies, while praying they didn't sue.

Somebody, though, killed those people, Reese mused. *Why?*

He ate mashed potatoes and corn, adding plenty of gravy.

If I can't find a motive, then maybe I need to find a pattern. If there's a pattern, that might lead us to a motive.

"You see any patterns in these killings?" he asked.

GJ wiped her hands on a napkin and drank iced tea. "The first two were at night. Vonnie was in the early morning, as was Cally. The basketball player was at night. So it seems this killer prefers the night and the dawn."

"The usual. At least as far as time is concerned."

"All were killed with a knife. Other than Lila, no one fought back. So the perp is killing people he knows."

"Which means all the killings are personal."

"Hate to have this person for a friend," GJ said.

"So why would this killer start killing his friends and acquaintances? What triggered him to start?"

"Good question Sarge. And look at the mix of ages: high school, college, upper end of middle age, and a senior. That's a wide age range. Who has friends in all of those age groups?"

"Good point. But they might not be friends exactly. Might just be people he knows. But knows well enough that the victim isn't going to suspect anything. So who would fit the picture?"

GJ nodded. "What person would know Lila and Vonnie? Dwayne and Zelmo? Zelmo and Cally? Vonnie and Cally? And going over the list of family, friends, and contacts, lots of people crossed over, but we didn't find one who was on all five."

Reece repositioned his glasses on the bridge of his nose. "Then it looks like we missed somebody. And that's the person we need to find."

48

FRIDAY, 16 FEBRUARY 8:38 PM

EMBER PUT THE PHONE DOWN. "THAT WAS CLAIBORNE." SHE'D slipped into a set of sweats after supper and was stretched out on the sofa.

"What's going on now?" Harry asked. He was wearing a robe and sitting next to her feet.

"He said he heard Cally's supporters are going to ask the bishop if he can bring in another minister to do her funeral service."

"Doesn't the family have a say in this?

"Of course they do. They have complete say. This is totally uncalled for."

"Take a deep breath. Power struggle. How about tomorrow we go visit Mr. Taylor and his daughter and confirm everything?"

"Good idea. Thanks, Harry."

"Don't mention it."

"So, where do we start with finding Cally's killer? We really need to jump on this so we can shut down this revolt."

"Revolt, eh? I think it's more like a coup. But in any event, as for finding her killer, we need to look at motive. Why would someone want to kill her?"

"Because she was a bitch?"

"Whoa, Rev. You're sayin' extra prayers tonight."

Ember laughed. "It's no wonder I love you. You always succeed in making me laugh."

"If you can't laugh, life becomes pretty doggone miserable."

"So, Mister, how do we figure out who had a motive to kill her and acted on it?"

"We have to figure out why someone wanted to kill her. Or needed to kill her. The police always start with the nearest and dearest."

"That says something about us as a species, doesn't it?" Ember said.

"I suppose so."

"So that means Reece should've talked with Owen and Clair-Ann."

"So let's assume they did. The fact that they're still walking around means Magnolia Bluff's finest and the DA both think they didn't kill her."

"What are their alibis? Do you know?"

Harry shrugged. "Haven't heard. They must be good, though."

"We are, however, looking at the Magnolia Bluff PD."

"And specifically Reece Sovern."

"Who immediately assumed I killed her."

"Right." Harry thought a moment, then continued. "It might pay us dividends to talk to those two ourselves."

"I think tomorrow would be a great time to make a pastoral call."

Harry smiled. "I think you're right. You ascertain their intentions regarding the funeral. Minister to their spiritual needs. And get them to disclose their whereabouts."

"That's a lot of work."

"I'll be there with you."

"What about the Really Good?"

"That's why I hired Jack and Estrelita."

"Then we'll make a pastoral call tomorrow."

Ember stood, pulled her sweatshirt over her head, and dropped it on the floor. She undid the tie and let her sweat pants fall to the floor, and stepped out of them. She was once again clothed only in her birthday suit.

"In the meantime, how about ministering to my spiritual needs?"

"Do I need to be ordained?"

"You already are for this particular biblical injunction."

"Then let's get ministering."

Ember giggled and ran to the bedroom, with Harry in pursuit.

49

SATURDAY, 17 FEBRUARY 11:03 AM

WITH THE HIGH TEMPERATURE PREDICTED TO BE NEAR SEVENTY, Harry and Ember decided to walk to the Taylors. While they walked and talked, he smoked an old Jobey Prince-shaped pipe.

"The frozen custard launch has brought in quite a few people, don't you think?" Ember said.

"I think so. Not as big a turnout as I'd hoped for, but the traffic thus far is encouraging. Elisha is certainly tickled pink."

Ember laughed. "Yes, he is. Bragging all about how this was his idea."

"Well, he was a big encourager of the idea. So let him brag."

"That's a good thing you're doing, Harry. This will be good for the boy."

"I hope so. He told me he'll be glad to work at the shop during the summer."

"Even better. Maybe he'll give up that dumb idea to be a boxer."

"He just might if he sees money being made from the frozen custard."

She smiled, then leaned over and kissed his cheek.

Harry returned her smile. "What's that for? Not that I mind."

"You're a good man, Harry Thurgood. Elisha needs this.

His smile faded slightly. "I hope you're right, Em. But more importantly, I hope I can get him out from under the influence of his evil sister."

"Oralene truly is evil. No doubt about that. Planning her father's death and then getting her brothers to do her dirty work. That's as bad as one can get. I believe she will pay for what she did."

"I hope you're right, Em. I hope you're right."

They walked the rest of the way in silence, holding hands.

When they arrived at the Taylor residence, Harry pressed the doorbell. The chime indoors was clearly audible.

In a moment, the door opened and they were looking at Clair-Ann.

She's pretty tall for a female, Harry thought, *and has a good build. Not wimpy. But not masculine, either. Attractive.*

"Oh, hello, Reverend, Mr. Thurgood."

"Good morning," Ember said.

Harry smiled and lifted his hat.

Ember continued. "We thought we'd stop by and see how you and your dad are doing."

"Uh, sure. That's very nice of you. Come on in."

She stepped aside, and Ember and Harry entered. He removed his hat.

"Dad's in his study. This way."

While Ember and Clair-Ann walked and made small talk, Harry let his eyes roam the entryway and a room they passed through. All was very tidy. A finger sliding along a surface produced no dust.

I wonder if this is the work of Clair-Ann or Cally? I'd say Clair-Ann, since Cally spent her time at church. Wonder if the daughter also cooked all the meals?

Clair-Ann knocked on the door frame. "Dad, Reverend Cole and Mr. Thurgood are here to see you."

"You, too," Harry said. "Your mother's death must have affected you as well."

"Uh, sure. It's affected a lot of people."

And not all are grieving, Harry said to himself.

"Come in, Reverend. You, too, Mr. Thurgood," Owen Taylor said. "Coffee? Tea? I'm going to have tea."

"Tea is fine, Mr. Taylor," Ember said.

Owen Taylor looked at his daughter. "Would you be so kind, Clair-Ann, dear?"

"Sure, Dad. I'll be right back."

Clair-Ann left and Harry and Ember sat on the sofa.

Harry let his eyes sweep the room. It was rectangular. Windows on two of the walls with a fireplace on the wall opposite the large dark wood desk, which faced a window.

At right angles to the desk and fireplace was the old, brown overstuffed sofa. It had seen better days, but was still comfy.

Bookshelves, crammed with books, lined every bit of space not taken up by the windows, fireplace, or door.

The room was bright, and Harry thought it would be a cheery place to work and relax.

Owen Taylor swiveled his desk chair in their direction. "Working on my book has helped to keep my mind off of, off of…"

Ember nodded. "Yes. Work helps. It keeps the mind from dwelling too much on the unpleasant."

"That it does. And my wife's untimely death is very unpleasant."

"You must have loved her very much," Harry said.

"I did. Still do. Her memory, at least."

"Did you get to kiss her goodbye before she left to go to the church?" Harry asked.

"That was the problem," Clair-Ann said from the doorway.

She walked into the room and set the tray on the coffee table. Harry admired the china tea set. *That is not something you'd find at Walmart or get off Amazon.*

"What was the problem?" Harry asked.

"My mother was never here. She failed doing her duty as a wife and a mother."

"Now Sinclair," Owen said, "you're being harsh."

"Is the truth harsh, Dad? It's true and you know it. Your wife did not want to be a wife. My mother did not want to be a mother. All that mattered was Saint Luke's."

Harry noticed that while Clair-Ann's voice was calm, there was a strong undercurrent of disapproval. Even intense anger.

"Cally was lay leader for a long time," Ember said.

"Thirteen years," Clair-Ann said. "And she chaired the church council for fifteen years before that."

"Isn't that a step down?" Harry asked. "To go from church council to lay leader?"

"No," Clair-Ann said. "The lay leader is the most important position in the church. More important than the pastor. Sorry, Reverend."

"You're right," Ember said. "No need to apologize."

"Did you get to say goodbye to your mother?" Harry asked.

"Say goodbye?" Harry watched her face harden into a look that spoke of intense hate, and her voice became a bit more strident. "The last thing she told me was to move out of the house. She never said hello or goodbye. She was a bitch and I hope there is a hell and that she's suffering horrible agony."

"Sinclair! That's a terrible thing to say about your mother."

"She didn't care about us, Dad. She was a nasty bitch and deserved what she got."

"I can't let you speak that way about your mother and my wife."

"Why do you defend her? She despised you and told me she wished I'd never been born. I'm glad she's dead. Now, if you'll excuse me."

Without waiting for anyone to say anything, Clair-Ann turned and stormed out of the room.

"Please excuse my daughter. She is... Well, she's never gotten along with her mother. She's always been a daddy's girl. Not that I mind. Especially as my wife pulled away from the family, Sinclair, or Clair-Ann as she prefers to be called, stepped in and more or less assumed the role that should have been her mother's. Now that Caldwell is gone... Let's just say I'm glad I at least have my little girl."

Harry mentally shook his head. *None of these people are healthy. This is one messed up and sick family. But if Owen and Clair-Ann alibied each other, then it's no wonder the police are ignoring them. And they each have a strong motive to cover for each other.*

"I'm sure she's a comfort to you," Ember said while pouring tea.

"Look at me. Making my guests pour their own tea."

Ember smiled. "Here you go, Mr. Taylor. And that's perfectly all right. I live to serve, as they say."

"I think you're a wonderful pastor. Sinclair thinks so, too. I just don't understand why Caldwell was so opposed to you."

"It was a puzzle to me as well. But right now, I want to know how *you* are holding up."

"It's difficult, Reverend. It's very, very difficult."

Harry saw the tears glistening in his eyes.

Ember continued. "Dr. Mike Kurelek is a wonderful grief counselor. You might want to consider talking to him."

"He's the fellow down at the college?"

"He is. And he's very good."

"I'll think about it, Reverend."

"I'm not a therapist, but if you just want someone to listen, I have good ears."

"Thank you."

"And you can call anytime. You are experiencing a major change in your life, and I am here for you."

"I just don't understand why a loving God would do this."

"I don't have an answer for you, Mr. Taylor. God's ways are not our ways. I know that's no comfort now. In time, though, you may see something good from this. What it will be, I can't say. However, I can say I've been through some very hard times. I asked God why would He do that to me. And at some point, sometimes years later, I finally gained some understanding."

"I don't know if I can wait years. I'm not well. I might not live that long."

"If that's the case, you'll undoubtedly find out when you join your wife in heaven."

"Do you believe that? Sinclair said she'll be in hell."

Ember smiled. "Would it shock you terribly much if I told you I don't believe in hell?"

"Truly?"

Ember nodded. "Heaven and hell were imported into Judaism by the Pharisees. They got the concept from the Zoroastrians, a Persian religion."

"I didn't know that. Do you believe in heaven?"

"Well, the ancients believed there were successive spheres surrounding our world. Each sphere was a 'heaven.' Hence, the idea of 'heavens.' Plural. I believe that today we'd call these 'heavens' parallel universes. So when we die, I think our souls move on to one of these parallel universes."

"That's very modern of you, Reverend. Do many ministers believe like you?"

"No, I don't think so. The notion of heaven and hell and a historical Jesus is solidly entrenched in Christianity."

"You mean to say you don't believe in Jesus?"

Ember laughed. "Oh, I very much believe in Jesus. Paul's Jesus."

"Wasn't Paul's Jesus the one crucified?"

"Yes, he was. Just not here on Earth. He was crucified in Satan's realm, which is the first sphere around our world. Up by the moon. Or so the very first believers believed. I think it was in a parallel universe."

"I'm shocked."

"That's why I don't broadcast my beliefs. But if you read the genuine letters of Paul, he always reports he got his information directly from Jesus or from the Scriptures. He never wrote of talking to eyewitnesses, or Jesus's family, and doesn't mention Jesus's birth. None of that. Why? The most logical explanation is because they didn't exist. Jesus is a spiritual being who fought another spiritual being to free us from our enslavement to that being."

"You have given me much to think about. Will you pray for me?"

"Of course."

While Ember prayed for Owen Taylor, Harry found himself thinking about what Ember had revealed concerning her beliefs. Some of it she'd hinted at previously. But hearing a fuller description, all he could say was that her views were truly out of the mainstream of even liberal Christianity.

I just might have to read Paul and see this for myself. And I hope Mary Lou doesn't find out about this. That would be the coup de grâce for sure.

"In the name of Jesus Christ, our Lord. Amen."

Ember stood, and Harry did as well. "Just remember," she said, "call anytime if you need me."

"I will. Thank you."

On their walk back to the Really Good, Ember said, "Clair-Ann is a very angry young woman."

"That she is. She has also effectively replaced her mother in the household dynamic."

"Do you think she could have killed her?"

"Possibly. Any of us can kill anyone given enough provocation. The question we have to ask is, was she provoked to the point of acting on the animosity she felt towards her mother."

"She did say Cally had thrown her out of the house."

"That she did. So was that the inciting incident?"

"It would have separated Clair-Ann from her father."

"Very true. But most of us don't kill the people we hate. We just hate them and treat them like crap or avoid them."

Ember was quiet for a moment and then Harry noticed the excitement on her face. "It's that play we saw, Harry. Clair-Ann is Elektra!"

50

SATURDAY, 17 FEBRUARY 12:38 PM

WHILE THEY WALKED, EMBER TALKED ABOUT THE TAYLORS AND that both Owen and Clair-Ann should make appointments with Mike Kurelek to work through their grief.

Harry smoked his pipe, and only half listened to what his wife was saying. His mind was pondering her bombshell revelation. Was Cally's murder a playing out of the Elektra story? Cally hadn't literally murdered her husband, but she had put him out of her life. A metaphorical killing, one might say. She'd put Clair-Ann out of her life, as well, from the tidbits he'd gathered.

Upon reaching the coffee shop, Harry checked in to see how the frozen custard launch was doing. To his surprise, he counted twenty-five people in the shop and all but three were eating custard.

Elisha was excited. "Business has been booming, Mr. Thurgood. Mr. Bonhoffer said I should talk to you about becoming a partner."

"Oh, he did, did he? Well, I'll have to think it over. In the meantime, if you want it, you have a job this summer running the custard side of the shop. What do you say?"

"Are you for real?"

Harry nodded.

"You betcha, sir! I'd love to run the custard business. The money will help me to get the equipment I need for my boxing career. Can Samuel help me?"

"Tell you what. You can hire him as your assistant, and the two of you can share your portion of the profits."

"How much will that be?"

"Thirty-five percent. Deal?"

"Can I talk it over with my mom first?"

"You sure can. Just let me know as soon as possible."

"I will, sir."

Harry looked over at Jack Bonhoffer. Jack had a smile on his face. Harry smiled back.

He and Ember walked through the shop, greeting Miguel as they passed by, exited the shop and got into the Alfa Romeo, which was parked in the alley.

"Where are we going?" Ember asked.

"Storm's Drive-In. That okay?"

"Sure."

At the drive through, they ordered burgers, fries, fried pickles, fried okra, breaded mushrooms, hushpuppies, and malts. A cherry for Harry and a pineapple for Ember.

With food in hand, Harry drove them to the park where they ate in the car while enjoying the view of the reservoir.

Ember took the food out of the bags, handing Harry his burger and fries, putting the sides on the dashboard and the malts in the cup holders.

Harry took a bite of his half-pound burger. Chewed it thoughtfully and swallowed.

"You've been awfully quiet, Mister."

"I'm digesting. Both this burger and your deduction."

"About Clair-Ann?" She sucked on the straw in her malt.

"Yes. It's quite a leap. You might call it a divine revelation."

"Now you are poking fun."

"Only a little bit. This Elektra thing is a bolt out of the blue, that's for sure, but you may have hit on something."

"You think so?" She ate a fried pickle.

"It makes a lot of sense. It's certainly possible. The question is, is it probable?"

"To make it probable we'd have to find out if there was some event that pushed Clair-Ann over the edge to commit murder."

"That's it in a nutshell."

"What about her statement that the last thing her mother said to her was to get out of the house?"

"Difficult to say. It might have been the straw that broke the camel's back."

They ate their burgers, fries, and sides in silence.

Harry watched a sailboat tacking into the wind. *Arduous work that. Although persistence pays off. A lesson there.*

Ember finished her malt with a big slurping sound and giggled.

She was wearing her saturno and an ankle-length black dress with long sleeves and a white clerical collar. In addition, she wore a gold pectoral cross and the necklace he'd give her for Valentine's Day.

Persistence sure paid off in getting Em to be my wife. And persistence will solve this case and put to rest the discord in Emmy's church.

"A penny for your thoughts, Mister."

"Not worth a penny. Just watching that sailboat. Tacking into the wind is hard work. And it's persistence that pays off."

"That applies to most things."

He took her hand and kissed it. "I know."

"I was so scared we'd never be together. I'm glad you were persistent, Mister. Very glad."

"You were worth the wait."

"I hope you feel the same a year from now."

"I will."

"You can't know that."

"I know me. My feelings won't change."

"I'll pray that they don't."

"You do that."

He reached into his coat pocket and pulled out a folded sheet of paper. "Here. I wrote this for you some time ago and just never found the right time to give it to you. Now is probably that time."

Ember took the paper, unfolded it, and read:

I'll Not Want Another

I'll not want another to stand by my side
In this life, or any other life that may
Be granted you or me. The night, the day,
They'll come, they'll go, and each we'll ride

Until nights and days for us rise never more.
In the meantime, we hold our hearts in our hands:
Yours in mine and mine in yours, they our bands
That bind you to me and me to you. Your

Doubts are unfounded. Your breath beats in my breast.
My eyes open and you are there. They close
And it's only you who they ever see.

What more can I say? With you I'm obsessed.
You ask me why; it's God, not I, Who knows.
All I want is for you to stand with me.

When she looked up from the paper, Harry saw the tears in her eyes. He reached over and ran his finger down her cheek to her lips.

She kissed his fingertip, and he touched it to his lips.

"We were meant for each other, Emmy. Forever and ever. In this universe, and whatever parallel one awaits us."

He watched the tears spill from her eyes and roll down her cheeks.

"Mister, I am so blessed. Kiss me."

Harry leaned over and kissed his bride, and he felt incredible joy at being able to do so.

And when they at last pulled apart, there was a knock at Harry's window.

51

SATURDAY, 17 FEBRUARY 1:14 PM

HARRY ROLLED DOWN HIS WINDOW. "HI, TRINITY."

"Hello, Harry. Ember. I'm sorry to disturb you, but I've been trying to find Ember all morning."

"Back door's open. Get in."

Harry didn't go in for spiritualism, although Trinity was apparently the real deal; and her shop, Spirit of the Shaman, did plenty of business. More than his coffee shop.

She was, as usual, wearing a brightly colored caftan, and a purple band secured her dreadlocks.

He loved her Jamaican accent.

Ember said, "What do you need to see me about?"

"I dreamt about you and Harry the past two nights. The same dream. Ember, you are in a dark place, and a shape blacker than the night looms over you. You are radiating white light, but the shape has the power to snuff out the light. Then you, Harry, appear. You also radiate white light. You spread your arms wide, and from the palms of your hands energy surges towards the shape."

"And what happens?" Ember asked.

"I don't know. I always wake up. So this morning I did a

reading. There are powerful forces working against you, Ember. They draw strength from your past."

"And?" Ember said.

"You must look to your future, for that is from where your deliverer comes."

"That's it?" Harry asked.

"It is enough," Trinity said.

"Will Em triumph?"

"She will. But only if she triumphs over her doubt."

"That's as clear as mud," Harry said.

"Each reading is a path. It is not necessarily the only path. There is danger, and the powerful forces arrayed against you, Ember, will win if you do not conquer your doubts, defeat your fears. But that is only the first step. You will still need to cling to your savior. The one who will enable you to triumph."

"Thank you for seeking me out, Trinity. As the hymn writer wrote: 'God moves in a mysterious way, his wonders to perform.' I believe you've been sent by God to warn me. And for that, I am very thankful. Job received no warning."

"You are a beautiful soul, Ember Cole. And you can win this battle. Now, I've interrupted your day long enough." She opened the car door.

"May God be with you, Trinity Williams," Ember said.

"And also with you, Ember Cole."

Trinity got out of the car and walked towards the Green.

"Well, what do you think of that?" Harry asked.

"I think something not at all good is about to happen."

52

SATURDAY, 17 FEBRUARY 1:52 PM

Harry dropped Ember off at the church so she could finish getting ready for tomorrow's worship service. He continued on to the Really Good and hoped that the frozen custard launch was still bringing in the customers.

"Be nice if the shop began turning a profit. Can't subsidize it forever."

He parked in the alley behind the shop, walked in by the back door, and as he entered the kitchen, Miguel, with a big grin on his face, gave him a salute and called out, "Boss on deck."

Harry laughed, returned the salute, and asked if everything was all right.

"Everything is fine, Mr. Thurgood. We're having a busy day today. Do you want me to make supper for you and the Reverend?"

"That would be wonderful. Em will appreciate it."

"Anything in particular?"

"No. Surprise us."

"Will do."

Harry walked on through to the public area.

Jack Bonhoffer, sitting by the cash register, stuck his finger in his book to mark his place, rested the book on his thigh, and said, "Afternoon, Mr. Thurgood."

"And a very good afternoon to you, Jack. How busy have we been?"

"Fifty-eight customers."

"All paying?"

Jack laughed. "Of course. You weren't here for most of the day."

Harry chuckled. "Got me there."

"Had two folks in asking about your loan service. Told 'em I'd text when you got back. Hope you don't mind."

"Nope. You did just fine."

Estrelita was at a table and winked at him. Harry smiled back. He walked over to where Elisha was standing.

"How's it going?" he asked the boy.

"Great, Mr. Thurgood. Got quiet about fifteen minutes ago. But it's a nice day. We should get more customers in before you close."

"Hope so."

Estrelita came up to the counter and gave an order to Elisha.

Harry asked her, "Are you having a good day?"

"Very good, Mr. Thurgood. Tips only so-so, but no one was demanding."

"No one demanding is good. Hopefully, the tips will improve."

"They are nice. But what you pay me takes care of my needs."

"That's good to hear. I'm glad you're working for me. You're top drawer."

"Is that good?"

"Yes, it is. It's the best."

"Thank you, Mr. Thurgood."

Elisha gave her the dishes of frozen custard and she was off to deliver them.

Harry poured himself a cup of Rwanda Nyamasheke light

roast, snagged a couple of doughnuts, and headed for his table in the corner.

He got seated, took a sip of coffee, and smiled. *Miguel is an outstanding roaster. He knows exactly when to remove the beans.*

The bells above the door rang. Harry looked up and saw Gunter Fight walk in. He watched the man cross the floor and take a seat at his table.

"Hello, Gunter. Have a seat. What can I get you? Coffee?"

"What does that sign in your window mean?"

"Which one?"

"You only have one. The one saying you're in the loan business."

"Ah, that one. It means exactly what it says. I'm in the lending business. Asset-based lending. You need a loan?"

"No, I don't need a loan. I want you to stop."

"Stop what? I haven't loaned any money yet. Which means I'm in business but don't have any business."

"I want you to close your doors."

"On the loan business that doesn't have any business yet?"

"Yes."

"Sorry. Not going to do that. I need money. So I'm diversifying. So to speak. As soon as I get some business, that is."

Fight leaned forward. In a conspiratorial whisper, he said, "One hundred thousand if you take that sign down and stop this enterprise."

"Hm. That's a nice chunk of change. But no. Now if you were to make me a full partner in your bank... That I'd think about."

Fight stood. "You don't know who you're dealing with."

"Come on, Gunter. I'm not the one picking a fight." Harry put a grin on his face.

"I will bury you, Thurgood."

"It didn't work the last time, Nikita. I doubt it will work this time, either."

Fight stormed off.

Harry got up and walked to the window. He watched the

bank owner strut across East Main, the Green, West Main, and on into his bank.

"What a putz," Harry murmured, and return to his table.

He was no sooner seated when the bells chimed and in walked a man and a woman. They looked at Jack; he pointed to the corner, and they walked over to Harry's table.

"Are you Harry Thurgood?" the man asked.

Harry stood. "I am."

"Hello. I'm Telford Whitacre, and this is my wife and business partner Terall."

"Pleased to meet you." Harry shook hands with the Whitacres, then said, "How may I be of help? And please, have a seat. Coffee?"

"No, thank you," Terall said. "We're good."

They sat, and Harry couldn't help but think she had the most radiant smile.

"We're from Massachusetts," Terall said. "We've relocated to Texas because our home state has become far too draconian when it comes to tobacco."

"Yes, it has," Harry agreed.

She continued. "There's a lovely little place a block over on Water Street that we'd like to buy and renovate."

"But the bank won't lend us the money because our business is pipes and tobacco," Telford said.

Now I know why Fight was here, Harry said to himself. Out loud, he said, "Well, I smoke a pipe, so that won't be a problem. In fact, I'll do what I can to help you get established here."

"You will?" Telford said.

"Sure. Brothers — and sisters — of the pipe must stick together."

A big smile was on Terall's face. "Our business is solvent. We have a thriving internet business and we ship tobacco, pipes, and pipe supplies worldwide."

"We also sell cigars," Telford added. "A necessity in this day and age. But our actual interest is pipes."

"What's your business called?"

"T and T Tobacconists," Telford said.

"I like the alliteration. Okay, let's get down to business. How much do you need?"

Terall answered. "Five hundred thousand. The building needs work inside. We'll also need to restock some of our inventory."

"And to keep the customers satisfied," Telford added, "we need to restock like yesterday."

"Completely understand. I will loan you the five hundred K. Your building and business inventory is collateral for the loan. I will lower my interest rate from thirteen to ten percent just for you, and will extend repayment from one year to three. How's that sound?"

"Monthly re-payment amount?" Terall asked.

"One hundred per month. The remaining as a balloon at the end of the three years. Deal?"

The husband and wife looked at each other, looked back at Harry, and together said, "Yes."

Harry smiled as he shook hands with the Whitacres.

At the end of round one, it's Thurgood one, Fight nothing.

53

SATURDAY, 17 FEBRUARY 2:02 PM

EMBER SAT AT HER DESK AND STARED AT HER SERMON NOTES. SHE didn't write out her sermons. She made notes on file cards and then delivered her message extemporaneously.

This week's sermon was on love. Her text was 1 Corinthians 13:4-8a. She had made her own translation.

> *Love suffers long.*
> *Love is kind.*
> *Love does not envy.*
> *Love does not boast about itself, and is not puffed up.*
> *Love does not behave inappropriately, nor does it seek*
>   *its own.*
> *Love is not happy about wickedness, but rejoices in the*
>   *truth.*
> *Love supports all things.*
> *Love believes all things.*
> *Love endures all things.*
> *Love never fails.*

The text, though, was too long. Too many subjects. There was little that was abstract. Most of what Paul had written was practical and to the point. Nevertheless, it covered too many topics.

Her eyes kept going back to the sentence, "Love is kind."

"There's been too much unkindness in our town of late," she said out loud. "If people were only kind to one another, we wouldn't have any problems. We might still have disagreements, but at least we'd be civil about them. There wouldn't be all this rancor, and in some cases out-and-out hate."

A knock on the doorframe brought Ember out of her thoughts. Standing in the doorway was Tipper Duvall.

"Hi, Tipper. Please come in. Have a seat." Given Tipper's antipathy, Ember thought it best to remain behind her desk. She might need the authority it conveyed.

The woman entered Ember's office, but did not sit.

She said, "As chairwoman of the pastor-parish relations committee, I thought it charitable to let you know that a group of us are meeting with the bishop. We think it best that another minister performs Cally's funeral."

"Yes, I know."

"Oh, I see. Uh, news travels fast."

"Yes, it does. Please sit."

"Uh, I need to—"

"Why do you hate me?"

"Well, uh…"

Ember stood and walked around the desk to face Tipper.

"Well, you see, Reverend—"

"Why do you hate me? What have I done to wrong you?"

"Wrong you? Well…"

Ember stepped forward, saw Tipper stiffen, put her arms around the woman, and kissed her cheek. When Ember took a step back, she saw Tipper staring at her.

"Why did you do that? Hug me. Kiss my cheek. I am married, you know."

"Yes, I know. That is how Christians greeted each other in Paul's day. I'm not a lesbian. I kissed you because you are my sister in Christ. In Christ, I love you. I know we may never be friends. But do we have to be enemies? Do you have to hate me?"

"Well, uh, I don't hate you."

Ember took Tipper's hand, saw the woman flinch, and pulled her to a chair. Tipper sat and Ember turned a chair to face her and sat.

"You're a Christian and I'm a Christian," Ember said. "You and I need to prepare and tend and nurture the garden so that it bears much fruit in anticipation of Jesus's return. We can't do that if there is animosity and rancor between us."

When Tipper didn't say anything, Ember continued. "I loved Cally. In Christ. She didn't want to be my friend, although I would have gladly been hers. We need a new lay leader. I'd like that person to be you. But only if you can put aside your hate for me. So I ask again, what have I done to you? I want to make amends to end the wrath."

"You want *me* to be lay leader?"

Ember nodded. "But only if we can at least be friendly, if not friends."

The switch was sharp and surprised Ember. "You're trying to bribe me. Well, you can't. You don't fit here. You're not one of us."

Tipper stood. "Carpetbagger. You've been warned."

Ember watched Tipper storm out of the office and then shook her head. After a moment, she stood, gazed at the empty doorway, and then resumed her seat behind the big oak desk.

I tried, Lord.

She looked at her notes and read, *Love is kind.*

Closing her eyes, she whispered, "Please make me kind, Lord. For then I will know I love."

When Ember looked up, she saw standing in the doorway Mary Lou Fight.

54

SATURDAY, 17 FEBRUARY 3:41 PM

REECE SOVERN PITCHED HIS SOGGY STOGIE INTO THE STREET, repositioned his glasses on the bridge of his nose, got into his car, and slammed his hand against the steering wheel.

He wasn't going to get them to budge. Owen and Clair-Ann alibied each other six ways to Sunday.

Talking to them individually, talking to them together, didn't matter. They stuck to their story like melted cheese on a hamburger. And if any were running off, it wasn't doing so in his direction.

When Clair-Ann started talking lawyer, Reece knew his time with them was over.

He'd followed Thurgood's line of reasoning, that there was only one intended victim, and had questioned the Taylor's again.

He'd gotten nowhere with them, but people were usually killed by their nearest and dearest. And if not by them, they were usually dispatched by at least someone they knew.

Sure there were exceptions. There are exceptions to everything. But as far as murder was concerned, nearest and dearest ruled.

So if Cally was the intended victim, he mused, *and her husband and daughter didn't do her in, who did? Who were her closest friends?*

Who were her rivals? Was she in the way of someone climbing to the top?

Reece got out a fresh cigar, disposed of the cellophane, and stuck the green corona in his mouth.

Cally's murder stood out. That seemed to be a no brainer. The others were too… He thought a moment, searching for a word, and finally said, "Perfunctory." He chuckled. A Thurgood word.

But it fit. Nothing stood out about the other murders. They were all simple. Stab and slash. Lila's would have been too, if she hadn't fought back.

But Cally Taylor… Reece shook his head. That one was gruesomely brutal.

"Yep. Ol' Harry Thurgood is right again," he said out loud. "So, we focus on everyone who knew Cally Taylor. Even if it's half the county."

———

Harry slipped the phone back into his pocket.

The call had been from Elmore. Both he and Mary Lou's detective were flying back to Texas. His news was disturbing. If Elmore was right, then… His mind drifted back to Trinity's words of warning and advice.

Something big's going down for Em. And this just might be it.

He looked around the coffee shop. It was quiet now. The frozen custard launch rush having died down.

This and Em are my life. And it's a good life. One that will only get better.

Except Harry knew the wicked Crimson Hat Queen just might have the wherewithal to take it all away.

What bothers me the most is that I may be powerless to stop her.

The bell over the door chimed and a man walked in. Harry saw Jack point in his direction, and the man made for his table.

"Hi, Mr. Thurgood. I'm Ronald Finseth."

Harry stood, shook hands with the man, and indicated he should sit.

"What can I do for you, Mr. Finseth?"

"I'm looking for a home mortgage loan."

"I don't do those. My loans are short term. No more than a year. And I take the property as collateral."

"Oh, I see. You don't do a good faith loan?"

Harry smiled. "I'm not a loan shark. I don't bust knee caps if you can't pay. I'm a hard money lender and I take assets as collateral. Sorry, I can't help you."

"Very well. Thank you for your time."

Harry nodded to the man. His phone rang at the same time, and he pulled it from his pocket. *Wonder what Graham wants?*

"Afternoon, Graham. What's cookin'?"

"Glad you didn't say 'good lookin' because then I'd know you were lyin'."

"Honest Abe Thurgood."

"Ha! That's a Pinocchio for sure."

"So, what can I do you for?"

"Monika's out and so are Rob and Landon. I have something to tell you, so why don't you hop on over?"

"On my way."

Call ended, Harry slipped the phone into his pocket, told Jack where he was headed, and left the coffee shop.

Huston was at his desk in the back of the small office of the *Magnolia Bluff Chronicle.*

"Have a seat, Harry."

Harry sat in the straight-back chair. "What's so hush-hush?"

"Two things. Mary Lou's making a move to oust your wife. Possibly as soon as tomorrow."

"Okay. Next."

"You know. Impressive. Okay. Next is this little gem: someone saw Clair-Ann at the church the morning her mother died."

"How soon after her mother arrived?"

"Don't know. The person didn't check the time. Just saw Clair-Ann. Didn't think anything of it."

"Why don't they want to go to the police?"

"Bad experience."

"I see. So they tell you instead."

"I'm not the police."

"But this information is pretty much worthless if he or she doesn't come forward."

"It has its limits. But you and I know that Clair-Ann lied to the police, and that is very valuable. For us, that is. Probably not so valuable to the police."

"So why tell me?"

"Because you're checking things out. And if you tell Reece, fine. If he asks where you got the information, you can tell him some story. Me? He'll want to know my source, and I want to protect my source. You can blow him off with a story easier than I can."

"Thanks for the info, Graham."

"You're welcome. I appreciate doing business with you."

Harry chuckled. "I'm sure you do."

On the way back to the Really Good, Harry pondered how he could use the information.

Just might have to do an I-know-what-you-did-last-summer campaign. See if she cracks.

But more importantly, word was getting around that Mary Lou was making her move to get rid of Ember. That meant Saint Luke's would be packed tomorrow and it would probably be best if some of those packing the church were friends.

55

SUNDAY, 18 FEBRUARY 10:54 AM

HARRY SAT IN THE LAST PEW ON THE RIGHT AND WATCHED THE
people filing in. And there were a lot of them.

He'd attended often enough to know who was a regular and
who wasn't. This morning there were an awful lot of visitors.

His mind drifted back to last night. Em had been very quiet.
He'd tried to get her to talk, but she had politely, yet persistently,
refused. Her cryptic remark was, "Tomorrow all things will be
revealed. For better or for worse."

And that was that. She refused to say more.

Harry finally said to her, "Okay, Emmy, we'll talk tomorrow."

Then she asked him to make love to her, which he did.

This morning she was quiet. She'd taken an early phone call,
but did so out of earshot.

They made small talk until she left for the church.

Now he was sitting in the sanctuary. Waiting. Waiting with
the scores of people filling up the pews.

He nodded to Graham Huston and Monika Crow when they
walked in. Returned the waves of Joetta Reston and her mother,
Jearlene. And nodded his head in acknowledgement of Landon
Pace's casual salute.

When Tipper Duvall and her husband walked by, he did his best to give them a warm smile. And the same when he saw Tiffany Graceson and Pearline Applewhite and her husband.

With Tiffany and Pearline in attendance, Harry knew Mary Lou was going to make her move.

Harry gave a nod to Stanton and Scarlett when they walked in.

At least he wouldn't be going into battle alone.

However, he couldn't help but think this was how Roland felt at Roncevaux Pass, outnumbered and in a bad position, when he and his troops were ambushed by the Moors. Although, the Frankish leader didn't have Scarlett blowing him a kiss.

The next hour was a great big unknown. And all he could do was wait and play it by ear.

––––––––

The organist was playing soft, meditative music. But the general tenor of those in the pews was anything but meditative.

The Reverend Ember Cole and Assistant to the Bishop, the Reverend Doctor O. Karen Dinsmore, came out of one of the back doors, walked to the chancel, and sat.

At eleven o'clock, Doctor Dinsmore stepped up to the pulpit. "Good morning. I'm Karen Dinsmore, assistant to Bishop Cobb. This morning, before worship, the Reverend Ember Cole is going to tell you a story. She told her story to me yesterday, and it is quite a story. After consulting with Bishop Cobb, he and I want to reiterate our support for your pastor. Reverend Cole?"

Ember stood and when Doctor Dinsmore had returned to her seat, Ember took the pulpit.

"I am going to tell you a story. My story. It is not pretty. And I have told it to no one before now. But it has come to my attention that my past has been discovered. And rather than have you hear it from others, I want you to hear it from me. If, after you've heard it, you have no confidence in me to be your pastor, I will accede to your wishes.

"Many years ago, when I was young, too young, really, I married a man who I thought was the love of my life. He turned out to be a horribly abusive man, both physically and mentally. I ran away from him and my marriage. And ended up in Las Vegas. I was without a job and had very little money. It is, however, quite easy to get money in Las Vegas. At least for a woman. And I took the easy route. I became an actress in the porn industry and quickly became a porn star. But pornography doesn't pay a lot, although women get paid way more than men. So I moonlighted as a high end prostitute at one of the casinos.

"I developed a significant following both as a film star and as a prostitute. My income increased, and I spent the money as fast as I made it on drugs, booze, and fast living.

"One morning, I woke up, looked in the mirror, and asked myself what was I going to do when I was no longer young and pretty. I had no answer. A worn out whore is a truly pathetic sight, and I'd seen enough of them to know I didn't want to become one.

"Not long after that morning I was channel surfing on the car radio and I heard a Christian speaker quoting a verse: 'His yoke is easy. His burden is light.' And a voice said to me, 'This is what you are looking for. You've found the way home.' I remember pulling over to the curb crying. Sobbing. The radio preacher then quoted, 'Come unto Him all ye who labor, and He will give you rest.'

"Right then, I knew I could never again turn another trick or have sex in front of a camera. That life was over. I had become a new person.

"I left Las Vegas, ended up in Minneapolis, where I went to college and got my bachelor's degree, and then went on to seminary.

"That is my story. I pray you will let me continue to minister to you. And I'm sorry I didn't say anything before now, but I was ashamed of my past life and wanted it to remain buried forever. Please forgive me."

Ember saw Mary Lou Fight get to her feet. "What a tale our strumpet in the pulpit has told us. It's time—"

A lilting baritone filled the sanctuary, drowning out the strident voice of Mary Lou. Ember saw Harry standing and singing:

> *Amazing grace! (how sweet the sound)*
> *That saved a wretch like me!*
> *I once was lost, but now am found,*
> *Was blind, but now I see.*

As Harry began the second stanza, Ember watched Jearlene and Joetta Reston stand and join in. Then Scarlett Hayden, Stanton Lauderbach, Graham Huston, and Monika Crow stood and joined in singing the hymn.

One after the other, she saw church council members Claiborne Allen, Ruth Ann Covington, Jane Jackson, Blake Hillwood, and Marveen Smalls stand and join the singing.

And Ember, who'd been so afraid of what Harry's reaction would be, watched him walk down the center aisle towards her. She stepped out from behind the pulpit and joined him in front of the communion table, where, together, holding hands, they faced the congregation.

Mary Lou and Gunter Fight walked out, followed by the other Crimson Hat members, except for Goody Preminger and her husband. They remained standing and singing.

As Ember sang

> *Through many dangers, toils, and snares,*
> *I have already come;*
> *'Tis grace hath brought me safe thus far,*
> *And grace will lead me home.*

. . .

she knew in her heart of hearts God had poured out His grace on her.

56

SUNDAY, 18 FEBRUARY 2:21 PM

HARRY AND EMBER GRABBED LUNCH TO GO FROM LUBY'S HOT Chicken and then headed out of town.

"Where are we going?" Ember asked.

"Some place nice and quiet."

They ended up at Enchanted Rock State Natural Area, where they ate their chicken sliders and fries.

When finished eating, Harry filled his pipe with Holiday mixture and they went for a walk.

"Harry, I have to know: are you going to stay with me?"

He took hold of her hand. "Emmy, I love you. Do you remember the poem I gave you?"

She nodded and touched her dress pocket. "It's right here."

"Then that says everything. Yes, I'm going to stay with you. And I hope that we get to raise a family together and grow old together."

She stopped walking and pulled him into a hug. "Thank you for loving me. I love you so much. I was scared to death you were going to leave me."

"Why?"

"Because of all the men and women I've been with. All the things I've done. The drugs. The booze."

"Emmy, you haven't done that stuff for quite a while now. You are a different person. The Ember who did those things is dead. Yes, they are in your past, but you don't have to let them control you."

He took her hand, and they continued walking.

"You're a new creation in Christ, are you not?"

"I am."

"Then your past lies in the old creation that is no more."

"Thanks for the reminder. I needed that."

He smiled. "Of course, that does explain why you are so accomplished in bed."

"You would think of that."

"Hey, I'm a man. We men do think about that."

Ember chuckled. "Yeah, we women do too. Although we want sex with the man we love. And I'm so glad God blessed me with you. I have everything now."

"I'm glad you think so, because I think the same."

"You succeeded in chasing Mary Lou out of the church."

"A little ploy I learned from an old political science teacher in college. Make sure your side is spread out in a group meeting. Then cheer on your proposals so that the others think they are outnumbered because there isn't one little cluster of people advocating for the issue. The advocates are everywhere. And most people don't want to be on the losing side."

"That's pretty clever. It sure seemed to work this morning."

"Yes, it did."

"I think today was a big setback for the Queen. The bishop still supports me, and then the people in the church stood behind me."

"True. Although, I don't think we've seen the last of her. But I daresay she's finished on this front. Your confession stole her fire."

"And your singing rallied the troops."

Harry laughed. "That it did."

"Credit, though, needs to be given to Doctor Dinsmore. She

was not in the least put off when I told her that Mary Lou had found out about my past. In fact, Doc Dinsmore wanted to go big. You know, 'High-Class Call Girl Finds Christ.' But I said no. I don't want to be a poster girl and I don't want my past to be the talked about subject anymore than it is."

"Well, I think you just might want to rethink your position. Because your past may be just the thing to bring in some of those college kids and those who are involved in all kinds of destructive behaviors. You can show them hope from your own life."

"Hm. I suppose so. I'll have to think about it. But more importantly, we need to find Cally's killer. That is the last thing to put to rest the current unrest in the congregation. And then the crooked will be made straight."

"And the potholes filled in."

Ember giggled. "Not very bible-speak, but true."

Harry told Ember what Graham Huston had told him.

"Oh, my God, Harry. That's like proof positive."

"Yes, and no. It makes Clair-Ann a likely suspect. But if the person who saw her refuses to come forth, it doesn't do us any good."

"And if we confront her, she'll just deny it. So what else can we do?"

"I think we need to do an I-know-what-you-did-last-summer play."

"We aren't going to kill her."

"Of course not. We simply want her to confess."

"I don't know. It might work. Although she just might blow it off."

"She might. But if she feels the noose tightening, she may decide to tell all. I don't have any other ideas. Do you?"

"No. I don't. But I'm not convinced it will work. And what if she isn't the killer? I mean, we don't actually know who the killer is. We're just guessing."

"That's very true. It's just a guess. Someone with an onus against Clair-Ann could be framing her." He paused a moment, then continued. "The church doesn't have security cameras, correct?"

"That's correct. Small town. The council hasn't seen any need. They might now, though."

"No help there, then." He puffed on his pipe. It was out, so he re-lit it. "What do you think? Are we going to do an I-know-what-you-did-last-summer campaign or not?"

"I don't think we have any choice. I just hope that if she's innocent, we don't end up driving her to do something we'll regret."

"We can leave it and try to come up with something else."

"Cally's death is a big issue. We need to resolve it by finding who killed her. When we do, I think we'll finally have peace. My church will have peace."

"Okay, then. We're on. Let's hope she's guilty and Cally gets justice."

57

SUNDAY, 18 FEBRUARY 2:21 PM

A DOG WITH A NEW CHEW TOY WOULDN'T HAVE BEEN HAPPIER THAN Graham Huston. The bombshell Ember Cole dropped on her congregation was worthy of a ninety-six point headline and a special edition for Monday morning reading.

He'd sent Rob Carter to interview Claiborne Allen. Landon Pace was off interviewing Tipper Duvall. Monika Crow was tracking down Clair-Ann Taylor for an interview.

And he, himself, was ringing the doorbell of the one and only Mary Lou Fight. With a finger on the button, he once again thought how apt her name was.

"Surprised she's not Baptist," he muttered.

The door was opened by a tall and slender young woman. She wore a black maid's uniform, complete with a white cap set atop her short and straight blonde hair.

"I'm Graham Huston. I have an appointment with Mrs. Fight."

"She's expecting you. Come in, please."

The maid's voice, while pleasant, was heavily accented.

Some Eastern European language, he thought. *Slavic, but not Russian.*

He entered the house, and let his eyes roam the entryway.

Gaudy. For all their money, the Fights have no taste.

Following the maid, he ended up in a large room. A fireplace dominated one wall. The opposite wall was solid glass and afforded a view of the Reservoir. At the far end of the room was a white grand piano.

Mary Lou was sitting on a sofa. Her husband, Gunter, was sitting in a chair by the fireplace. He was reading a hardback book and smoking a cigar. There was a square decanter of some brownish liquid and a tumbler on a small table next to the chair.

The maid announced Graham and withdrew.

Gunter stood. "Come in, Mr. Huston."

He met Graham halfway, shook hands, and motioned towards a chair. "You've met my wife, haven't you?"

Graham indicated he had. Mr. Fight nodded and returned to his seat by the fireplace.

"Have a seat, Mr. Huston," Mrs. Fight said.

"Good afternoon, and thank you." He sat in an overstuffed chair facing the sofa.

"I suppose you're here to get my views on the latest travesty befalling my church."

"What's happened at the Presbyterian Church?" Graham hoped his face was the picture of innocence.

Mrs. Fight blinked at him. Four times, before she said, "I was referring to Saint Luke's. Saint Luke's is my church. But as long as there is a strumpet in the pulpit, I, and many others as well, are part of the congregation in exile."

"Congregation in exile?"

Mrs. Fight nodded.

"But you were there today, and Reverend Cole was in the pulpit, with the bishop's blessing. I'm assuming she's the strumpet of whom you were referring."

"She is. And it is a shame that today's ecclesiastics are so very tolerant of open sin, such as that displayed by the woman occupying the pulpit at Saint Luke's."

"Your church."

"Yes, my church."

"But you were in attendance today."

"I was. I was going to make an announcement."

"I didn't notice your name on the order of worship. Were you going to interrupt the service?"

It was all Graham could do to prevent the smirk from appearing on his face. There was no expression on Mrs. Fight's, but her eyes were pools of ice.

"Yes, I suppose I would have had to interrupt the service to make my announcement."

"In fact, you started to do so, but were stopped by Harry Thurgood's singing. Isn't that right?"

"Yes. The lounge lizard rallied the strumpet's supporters so that I couldn't be heard."

"But didn't Reverend Cole, in fact, steal your thunder by her confession of her past?"

"Not really. You see—"

"Come on, Mrs. Fight, Reverend Cole made an end run and derailed your plan, to mix metaphors. But you get my point, I'm sure."

"I *get* your point, Mr. Huston. I had a very fine private school education. I'm not like most of the people who live here."

"Ah, well, that's good to know. So, Reverend Cole made a full disclosure of her past. She asked for forgiveness for not being up front from the beginning, but explained that her feelings of shame had held her back. So, now that she has confessed and has the congregation's and bishop's support, are you going to forgive her? Will you be returning to your church, as you put it?"

"Really, now, Mr. Huston. How can you expect me to forgive someone's past who is still an open sinner here in the present?"

"What do you mean?"

"Why her relationship with that coffee shop lothario."

"I don't understand. Ember Cole and Harry Thurgood are married."

"You mean that common law nonsense?" She made a disapproving noise. "They did not have a real wedding in a church. They didn't even have the decency to have Wylie Garrison or Judge Jones perform the ceremony. She and the lounge lizard just went ahead and started rutting like cats in heat. You call that a marriage?"

"The state of Texas does recognize their union as a legal marriage."

"That may be, Mr. Huston, but it doesn't mean that a servant of God can lower herself to act like the *hoi polloi*."

"The Reverend has the backing of the bishop and a sizable number of members of the congregation."

"Your point?"

"Perhaps it's time you accept what is."

From the direction of the fireplace, Graham heard, "That's the problem with this country. No stomach for change. Good change. Not the stuff spouted off by the current batch of rabble-rousers. No respect for culture or tradition."

"You see, Mr. Huston," Mary Lou began, "ministers are to behave in a manner that is consistent with the tradition of the office. Reverend Cole does not behave appropriately. Not now. Not ever. She should not be occupying that sacred office. Now that she's taken up with the coffee shop man, perhaps she should use her talents there: serving coffee and such."

Mr. Fight chimed in. "And where does he get his money? He has virtually nothing at my bank. Can't be legal."

Graham didn't want to get distracted talking about Harry Thurgood, so he asked, "In spite of your desire to replace Reverend Cole, it doesn't appear that's going to happen. At least in the near future. Do you intend to continue your campaign to try to get her to leave?"

Mary Lou smiled, and the smile contained not one bit of mirth. "That, Mr. Huston, is my business. Not yours. Not your readers. No one's." She rang a bell. "Eliška will show you out."

58

SUNDAY, 18 FEBRUARY 2:25 PM

ROB CARTER SAT IN A VERY COMFORTABLE, TUB-STYLE CHAIR. Claiborne Allen sat in a rocking chair across from him, smoking a pipe. The smell of the pipe tobacco was quite pleasant.

"How can I help you, Mr. Carter? What do the readers of the *Chronicle* wish to know?"

"Were you surprised by Reverend Cole's revelation of her past?"

"Well, who wouldn't be? But I don't hold it against her. She was a lost soul, escaping an abusive husband. She made her trek through the Slough of Despond and came out the other side a fine example of what Christ can do for a person."

"Are you still going to support her as your pastor?"

"Of course I am. She's a wonderful person. She's a dedicated servant of the Lord. I think her marriage to Mr. Thurgood will soften some of the seriousness that may have put some people off."

"Are you saying she wasn't fun-loving?"

"I wouldn't say that. There was a gravitas about her. An all business attitude. I think we'll see more laughter and light-heartedness."

"Will Reverend Cole's past work against her in the community?"

"Here in Magnolia Bluff?"

Rob nodded.

"Someone will always take exception to something. But if Christ can produce a marvelous woman like Ember, well, in my book, that's the best testimony a church can have. Might even lead to a genuine revival."

"You think we need one?"

"Given the amount of sin one sees on a daily basis, I'd say so."

"But isn't a revival tantamount to stuffing religion down people's throats?"

"Christ offers peace. He's not forcing it on anyone. And neither are we his servants. If you aren't a believer, then all we're doing is offering you an alternative to your current belief system. And given Reverend Cole's transformation, I'd say that's a powerful change that can happen to anyone. A powerful change for the better."

"What about the dissension in the church? Do you think it will go away?"

"Difficult to say for sure, but I do have my doubts about that. Just too many ornery people at St. Luke's."

Landon Pace was very impressed with the Duvall home. From what he'd seen, it was tastefully furnished. It spoke of money, but very subtly. And he liked that.

He and Tipper Duvall were seated in the living room.

"That's a lovely painting," Landon said.

"It was painted by Arnold Duvall, the famous Hill Country artist."

"Any relation?"

"My husband's grandfather."

"He was very talented."

"Yes, he was." Tipper took a cigarette from a box on the coffee table. "Would you like one, Mr. Pace? They're Turkish tobacco. I have them specially made for me by a tobacconist in Greece. I get one thousand every month. I smoke no more than half. The rest I sell or give away."

"I smoke an occasional cigar. Never smoked a cigarette."

"The taste is very strong. Try one. Smoke it like a cigar."

Landon took the cigarette. Tipper put hers in a cigarette holder, lit it, and passed the large crystal lighter to him.

He lit the cigarette and puffed on it. The smoke was thick, spicy, and sweet. It certainly wasn't anything like a cigar. And it was strong.

"So, what do you wish to talk to me about?" She took a deep drag on her cigarette, held it, then exhaled.

"Reverend Cole. What's your take on her confession?"

"It's quite a little secret she's been sitting on. I'm not sure there's much we can do. She has the backing of the bishop and a large portion of the congregation."

"But you're the chair of the Pastor-Parish Relations Committee. Surely, you have some say in the matter."

"Not as much as I'd like. We have requested of the bishop that someone other than Reverend Cole perform Mrs. Taylor's funeral."

"Have you gotten an answer to your request?"

"Not yet. But after today, I'm not very hopeful we'll get the answer we want."

"Who are *we*? The committee?"

"No. A group of us in the church who feel that because of the animosity between the Reverend and Mrs. Taylor, it is inappropriate for the Reverend to conduct the service."

"I see. How does Reverend Cole feel about your plan and what do the Taylors want?"

"You'll have to ask them."

"In other words, you don't want Reverend Cole to conduct a

funeral service even if the family is okay with her doing so. Is that correct?" Landon favored her with a big smile.

Tipper inhaled smoke from her cigarette and blew out a long, slow stream towards the ceiling. "If the Taylors insist on the Reverend conducting the service, then that is what should happen."

"What about her revelation of her past? What sort of impact do you think it will have on her work at the church?"

"I don't know. It is a concern. Her ministry here started well and then it just seemed to become fraught with problems."

"So you don't think she's good for the church?"

"No, I don't. Not anymore."

———

Monika Crow drove all over town before she finally found Clair-Ann Taylor leaving the cemetery.

She rolled down her window, waved her hand, and called out, "Clair-Ann! Do you have a few minutes to talk?"

The young woman walked over to Monika's car. "What do you want to talk about?"

"What was the issue between your mother and Pastor Cole?"

"I haven't had lunch yet."

"Hop in and we'll get something to eat."

Clair-Ann got into Monika's car. "Is Storm's okay with you?"

"Sure. Let's go."

Monika put the car in drive and headed off toward the fast food place.

"I was talking with my grandmother," Clair-Ann volunteered. "She's buried in the cemetery. Almost all of my family is. A few were cremated. Some were killed in wars. I have a great-great-granduncle whose position was hit by German artillery in World War One. There was nothing left to bury."

"Is there a plaque or something?"

"I don't know if there was or not. Maybe a flag. You'd have to ask my father."

"That must've been tough for those at the time."

"I suppose. When it came to Saint Luke's, my mom was a control freak."

"Why was that?"

"Because she didn't like anyone."

Monika pulled into the parking lot. "Eat here, okay?"

"Sure. That's fine."

Monika parked, they got out, and went into the restaurant. They ordered their burgers and drinks and found a place to sit.

"Your mom didn't like anyone? What do you mean by that?"

Clair-Ann sucked Dr. Pepper through her straw. After she swallowed, she said, "Just that. Her lover was Saint Luke's. She lived for that church. Not the people. The building, the organization, the power."

"What about her faith?"

"I'm not sure she had any. My mother was a control freak. Early on, she found she couldn't control me or Dad. So she lived for Buck, my brother, and Saint Luke's."

"Do you have any idea why your mother would be part of this current string of murders?"

Clair-Ann shrugged. "I don't know. Maybe those other people were doing what was wrong. Just like my mother."

Their burgers arrived and they took a couple minutes to get situated; after which they ate in silence for several minutes.

Clair-Ann dipped a French fry into ketchup. "So what is Monika going to hear about me on Tuesday?" She popped the fry into her mouth.

Monika chuckled. "Don't know if she'll hear anything about you. But Graham wants to put out a special edition tomorrow."

"He's going to put Reverend Cole on the hot seat? He shouldn't, you know. What she did today was very brave. It shows what the church is all about."

"I don't know what his angle will be. He does like Ember, so I doubt he's going to roast her. Besides, Harry's a big advertiser."

"Money talks, doesn't it?"

"Well, it certainly does when you're trying to keep the lights on. Small town newspapers are making a desperate and not so successful attempt to fight extinction."

"The business version of the dodo."

"Something like that. So what do you think these other people were doing that was wrong?"

"Other people?"

"Yeah. The ones that were killed. The police think there might be a race aspect to the murders."

Clair-Ann shrugged. "That might fit Zelmo. A jock for Jesus that was putting one through the uprights of every white girl he could get to say yes."

"Not very religious."

"He was a jock. A basketball player. All they think about are balls and what they're slapping against."

"Certainly true of some."

"Ha. Not some. All. Disgusting, immoral pigs. Not crying any crocodile tears over Zelmo the pig for Jesus."

Some strong feelings there, for sure. Wonder what her story is. Out loud, Monica said, "Does that go for DeWayne as well?"

"He was a jock, wasn't he? And he wasn't dating a black girl."

"But race doesn't apply to Vonnie Vebelsteadt or your mom."

"No, it doesn't. But religion does. Religion also applies to the others. Lila was Catholic and DeWayne was Baptist. Vonnie was Lutheran. Very devout. My mother was married to the church. Zelmo was with Holy Crusaders for Christ."

"That's interesting. Hadn't thought of that. Religion's involved with all the victims."

"And they all got religion screwed up. Reverend Cole is such a nice person. If I were her, I'd leave that messed up church and work in the coffee shop with that movie star she married. Everything would be so much better. I gotta go. My dad's been alone too long. He needs me there."

"Sure. I'll drop you off." On the way to Clair-Ann's house, Monika couldn't help but think she'd uncovered something significant.

59

NOT FOR THE FIRST TIME, GRAHAM HUSTON THOUGHT ABOUT putting the *Chronicle* online behind a pay wall.

It would be a lot cheaper and easier, he said to himself, *and we might actually get younger people to read it. Especially if there was an app.*

He made a change in Rob Carter's story. *I wonder how kids these days take a crap, because as far as I know there's no app for that.* He paused in his rumination, then continued, *At least I don't think there's an app. Wouldn't be surprised if there was, though.*

His mind drifted back to Monika's story, which was doggone good, along with the separate sheet of notes she'd made for him.

Monika's observations were insightful. In Graham's opinion, significantly so.

Probably need to share these with Harry and Ember, he thought. *I doubt they're in danger, but in the end, who knows? More and more it's looking like Clair-Ann's breakfast is missing the biscuits and gravy. No telling what she might end up doing. That is, if she's guilty.*

Harry felt Ember snuggle next to him. They'd just spent the past thirty, forty minutes making the most delicious love.

He was the luckiest man on earth. A smile touched his lips. *Probably every man who's just made love to the woman of his dreams has thought that.*

And Ember was indeed the woman of his dreams. She was beautiful. And what man doesn't think his woman is beautiful? Whether she is or not. But Ember was beautiful.

She was also witty. Bright. Devoted. And had her own mind.

Harry knew, in his heart of hearts, he was going to enjoy growing old with this woman by his side.

His only concern was that it was now just he who had the secret life, and would she want him to tell her what it was? For her own sake, he hoped she would leave it be. Unfortunately, he had his doubts that she would.

But I'll cross that bridge if or when I need to, he told himself.

He turned his head and saw her looking at him. "Like what you see?" he asked.

"I do. And I have from the first time we met. You're very handsome, you know. Kind of like a movie star."

He chuckled. "I thought the same of you."

"That silent film star, right?"

"Yes. Louise Brooks. The most beautiful woman. Next to you, of course."

"Go on. You're just saying that."

"I am just saying that because it's true. And you are so much better than Louise. At least to me. I can hold you, kiss you, look at you, and talk with you forever."

"We'd never get anything done. And we do need to get a few things done every now and then."

"Burst a guy's bubble, why don't you?"

"Can't help it, I'm practical. Had to be. Otherwise, life would have totally crushed me."

"What about God?"

"What about Him?"

"Isn't he supposed to be there for you?"

"He is. But He also gave us brains, and I believe He expects us to use them."

"That's quite incredible."

"What is?"

"That God expects us to think."

Ember smiled. "Isn't it, though?" She sat up. "After that work out, I'd like something to eat. How about you?"

"My mouth says yes. My waistline says no."

"And the winner is?"

"My mouth."

She laughed. "Okay, tubby, follow me."

Harry sat up and watched her get out of bed and leave the bedroom. God, she was beautiful.

She poked her head back into the room. "Hey, Mister, I said, 'Follow me.' What the heck are you still sitting there for?"

Harry smiled and got out of bed. *Oh, yeah. I love this woman.*

60

MONDAY, 19 FEBRUARY 2:21 AM

THE AIR WAS DRY AND CHILL. THE THERMOMETER WAS HOVERING around the 42°F mark.

At least the wind is calm. Harry Thurgood comforted himself with the thought.

The moon and stars were out there somewhere, but the cloud cover was a black blanket pulled across the night sky.

To match the night, Harry wore black sweats, black shoes and socks, black gloves, and a black balaclava.

His pencil flashlight threw a thin beam of yellowish light on the sidewalk.

No one was about.

He chuckled. *It's a lie. They don't roll up the sidewalks after dark. I'm walking on one.*

He stood in front of the Taylor home and let his eyes roam the house, the homes of the neighbors on either side, and then he turned around and surveyed the homes and yards across the street.

In his pockets, he had the envelope containing the note and four tiny surveillance cameras.

The wonders of modern technology. For a few bucks, we can spy on our neighbors, our spouses, our significant others, our friends, our enemies. We can all be Gladys Kravitz on steroids.

And that was a very scary feeling. Everyone spying on everyone. And the government, the biggest spy of them all.

Harry pulled himself out of his reverie and went to work.

He slipped the envelope through the mail slot in the door. Two of the cameras he fixed to trees across the street. They covered the front door. The other two cameras he positioned to cover the back door.

He checked the app on his phone. The cameras were live and sending video to the cloud.

All's well that ends well. And tonight has gone well thus far. Hopefully tomorrow will tell if my guess is correct and we can end this. Now, though, I have to make it home without being detected. Reece had better be asleep. I don't need his car pulling to the curb and him asking me what I'm doing.

And with that hope foremost in his mind, Harry headed for home.

61

MONDAY, 19 FEBRUARY 5:51 AM

BEING THAT IT WAS HER DAY OFF, EMBER DECIDED SHE'D WALK TO the Really Good with Harry and perhaps spend the day there. The idea being to see how her husband ran his store. To learn firsthand what her husband did all day.

They were holding hands, walking down the street, enjoying the morning. Harry was smoking his pipe. Some nice smelling blend he called Barking Dog. The aroma was like the smell of a campfire in the distance.

She'd smoked cigarettes some in her former life, but most of the time, if she smoked anything, it was weed. But that was years ago. She quit smoking anything when she left Vegas.

In fact, when she left Vegas, she left behind a lot of things. The drugs. The sex. The booze. The fancy clothes. The parties. At first, it was freeing. But as time went on, her self-imposed asceticism felt more and more like a cage. And now, married to Harry, she once again felt free.

Today, she left her clerical garb at home. She was wearing an ankle-length, long-sleeved A-line dress in dark brown, with a red and gold paisley pattern. On top of the dress, she wore a beige cardigan sweater.

On her head was a dark red, wide-brimmed fedora-style hat. And on her feet were dark brown Mary Janes.

Harry was wearing a dark gray, three-piece suit. The gray having a slightly brownish cast to it. The suit was custom made by Brooks Brothers.

His tie was an intricate red and brown pattern overlaying a yellow background. His hat was a charcoal gray pork pie. Black socks and Oxfords completed his outfit.

She thought they made a handsome couple and giggled at the thought.

"What's so funny?"

"If I may say so, I think we make quite a couple. Look at us. We're totally the style mavens."

"I guess we are. When it comes to clothes, I have to admit to a bit of vanity. I like a good set of threads. But what surprises me is your secret wardrobe. Who would have guessed?"

"And all I did was wear them in the house."

"Why not in public?"

"I was maintaining an image. It was like I had to remind everyone I was the pastor. I was a servant of God. Perhaps I was overcompensating for my past life."

"And you don't feel you need to prove it now?"

"Since you and I, well, since we decided to get married, it's like I don't need to prove anything anymore. Your steadfast commitment, even when I didn't give you a lot to hope for, has given me a freedom. I'm a woman first. That's how God made me. Secondarily, He chose me to be His servant."

"God actually chose you?"

"Yes, in a dream. Jesus said the words of the Great Commission to me. So I went to seminary and became a Methodist minister."

"Interesting. He actually spoke to you?"

"He did. It was a shock the first time. Two nights later, he repeated the commission. Only he used my name that time."

"Has he talked to you since?"

"He has." Ember stopped walking. "Do you think I'm nuts?"

"No, I don't. To be honest, I'm not sure what to think. Obviously, you believe Jesus spoke to you. Who am I to say he didn't? Henry James said that the visions of the mystic are the most convincing of religious experiences. But only to the mystic. I've never had a mystical experience. I've never seen or experienced a ghost. But others have. How can I say they didn't, even though I may not think it's even possible? Belief is just that: belief. At the end of the day, even science is a belief system. Belief that the facts we think we observe, and our interpretation of them, are truth."

"I grew up in a nominally Christian home. We didn't go to church, and religion was seldom talked about. My abusive husband and Vegas showed me two aspects of myself I didn't like. I looked at my life and said to myself, there has to be more than this. And I discovered there is."

They resumed their walk. In the distance, she heard the sound of a car engine and, just above their heads, the light wind in the bare branches.

"I rather admire that about you, Emmy. That you have a purpose beyond eating and sleeping and just getting through the day to once again eat and sleep."

"What's your purpose?"

He shrugged. "Not sure I have one. In fact, I don't think we human beings have any ultimate purpose. Other than perhaps reproduction. Just like nature, we're simply here. I try to live by the Golden Rule and to live simply. I don't think keeping up with the Joneses gets us anywhere. Consumerism just creates a lot of unhappiness."

"Living simply isn't bad. In fact, it's pretty good. But no purpose other than reproduction? I find that a bit depressing."

"It's the only thing all living entities have in common. So, to my way of thinking, it must be the baseline. Anything beyond that is ultimately up to the entity."

"I think that only applies to us humans. I can't imagine trees doing anything other than just living and ultimately dying."

"Reproducing in between."

"I suppose. Do you have any children?"

"No. You?"

"No. And, in case you're wondering, I'm not taking any birth control. I hope that's not a problem. We probably should have discussed it."

"Well, in case you hadn't noticed, I'm not doing any preventive measures either."

"I guess we're on the same page then."

"Seems we are."

"I love you, Harry. Heart and soul."

With a smirk on his lips, Harry began singing:

> *Heart and soul, I fell in love with you*
> *Heart and soul, the way a fool...*

And a familiar black sedan pulled to the curb next to them.

62

MONDAY, 19 FEBRUARY 6:04 AM

REECE ROLLED DOWN THE CAR WINDOW. "GOOD MORNING. YOU two out for an early morning stroll?"

"Walking to the Really Good," Harry answered. "It's a workday."

"So it is. Why don't you get in and I'll give you a lift."

From the looks on their faces, Reece could tell they weren't too happy with his suggestion. But in spite of the looks, they got in the car. Harry in the front seat, and Ember in the back.

To keep the mood light, Reece said, "You're lookin' mighty smart there, Reverend. That's a very attractive outfit."

"Thank you, Mr. Sovern."

She sure has a pretty smile. That Thurgood is a lucky guy.

He put the car in drive and stepped on the gas.

"Well, Reece, anything in particular on your mind?" Thurgood asked.

"I know you and Huston are sniffing around these murders, and I was wondering if you found out anything that might be helpful."

"Did you ask Graham?" the Reverend asked.

"I did. He was very tightlipped. Told me to read the paper. Guess there's a special edition coming out this morning."

"I doubt we can be of help, Reece," Thurgood said. "I already suggested a line of inquiry. We have nothing more to add."

Nothing more to add, my foot, Reece thought. Out loud, he said, "Well, we're here. If you come across anything, will you please pass it my way? I'd appreciate it."

Thurgood got out of the car. "Will do, Reece." He opened the back door for the Reverend, and she got out.

"Hope you have a good day, Reece," Reverend Cole told him, and then she turned and he watched the two enter the coffee shop.

I'm willing to wager my pension that those two and Huston have something under wraps. I have half a mind to start monitoring those three. Save me and the DA's investigator a whole lot of time.

———

"What was that all about?" Ember asked, as they entered the coffee shop.

"Reece is desperate, methinks."

"But why pick on us?"

"The police are basically bureaucrats. They have to get results to justify their budget. It's a fact of life for all government agencies. So, in Reece's case, he's going to pester us and Graham because he suspects we have the answers, so he can close the book on this case."

"Well, I'm getting tired of it. I don't have anything against him, personally. I think he's basically a nice guy. However, I'd like him to quit being a yo-yo. Pick a position. We're bad, or we're good."

"Nice thought, that. But don't hold your breath."

"You're probably right."

"Ah, I hear Miguel in the kitchen. Why don't you see how he sets up, while I go get a paper."

"Okay."

Harry left the shop, jogged across East Main, the Green, West Main, and entered the *Chronicle* office.

Monika was all smiles. "Come to get a paper?"

"I did."

"I have one right here for you."

"Why, thank you.'

"Always happy to be of service to one of our best advertisers."

"Ha! I knew there was a catch."

"There always is, Mr. Thurgood."

"That there is, Ms. Crow. Catch you later."

Harry headed back to the coffee shop; and, when he arrived, he dropped the paper on his table and did a quick check to make sure everything was ready for the opening bell.

Ember was talking with Jack Bonhoffer and Estrelita. From the kitchen, Harry could hear Miguel singing a song in Spanish. All was well in this little corner of the world.

He grabbed a cup of coffee and a doughnut and sat at his table. The newspaper headline was huge.

Rev. Cole Makes Pulpit Confession

The secondary line was the size of normal headlines.

From Porn Star to Preacher

Harry skimmed through the articles on page one and called Ember over. When she was seated next to him, he said, "Here. Take a read."

She read through the stories, folded the paper, and put it on the table. "Well, now everyone knows my past. Although, I have to say, Graham was very nice. He painted quite a sympathetic portrait of my life. I'll have to thank him."

Harry picked up the paper. "I wonder what Monika heard

today?" He opened the paper. "Ah, here it is. Page two. Let's see."

He read the column, then handed the paper to Ember.

She read through "Monika Hears"; then showed the paper to Harry and pointed to the third paragraph.

Harry nodded. "Yes," he said, "it seems Monika heard a lot in her interview with Clair-Ann. I wonder what she heard that Graham didn't print?"

"That is a very good question. Although, if it's important, he'll probably share it with us. He wouldn't want to upset one of his advertisers."

Harry laughed. "No, he wouldn't."

Ember read out loud, "And about the current spate of murders in Magnolia Bluff, Monika hears that religion gone awry is the reason the victims died. Perhaps there's a holy crusader righting wrongs or at least thinks he's doing so."

"Of course, we don't know if that bit of information came from Clair-Ann," Harry said. "Although Graham did let me know he was sending Monika to talk to the Taylors."

"So if we say that Monika's information came from Clair-Ann, then the question begs to be asked: how does Clair-Ann know what Monika reported?"

"Idle gossip?"

"Possible."

"A cathartic confession?"

"That's possible, too. In any event, we'll know one way or the other soon enough."

63

MONDAY, 19 FEBRUARY 6:45 AM

MBPD Investigator Georgia Jean Riggins set the pot of coffee on the table.

Reece had already set out mugs and opened a box of Bluff Bakery donuts.

"Anything else you need, Sarge?" GJ asked.

"I think we're good. Take a seat."

Assistant District Attorney Chuck Dillon cleared his throat and began talking.

Reece didn't like the man. He was bossy. And a lawyer. And Reece hated lawyers. *Just about all of the world's problems are caused by lawyers,* he told himself.

Dillon said, "We have five victims all killed with the same MO."

"Not quite," Reece interrupted. "Cally Taylor is different."

DA Investigator David Scott said, "But she was killed with a knife. Stabbed in the back, then stabbed in the stomach. At least that's how the ME sees it."

"And that's my point," Reece said. "The MO is actually different with Cally."

"Explain," Dillon said.

Reece smiled to himself. *One for me.* Out loud, he said, "Cally was first stabbed from behind; then stabbed in the stomach from the front, not the throat, and then she was bludgeoned, probably to death, with the altar cross. After which, the victim was mutilated—"

Dillon held up his hand. "Okay, I get your point. Where are you going with this?"

"Caldwell Taylor is the one we should be focusing on."

Chuck Dillon sat back in his chair and pinched the bridge of his nose.

GJ said, "The others are decoys. We find who killed Mrs. Taylor, we'll have found who killed the other four."

Dillon sat up. "Yes, Ms. Riggins, I'm not a complete idiot." He poured himself a cup of coffee and took a doughnut out of the box. "So, Sergeant, who killed Mrs. Taylor?"

The assistant DA bit into the doughnut and jelly squirted out all over his shirt. The expletive he didn't say was written loud on his face.

Dillon stood. "I'll be back," he said, and left the room.

A belly laugh rolled out of Georgia Jean. David Scott chuckled. And Reece permitted himself a big smile.

When Dillon returned, everyone was straight-faced, drinking coffee, and eating doughnuts.

He sat, cleared his throat, and said, "Now that you've had a good laugh at my expense, the fun and games are over. I want results. I can't take these five cases out the door, let alone to the grand jury. I need a killer and solid evidence to convict the scum. You got it?"

There were nods around the table.

"Good. If you think the murder of Caldwell Taylor is the key to it all — then find her murderer. We're running out of time. These cases are getting colder and colder. And before we know it, they'll be like some woolly mammoth locked in a glacier for the next fifty thousand years. Which won't do any of our careers any good."

Dillon stood. "Get me the killer," he said, and strode from the room.

David Scott said, "The DA's getting heat, and he's shoveling the coals on to Dillon."

Sovern nodded. "Horse crap falls from above. David, you mind talking to the family again?"

"Nope. On it."

"GJ, talk to all the church council members. See if you can't shake some of something loose. I'll see if I can get anything out of Huston, Thurgood, and Reverend Cole. We'll meet back here for a working supper."

"I'll cover the food, Sarge," GJ said.

"Thanks," Sovern replied. "Let's get some results."

64

MONDAY, 19 FEBRUARY 9:02 AM

MBPD Police Chief Tommy Jager stopped five feet inside the Really Good. It was so sudden, Reverend Billy Bob Baskin ran into him.

"What happened to you?" Tommy blurted out.

"Do you want to move?" Magnolia Nadine Roane said. "You make a better door than a window."

Graham Huston pushed his way forward until he was next to the police chief. "Well, I'll be...," he managed to say.

The two men stepped aside so the rest of the Niners coffee klatch could enter the Really Good.

Magnolia Nadine said, "Oh, my," and Caroline McCluskey's eyes opened wide, and then, a smile on her face, said, "You look lovely, Ember."

Ember blushed. "Thank you, Caroline." Then she did a little twirl and asked, "Y'all like it?"

"It is certainly a different you," Billy Bob said, and added, "Yes, I like it. As Caroline said. You do look lovely."

"Did you quit?" Graham asked.

"Quit?" Ember replied.

"The church."

Ember laughed. "Oh, no. Of course not. It's my day off and I'm spending it here with Harry."

"You do know he eats an awful lot of doughnuts and drinks a lot of coffee," Tommy said.

"And how do you know that?" Harry asked.

"Every cop worth his salt has informants."

"I see. Well, grab a seat and have coffee and doughnuts. I don't want to have to consume all this myself."

The coffee klatch members sat. Coffee was poured and doughnuts, croissants, kolaches, and cinnamon rolls were transferred to plates.

Tommy, a huge bite of cream cheese kolache in his mouth, said, "I hope you wear more dresses, Ember. You're lookin' really good."

A collective grown swept the table.

Tommy, his face the picture of innocence, said, "What?"

Graham, notebook in hand and pencil behind his ear, said, "So what's Reece up to these days? Doing a little fishing?"

Tommy snorted a laugh. "His line's in the water. Might even have a hook on it."

"I thought you just promoted him," Caroline said.

"I did. Deserved the promotion."

Caroline continued, "But you make it sound like…"

Tommy drank coffee and reached for another doughnut. "Reece is good at what he's good at."

And when nothing more was forthcoming, Magnolia Nadine said, "Which is?"

Tommy, around a big mouthful of doughnut, said, "Still trying to figure that out."

Ember said, "That's a bit unfair, don't you think?"

Coffee cup halfway to his mouth, Tommy said, "I'm surprised to hear that coming from you, Mrs. Thurgood."

"I'm still Ms. Cole. Reece may be a bit one dimensional—"

Tommy nearly spewed coffee. "That's good. I'll have to remember that."

"I think what Emmy's trying to say, if I may, dear?"

Ember nodded.

Harry continued, "Is that Reece is a bulldog when he has all the puzzle pieces. He just lacks a bit of imagination in collecting those pieces."

"Reece is an asset," Ember added.

"I hope so," Tommy said, "because I have plenty of people chewing my tail end to get these murders wrapped up. And on that note, I'd best get going."

Tommy stood. "Hope y'all have a good day." He grabbed a kolache and was out the door.

"That's very noble of you to defend Reece, Ember, after all that he's done to you," Billy Bob said.

"I rather like him," Ember replied. "He's like a wheezing, panting, mean-looking bulldog. But you show him some kindness, and he's on his back wanting his tummy rubbed."

Billy Bob stood. "You are a picture of Christian charity, Ember Cole. I have to run. I have an appointment."

The Presbyterian minister left and was followed by Caroline and Magnolia Nadine.

Harry looked at Graham, a faint smile on his lips, and said, "You're still here. You must have something to tell us."

"I do. Pour yourselves more coffee."

65

MONDAY, 19 FEBRUARY 9:04 AM

DAVID SCOTT DECIDED THAT TALKING WITH THE TAYLORS, FATHER AND daughter, would be fruitless. They'd already demonstrated they weren't deviating from their previous statements. So Scott put in a call to Buchanan Taylor, son of Owen and the late Caldwell Taylor.

The man answered on the fourth ring.

Scott identified himself and asked if Taylor had a few minutes to answer some questions.

"Not really. But if I don't, you people will just keep pestering me. So go ahead. What do you want to know?"

What a pompous ass, Scott thought. He cleared his throat and said, "Did your mother have a best friend?"

"I thought I already told someone this. She really didn't have any friends. People always disappointed her. Probably the person she was closest to was Tipper Duvall at church. But I don't know that she thought of Tipper as her friend."

"There was no one outside of the church?"

"Look, the church was her life. There was no 'outside of the church'."

"I understand she had a lot of enemies."

"Who told you that? Wait. It was my sister, wasn't it?"

"I'm not—"

"Yada, yada. Look, Mom was a difficult person because she had exacting standards. Very few people met up to her standards. So, yes, she probably turned off a lot of people. Did she piss someone off enough that they killed her? I find that highly unlikely."

"Your mother, though, seemed unusually adept at pissing people off."

"Again, I don't know who you're talking to. Probably my sister or that minister. My mother wasn't perfect. But she was a wonderful mom, and she was dedicated to her church. Now, instead of badgering me, why don't you find her a killer?"

When Scott tried to reply, he realized he was speaking to himself. Buchanan Taylor had ended the call.

Scott shook his head and muttered, "Like mother, like son."

———

Police Investigator Georgia Jean Riggins knocked on the door of her second cousin once removed, Waymon Riggins, who was the chairman of Saint Luke's Finance Committee.

Even though he was a relative, she actually knew very little about the man. The only time she'd seen him was at a family reunion five years ago. He was four decades her senior, and they didn't travel in the same social circles.

The door opened. The woman who opened it stared at her for a moment, and then said, "Hello, Georgia Jean. Come in."

"You know me?"

"Of course. You're family. Come in. We're eating breakfast. How do you like your eggs? I'm Burdette, by the way."

The woman turned around and headed back into the house.

GJ said, "Uh, scrambled," and followed her cousin's wife, making sure she closed the door behind her.

Burdette pointed. "There's the dining room. Waymon's in

there." And the woman disappeared through a different doorway.

GJ entered the dining room. Waymon looked up from the Austin American-Statesman newspaper. "Hello, Georgia Jean. Have a seat."

She sat.

"What brings you here?" Waymon asked.

Burdette brought in a coffee cup, set it before GJ, pointed to the coffeepot, and went back the way she came.

GJ poured herself a cup of coffee. "I wanted to talk about Caldwell Taylor."

"Ah, yes," Waymon nodded. "Tragic. Wouldn't have happened had the pastor the decency to leave."

She drank coffee. *No dancing around the mulberry bush.* "How's that?" she asked.

"The Reverend Cole refuses to accept she's not wanted here."

"So why is she still here?"

"Because the bishop and a slim, and I do mean slim, majority of our members want her to stay. Members who rarely darken the door."

Burdette entered and placed a plate before GJ that was piled high with eggs, hash browns, bacon, and, from the smell, a freshly baked orange muffin.

The woman sat, and said, "Cally did more for our church than any pastor ever did. Now she's dead. I don't see how the church will survive."

GJ swallowed bacon. "So, who wanted her dead?"

"That's the mystery," Waymon said.

"It is indeed," Burdette concurred.

"Her death was brutal. Someone must've hated her awfully bad."

"Couldn't have been anyone in the church," Waymon said.

"Didn't have an enemy in the world," Burdette added.

Waymon drank coffee, set the cup down, and said, "Except for the pastor."

"Oh, yes," Burdette said. "The pastor. Yes."

"Reverend Cole killed her?" GJ asked.

"Who else could it be?" Waymon said with a shrug. "She hated Cally."

GJ ate eggs and bacon. After the bacon was gone, she said, "Reverend Cole has an alibi."

Waymon made a noise.

Burdette tutted.

Waymon said, "That coffee shop owner, I presume?"

"That's no alibi," Burdette said. "And it's very suspicious that they announce this marriage and then Cally Taylor is murdered." She nodded. "Very suspicious." She raised her coffee cup to her lips and drank.

"How are your parents?" Waymon asked.

GJ knew she wasn't going to get anything more from Waymon and Burdette. She ate, talked about her parents, drank coffee, and then excused herself.

"Don't be a stranger," Waymon said, picking up the newspaper.

Burdette walked GJ to the door. "Say hello to your parents for us. And as Waymon said, don't be a stranger."

GJ stood on the sidewalk for a moment digesting what her cousins had told her. Then she shrugged. *If Cole and Thurgood killed Cally Taylor, then this case is destined to be a cold file.*

66

MONDAY, 19 FEBRUARY 9:31 AM

REECE SOVERN PUSHED OPEN THE DOOR, HEARD THE BELL TINKLE, and stepped into the Really Good. He stopped. Did a double take, and said, "Ember?"

She giggled and said, "Hi, Reece. It's my day off."

Reece pushed his glasses up, rolled the green perfecto to the other side of his mouth, and said, "Well, I have to say, you look stunning."

"Thank you. Would you like a cup of coffee?"

"Too rich for my wallet."

"I hear you got a promotion. Congratulations. I'm very happy for you."

"You are?"

"Yes. You're a hard worker, honest, and you deserve it."

Reece cleared his throat. "Well, um, thank you. Where's your other half? I have a few questions."

"He's in back talking to Elder Smythe about today's vegetable delivery. Have a seat. I'll get him."

He took a seat at a table. A moment later, Estrelita put a cup of coffee in front of him.

"I didn't order this."

She smiled at him. "It's on the house."

"Thanks. Hope you don't get in trouble with your boss."

"I won't. You're on the list to get free coffee."

"I am?"

"You are. Enjoy."

She walked away, and Reece looked at the cup of Joe in front of him. *Well, I'll be damned. Me on the free coffee list. Huh.*

He took a sip. *Man, wish I could afford this stuff.* He took another sip and, over the rim of the cup, saw Thurgood and the Reverend approach the table.

"Good morning, Sarge," Thurgood said.

"Good morning, and thanks for the coffee."

"You're welcome. And congratulations on the promotion."

"Uh, thanks."

The couple sat, and Thurgood said, "I assume you are here on business. How can we help?"

"We still haven't found anyone with a motive."

"For which murder?" Thurgood asked.

"All of them."

The Reverend said, "That's too broad of a field, Reece. You need to focus on Elektra."

"Who?"

Thurgood chuckled. "The ancient Greek myth. Elektra killed her mother because Elektra's mother killed Elektra's father."

"You lost me. And what does ancient Greek stories have to do with this murder?"

"Who is Cally's daughter?" Thurgood asked.

"Clair-Ann. But Cally didn't kill her husband."

"No, she didn't. At least literally. But Clair-Ann believes her mother neglected her father and her for the church. Call it a symbolic murder."

Reece pushed his glasses up and rolled the cigar to the other corner of his mouth. "Symbolic murder? Neglect? That's not much of a motive."

"People kill for less."

"Yes, I guess they do."

"Did you see the *Mourning Becomes Electra* trilogy?" Reverend Cole asked.

"Those plays? No. Not my thing."

"If you had, you'd understand," she said.

Reece scratched his head. "So you're telling me Clair-Ann did it. She killed those people."

The two nodded.

"Where's the proof?"

"Don't have any," Thurgood said.

"I see. This is a guess. Based on a play."

"Nevertheless, she's the person you should look at."

"And I should do this on your say so. With no proof. All because of some play?"

"You're the one asking for our opinion. Then when we give it to you, you don't like it." Thurgood shrugged. "There's nothing more we can do to help. Take it or leave it."

Reece finished his coffee and stood. "Thanks. Appreciate the suggestion."

Ember said, "Get a copy of the play from the library and read it. You'll see."

Harry added, "It's all we have. If I was a detective, I'd start looking for evidence to prove my theory."

"If the theory is correct."

Thurgood nodded. "If the theory is correct." Then, after a moment, he added, "It is, though, the one on which you need to focus."

67

MONDAY, 19 FEBRUARY 10:01 AM

HARRY WATCHED REECE LEAVE THE COFFEE SHOP.

"Poor Reece," Ember said.

"He lacks imagination."

"But you don't."

"Flattery will get you everywhere." Harry kissed Ember's cheek.

She giggled. "Here? In public?"

"We're married. I can kiss my wife."

"I won't say no."

"That's good to hear."

"But back to the subject at hand."

"Which is?"

"Clair-Ann. Do you think Reece will read that play?"

"Probably not. And to his loss. However, concerning Clair-Ann, we're working on it. And with Graham's information, I think we're on the right track."

"I hope so, Harry."

"Don't worry. Your job is to pray. Remember?"

"Yes, you're right. So it's mostly a waiting game at this point."

"Correct. We gradually escalate the pressure and see what happens."

"I hope this doesn't backfire on us."

"Me, too."

Landon Pace ended the call with Monika Crow. He thought it a strange request, but being the intern at the *Chronicle* put him at the very bottom of the pecking order. Which meant everyone was his boss.

All in all, he didn't mind overly much. It was all experience. Experience he hoped would get him a job back home in Richmond.

"Who was that, Landon?" Joetta Reston asked.

Landon watched his very pregnant girlfriend enter the room. "Monika. She wants me to get some information. Anything you need while I'm out?"

"No. We're good. I hope you're home for dinner."

"What are we having?"

"Fried Chicken, succotash and greens, corn pone, fried okra, bread pudding, and sweet tea."

Landon took Joetta in his arms, kissed her, and said, "You're going to make me fat, you know that?"

"You've been so good to me. I want to make sure you know I appreciate your kindness."

"My darling, it's not kindness. I love you."

"Do you really? You hardly know me."

"I know you well enough to know you are my princess."

"Landon Pace. You are the kindest and sweetest man on this earth."

"You know, maybe we should do the common law thing. Like that coffee shop owner and the minister."

"Mr. Thurgood and Reverend Cole?"

"Yeah, them."

"They were so good to us after Pa was murdered. They're good people."

"What do you say, Jo? Let's do the common law thing. Let me make an honest woman of you. Will you marry me?"

Tears were streaming down Joetta's face. "Yes. Yes, I'll marry you, Landon Pace. But what about..."

"Our child? I guess we do what all parents do. We'll do our best to raise him or her to be a good person."

"You are an amazing man to accept another man's child as your own."

"It's you, Jo. You're the sweetest person. And you showed me a better path." He kissed her again. "If I'm to be home for dinner, I'd best scoot."

Landon left his future wife to run Monika's errand.

As he walked down the sidewalk, he thought about how lucky he was.

I was a selfish and self-centered prick. And at first, all I wanted to do was get into Joetta's panties. But she is such a kind soul. So different from that sister of hers, Oralene. Jo made me think twice about the way I was living and how my life would be better with her by my side. Who would've thought the death of a snake-handling, religious huckster would change my life?

———

Landon couldn't see the point, but Monika was insistent. And next to Huston, she was the top dog at the paper.

For two hours, he sat in the high school library studying every yearbook that had a picture of Sinclair Ann Taylor.

He dutifully took pictures with his phone of every photo and scrap of information that had something to do with the young woman. And there was a fair amount of material.

Wonder what she wants with all of this stuff? Probably something to do with her "Monika Hears" column.

He closed the cover on the last book, returned it to the self, and stood.

Mission accomplished. I'll send these to the Boss Lady and then get on home to dinner.

Walking home, he sent the photos to Monika. After a few moments, she texted him.

> The photos look good. Stand by for further instructions.

68

MONDAY, 19 FEBRUARY 10:37 AM

REECE SOVERN AND GEORGIA JEAN RIGGINS WERE SITTING IN A booth in The Cafe. Reece was trying to drink a cup of coffee and GJ was nursing a sweet tea.

He stared at the black liquid in the cup. *I'm either getting spoiled by Thurgood's coffee or this stuff really is like that barley crap my Aunt Beryl used to drink.*

"Why do we care what Thurgood thinks? He's not a cop, and he's shady to boot," GJ said.

"Yeah, there's something off about the guy. I'll give you that. But he has instincts. He's also friends with Huston and his gossip columnist. And their information network rivals Mary Lou Fight's Crimson Hat network. So buddying up to Thurgood may give us what we need, and that is information."

"You have a point, Sarge. I just hate working with the guy. And his common-law wife's no better: all Miss Goody Two Shoes, and then we find out she's a porn star and whore." GJ uttered an expletive and drank tea.

"Yeah, that was a shocker."

"Now that it's out, she'll probably start Hookers for Jesus and cash in."

"I don't think so. That was all in the past, and Ember's cut from a different cloth."

"Ember is it? You smitten?"

Reece cleared his throat. "No, I've just dealt with those two long enough to know what they're like."

"Maybe. But birds of a feather flock together. Look again, Sarge. She's as phoney as a three-dollar bill. Just like the smarmy movie star lookalike she's with."

Or maybe it's a case where they both have some redeeming virtues. Reece thought as he drank coffee. *Where on earth did they find this stuff?*

"Setting Thurgood and the Reverend aside," Reece said, "I want you to focus on Clair-Ann Taylor. I want to know everyone she's talked to since she learned to talk. I want to know everyone who likes her and who doesn't. Find out what she eats for breakfast and if she takes a crap every day. You know the drill. I want to know that girl better than she knows herself."

GJ shrugged. "If that's what you want."

"I do. And I want a thorough job of it. If I find you missed something, you'll be directing traffic."

"We don't have much traffic."

"Exactly."

"Oh. Gotcha. All right, Sarge, if that's what you want. I'll get it for you."

"Good. Now get out of here."

GJ gulped her sweet tea and left.

Reece took a sip of his coffee, wrinkled his nose, and set the cup aside. *That darn Thurgood is ruining my taste for coffee.*

He stood, put a ten on the table, and left.

Walking back to the police station, he thought about Harry Thurgood and Ember Cole.

I'm positive those two have deep wells. And of the two, Thurgood's is the deepest. Nevertheless, he's always willing to help. And on this case, he just might be on to something.

69

MONDAY, 19 FEBRUARY 11:08 AM

JAVIER HERRON SAT ACROSS FROM THE FRIGID ICE BLUE EYES OF Mary Lou Fight. Sitting next to her was a young woman Mrs. Fight introduced as her daughter.

He wondered how he'd missed that. As far as he knew, the Fights had no children. He'd have to double check his background information.

Mrs. Fight was not a happy person this morning. But then Javier wondered if she ever was.

"Your information was exceptional, Mr. Herron. However, we were outmaneuvered on the field of battle, so to speak. Nevertheless, not all is lost. We did uncover the fact that the strumpet is, in fact, a harlot, and that may yet work to our advantage."

Javier favored her with a smile, which he cut off by drinking tea.

"Now, what have you found out about her pre-harlotry days?"

"As with Mr. Thurgood, Ms. Cole apparently found a very good forger to create a synthetic identity for her."

"Doesn't that take a lot of money?"

"Yes, it does."

"Interesting. I wonder where she got the cash to pay for it?"

Javier smiled. "I'm working on that."

"Good. So what about that story the lounge lizard told Chief Jager? Some story about a Granville Finch in Minnesota. Is that true or not?'

"No, it isn't true. That was a fake synthetic identity created to give veracity to his actual synthetic identity."

"That would take an incredible amount of money, wouldn't it?"

"Probably something north of half a million dollars."

"Very interesting." She drank tea, set the cup down, and stared out the window. After a minute or so, she turned her head and Javier felt those frigid ice blue eyes focus on him. "Keep digging."

"On both?"

"Yes. On both of them. Dust bunnies accumulate in the corners. Don't neglect the corners."

"I won't, Mrs. Fight." *Not that I ever do*, he said to himself.

She rang the bell, and Javier stood. In a moment, Mrs. Fight's maid appeared.

"Eliška, please show Mr. Herron out."

"Yes, ma'am."

Javier followed the young woman to the front door and left the Fight home.

Once behind the wheel of his car, he wondered if it might be best to terminate the contract with Mrs. Fight.

It was obvious she had a vendetta against Cole and Thurgood. But as near as he could tell, the couple had hurt nobody. And definitely hadn't wronged Mary Lou Fight in any way whatsoever.

I think it's time to discuss this one with my boss.

———

"That is how it is done, Oralene. People are here to serve you. There have always been those who are the best people. And those who are here to serve their betters. We are the best of people. Do not forget this."

"I won't, Mother."

"Good. We are the ones who bring enlightenment and culture to the world. I hear you are doing well on your piano lessons. You already have a lovely voice. Once you've mastered the piano, you will have passed another cultural milestone."

"Thank you, Mother. Thank you for believing in me."

"You will be my successor, Oralene. I am very glad I found you. Very glad your family came to Magnolia Bluff and brought you to me."

"The Lord blessed us both when my father decided to come here."

"Indeed." Mary Lou lifted her teacup and watched Oralene do the same.

To herself, Mary Lou said, *You may soon be my legal daughter, but don't think I don't know you. You aren't one of us, at least not yet. So I have plenty of eyes watching you. One misstep on your part, my pretty, and you will be back in the gutter before you can blink.*

70

MONDAY, 19 FEBRUARY 1:47 PM

THE LUNCH CROWD AT THE REALLY GOOD HAD NUMBERED ELEVEN, including Harry's new friends Telford and Terall Whitacre. They chatted for a few minutes, and the Whitacres accepted Harry and Ember's invite to join them later for dinner.

With the shop now empty, Harry and Ember, along with Jack Bonhoffer, Miguel, and Estrelita, sat down to have a bite of lunch. Brisket Queso sandwiches and sweet tea.

After swallowing a big bite of his sandwich, Miguel said, "Today has been a good day. Murder is good for business."

"How can you say such a thing", Estrelita chided her cousin.

"It's true. Isn't it, Mr. Thurgood?"

"Seems that way," Harry answer.

"People are a perverse lot," Jack said.

"It's our propensity to sin," Ember added.

"Do you think you broke even?" Jack asked his boss.

Harry swallowed his bite of sandwich. "Possibly. And if we did, then, yes, I'd have to say murder is a plus for the shop. It's a sad commentary, but true, people seem to delight in the misfortunes of others."

"It shouldn't be that way," Estrelita said.

"No, it shouldn't," Ember agreed, "but it seems it is."

"We know you and the missus are trying to find the culprit who did these killings," Jack said. "I guess what we want to know is are you close to catching the person?"

Harry set his sandwich down. "Yes, and no. Em and I are pretty sure we know who did it, but we have no proof."

"And you can't do much without evidence," Ember added.

"So, what are you going to do?" Estrelita asked.

"We're going to try to get the person to incriminate themselves," Harry said.

"Who'd do that?" Miguel asked.

"No one willingly," Harry answered. "We hope to set up a situation where our person of interest does so before realizing he did."

"You're going to trap them," Miguel said.

Harry nodded. "Yes. Hopefully."

A groan escaped Estrelita's lips. Coming through the door were the members of the Crimson Hat Society.

———

Georgia Jean started with the church receptionist and secretary, Larrilyn Hammer.

"Clair-Ann, as far as I know, doesn't have many friends," the woman told her. "She spends most of her time taking care of her father. Although Mrs. Taylor thought it was all a show. That her husband wasn't really sick. Just wanted attention."

When GJ pressed her for names, Larrilyn provided the name of one of the elementary school teachers with whom Clair-Ann had worked.

The woman, Suzy Fern Roy, was on maternity leave, GJ found out after checking at the school.

Checking further, GJ learned the teacher and her husband lived on the north end of town in a small stone-faced house on Gregory Lane.

GJ pulled up in front of the house. The front door was

recessed between the garage and what she assumed was probably the living room, given the large window that looked out
onto the front yard and street.

"I hate those recessed doors," she muttered. "Like being in a
tunnel. Too claustrophobic for my taste."

She got out of the car, walked up to the door, and rang the
doorbell.

After a few moments, the door opened to reveal a woman GJ
guessed to be in her late twenties. She had light brown hair, fair
skin, and was holding a baby in her left arm.

"How may I help you?" the young mother asked.

GJ held up her badge and said, "I'm Investigator Riggins
with the Magnolia Bluff police. Are you Suzy Fern Roy?"

"Yes."

"I'd like to talk to you about Clair-Ann Taylor. May I
come in?"

"What's this about? Is she in trouble?"

"I'm not aware that she's in trouble, but in order to find who
killed her mother, we're talking to everyone who knows the
family. Even in the slightest."

"I see. Okay. Come in."

GJ entered and pulled the door closed behind her. She
followed the woman to what she took to be the living room. It
was the room with the big window.

"Nice home you have here," she told the woman.

"Thank you. Tom and I love it. Have a seat."

Suzy Roy sat in a rocker recliner and GJ sat on the sofa.

"If it's okay with you, Mrs. Roy, I'm going to record our
conversation."

Suzy shrugged. "That's fine."

"How long have you known Clair-Ann Taylor?"

"I'm not sure. Four or five years."

"And you knew her from school?"

"Yes. We're teachers at the elementary school. Well, she's now
a substitute. She has to take care of her father."

"What do you know about that?"

"Just what she told me. Her mother neglected her father. Even put him down."

"Did she ever say how her mother put her father down?"

"Told him he was a hypochondriac, that his interest in his family history was a waste of time, that he should do real work. Things like that. According to Clair-Ann, that is. I never met her parents."

"How did Clair-Ann feel about that? Her mother putting her father down."

"Oh, she didn't like it one bit. In fact, she never said one good thing about her mother, as I recall. Idolized her father, though."

"In what way did she idolize him?"

Susie shrugged. "Oh, I don't know. She just thought he was the greatest man. Couldn't do anything wrong. I sometimes wonder if she didn't date because no man could compare with her father."

"She didn't date?"

"Not that she ever talked about. A couple of the other teachers used to talk about her 'Daddy fixation.' Thought she was a bit nuts."

"Do you think that?"

Suzy shrugged. "She thought the world of her father. Kind of makes me wish I had a father like that."

"Do you think Clair-Ann could kill her mother?"

"Heavens no. She didn't like her mother. How many of us don't like one or both of our parents? Doesn't mean we kill them, does it?"

GJ smiled. "You tell me."

"That's ridiculous. Clair-Ann adores her father and didn't like her mother. From the things she told me, that woman was a witch. And no, I don't think she killed her mother."

The baby started fussing. GJ stopped the recorder and stood. "Thank you for your time. If you think of something, anything, here's my card. Call me, please."

Once GJ was behind the wheel of her car, she let a big smile spread across her face. "Sarge is gonna love this."

71

MONDAY, 19 FEBRUARY 2:16 PM

WITH THE ARRIVAL OF THE HATS, EMBER SLIPPED OUT THE BACK door of the Really Good. She'd asked Harry to text her when they'd left.

To make use of the time, she decided to visit Clair-Ann, and walked the several blocks to the Taylor's home.

In response to the pressing of the doorbell button, Ember heard Clair-Ann's voice through the door say, "Go away. We don't want whatever you're selling."

"Clair-Ann, it's Ember Cole."

The door opened a crack and Ember saw an eyeball looking her up and down, then the door opened fully.

"Hello, Reverend. Sorry. A lot of people have been pestering us since Mom's murder. Dad's taking a nap."

"That's okay. I actually came to see you."

"Oh, well, here I am."

"May I come in?"

"Uh, um, okay. Sure."

Clair-Ann stepped aside and Ember walked in.

"I was just finishing my lunch. Would you like tea? Coffee?"

"Tea would be fine."

"I'm in the kitchen."

Ember followed the young woman to the kitchen. Off to the side was a breakfast nook, and Ember saw a plate with a partially eaten sandwich and a cup of what she suspected was tea.

Clair-Ann indicated Ember should sit at the table opposite the plate and cup, and went off to fill the teakettle with water.

"Would you like a sandwich? Egg salad?"

"No, thank you. I've eaten lunch already."

"So what do you want to talk about?" Clair-Ann asked as she sat down. "Your tea should be ready in a minute."

I just want to see how you're doing since your mother passed."

"She didn't pass. She was brutally murdered."

"Yes, she was. How are you holding up?"

"She was brutally murdered. And I hope she suffered. I hope her last moments on this earth were filled with pain and agony. Payback for all the misery she caused."

The tea kettle whistled and Clair-Ann got up. In a moment, she returned with a teacup and saucer. A tea bag was steeping in the hot water.

Ember dunked the bag up and down. "You don't really mean what you said, do you?"

"Didn't you hate her?"

"No. No, I didn't. If anything, I felt sorry for her."

"Then you're a better person than I am, Reverend, because I hated her. I wished for her death ever since I was a child. Now she's dead and I'm glad. I just wish she'd suffered more. Suffered longer. Years would not be long enough."

Ember removed the tea bag from her cup. "I'm sorry you suffered, Clair-Ann. Your mother had a mean spirit—"

"She was vile, Reverend. Look at you. All the things you went through. Yet you curse no one. My mother was married to the most wonderful man. She had beautiful parents. And she was nothing but a self-centered, nasty bitch. I am not sorry she's dead. And when she's in the ground, I will dance on her grave."

Ember drank tea, and Clair-Ann took a bite of her sandwich. When Ember set the cup down, she said, "Will you talk to Dr. Kurelek?"

"Why? I'm not nuts."

"I didn't mean to imply you are. I think he can help you channel your anger in a positive direction."

"My anger — my hatred — doesn't need channeling. The wicked witch is dead. Now it's just my father and me. As it should've been all along. Whoever killed my mother did the world — did you — a service. God has answered my prayers."

Clair-Ann stood up. "I need to check on my father. Please see yourself out." She started to leave, paused, and said, "Thank you for stopping, Reverend. Everything is fine now. Truly. The wicked witch is dead. Death comes so easily. I wish I would've known years ago how easy it is for a person to die."

72

MONDAY, 19 FEBRUARY 7:42 PM

Harry and Ember did a bit of rearranging of the furniture to facilitate conversation with their guests. The sofa had now joined the two coastal-style wingbacks by the fireplace. The coffee table was in the middle of the ensemble.

Ember put the Whitacres on the sofa, and she and Harry took the wingbacks. On the coffee table was a decanter of Sercial Madeira, which served as the apéritif for dinner.

Harry thought the Whitacres made something of an odd couple. He was short and round. She was tall, taller than Telford, and slim. He was reserved. She was outgoing. But when it came to business sense, they were equals. And they had enough good sense to leave Massachusetts and move to Texas.

Telford sipped madeira. "What I don't get, and this wine is quite good, by the way; what I don't get is all the negative press regarding tobacco, but marijuana, which is far more dangerous, gets a free ride."

Terall added, "It's a known fact that daily marijuana use saps one's willpower to do anything. Makes the user unmotivated. Which, I suppose, is exactly what our growing nanny state wants."

"Makes the sheeple easier to control," Harry said.

"Precisely," Terall agreed. "What isn't talked about are all the health benefits of nicotine. It's far more healthy than marijuana."

"Exactly," Telford said, and took a sip of wine. "Starting with Jean Nicot in the sixteenth century, tobacco has been used to cure many ailments."

"We don't hear about that, do we?" Harry said. "If the government and health advocates were honest, they'd focus on cigarettes. Smoke inhalation is known to kill you and the chemicals in paper are known carcinogens. Seems like a no-brainer to me."

"If that's the case, then marijuana smoking is as dangerous as cigarettes because most marijuana is consumed as paper wrapped reefers and the smoke is usually deeply inhaled and held in the lungs for as long as possible," Ember said.

"Very true," Terall concurred. "Usually more deeply inhaled than cigarettes and certainly held longer in the lungs than tobacco smoke is. Which means more tar is deposited in the lungs than is common with cigarettes. Chronic bronchitis and bong lung are now issues."

"In actuality," Harry said, "it's not about health. It's about control."

"Touché," Telford said.

"One thing they haven't started passing laws against is food," Harry said.

Telford chuckled and patted his stomach. "Thank God."

"Maybe they should," Terall said.

"You always say that, my love, and then proceed to eat more than I."

"Metabolism," Harry said.

"You should see this guy and doughnuts," Ember said.

Harry stood. "Let's eat the wonderful food Miguel prepared for us."

"You have a chef?"

"My cook at the Really Good," Harry explained.

"He often prepares our dinner," Ember added.

"For which he gets paid extra," Harry said.

They moved to the dining room; and while Harry uncovered the dishes, Ember said, "We'll do this family style. Just help yourselves."

"What we have," Harry began, "is Pork Chops Olé for the meat dish. The vegetable is corn with tomatoes and peppers. We have a kale salad, with garbanzo beans, feta cheese, and a balsamic vinaigrette. For dessert, Miguel made us an apple pie, which you can have with frozen custard or cheddar cheese."

"Sounds wonderful, Harry," Terall said.

"Oh, and we have a Texas Zinfandel Rosé from a local winery for our beverage," Harry added.

They sat, dished up food, and after a couple minutes of eating and savoring the flavors, Ember asked if the Whitacres had found a church home.

Terall dabbed her mouth with her napkin. "We don't go to church. I grew up Methodist, but stopped going to church when I was in college. I just didn't see how Christianity was relevant in a modern world."

"The same with me," Telford said. "Except my family was officially Congregationalist. Rarely went, though."

"My history is much the same," Harry said. "However, whether religious or not, it does pay to be churched in small town in Texas."

"I see," said Terall.

With a big smile on his face, Harry said, "It's good for business. That's why I married the Methodist minister."

"I hate to tell you, Mister," Ember said, "it's not working."

"Probably because I actually married you for love, rather than money."

"So, in other words, no guarantees," Telford said.

"I can tell you, I was unchurched and the locals didn't darken the door. Since marrying Em, and attending church, I've started seeing a few drop in. So who knows?"

"In any event," Ember said, "I'd love to have you worship with us. I believe the Christian worldview is relevant for today."

"No promises," Terall said, "but we'll give you a chance."

"Thank you. That's all I'm asking," Ember said.

After dinner, the couples adjourned to the living room. Harry and Telford started filling their pipes, but when Ember saw Terall filling a pipe as well, she said, "Boy, I'm going to be the odd one out."

"Join us?" Harry asked.

"I don't know, Harry."

"Maybe we shouldn't," Terall said.

"No, no," Ember responded. "Harry smokes here all the time. Please."

"But I don't want you to feel uncomfortable," Terall said.

Ember looked at Harry. "In for a penny, in for a pound. Do you have one I can use?"

———

Eliška entered the small sitting room that Mary Lou Fight called her morning room and placed the tea service on the coffee table. She poured tea into the two cups and departed.

Mary Lou's eyes studied Tipper Duvall. The woman was picking imaginary pieces of lint off of her slacks.

"If you didn't smoke those foul cigarettes, you'd be less high-strung," Mary Lou said.

Tipper looked up and started to speak, but Mary Lou's look silenced her.

"Eliška made a pecan pie." She pointed to the two plates on the tray. "It is a wonder that she makes such a delicious pecan pie, seeing that she never heard of pecans back in her native Czech Republic. Try it."

Mary Lou watched Tipper pick up the pie plate and put a bite of pie in her mouth. After she'd swallowed, Tipper said, "Yes, this is very good."

"Isn't it, though?"

The two women ate pie and drank tea in silence. When the pie was eaten and tea drunk, Mary Lou refilled their cups.

"You are undoubtedly wondering why you are here."

"Uh, yes, I am, my Queen."

"I understand the strumpet asked you to be lay leader at my church."

"Yes, she did. But I refused."

"You didn't think to ask me first before making such a hasty decision? And a wrong one, I might add."

"Uh, well, I didn't think—"

"No, you didn't. I want you to accept the position."

"You do?"

"Yes, I do. What better way to get close to our enemy than to hold the most powerful position in the church?"

"Oh, yes, that makes sense."

"Of course it does. Caldwell Taylor did not understand this. She was far too belligerent. I want you in the position and I want you to make the strumpet believe you are her friend."

"But what I said to her..."

"It wasn't very nice, was it?"

Tipper focused on more of the lint that wasn't on her slacks. "No, it wasn't."

"You will apologize, ask for her forgiveness, and then tell the strumpet you would be honored to accept the position and put your differences behind you."

Tipper looked up. "Yes, my Queen."

"You will become her confidant, and when she lets the vital piece of information we need fall from her lips, you will be there to catch it and bring it to me. Understand?"

"I do."

"Good."

Mary Lou rang the bell, and in a moment the door opened and Eliška appeared in the doorway.

"Mrs. Duvall is leaving."

"Yes, ma'am," the maid said.

"Good night, Tipper."

"Good night, Mrs. Fight."

When Tipper Duvall was gone, Mary Lou poured tea for herself and took a sip.

By this time next year, that harlot will be out of my church.

73

LANDON PACE FOUND HIMSELF RINGING THE TAYLORS'S DOORBELL when he'd much rather be at home with Joetta. But Monika insisted he talk with Clair-Ann about a picture he'd found in one of the yearbooks.

"Can't this wait until morning?" he'd asked.

Monika's curt "No" put an end to his protest.

So there he was ringing the doorbell and hoping to talk with Clair-Ann.

"All because Monika wants a juicy tidbit for her column tomorrow."

Suddenly, the porch light went on and a voice said, "Go away. We don't want whatever you're selling."

"I'm not selling anything. My name's Landon Pace and I'm with the *Magnolia Bluff Chronicle*. I'm interested in your reaction to a picture that might be appearing in the paper tomorrow."

"What picture?"

"You're going to have to open the door. Can't show you through the wood."

He heard the deadbolt click, the chain slide, and watched the door open.

Clair-Ann was staring at him, holding a long slicing knife in her hand.

Landon watched her look at him, glance at the knife, and then set the knife on a table.

"There is a killer in our town," Clair-Ann said.

"Yes, there is."

"What picture?"

Landon handed her the photograph.

"Where did you get this?"

"Yearbook."

"Why do you want to put this in the paper?"

"Something to do with religion getting it all wrong. That is you, isn't it, with Jeremiah Brown, the Missionary Baptist preacher's son?"

Clair-Ann crumpled up the photo.

Landon continued, "For the record, is race mixing part of what people are getting wrong with religion?"

Before he could react, Clair-Ann slammed the door shut.

He heard the chain go back on the door and the deadbolt slide into place.

"I have to say that was definitely a demonstration of non-verbal communication."

He walked back to his car, got in, and told his phone to call Monika. She picked up on the third ring.

"How did it go?"

Landon told her.

"Very good."

"Did Monika hear anything?"

"Yes, she did. Did you?"

"I'm not paid to hear."

"True. Nevertheless, I'll recommend you get a check this week."

"Gee, thanks. Can I go home now?"

"Yes. See you in the morning."

Call ended, he started his car, put it in drive, and headed for home.

"Monika and Graham are up to something. Wish I knew what it was."

74

TUESDAY, 20 FEBRUARY 6:58 AM

HARRY WAS READING THE INSTRUCTION BOOKLET FOR HIS TWO NEW Bodum vacuum siphon coffee makers when Monika Crow walked into the shop.

"Here's your paper, Harry."

"Thanks. Personal delivery? Must be something good."

With a coy smile, she said, "Perhaps."

Harry, noticing her loose off-white blouse, ankle-length tie-dye skirt, and sandal-clad feet, said, "You're looking like a hippie right out of the sixties."

"It's my retro look. You like?"

"Hm. I have to say it is you. Not sure anyone else could pull it off."

"I'm going to take that as a compliment. Okay, gotta run. Make sure you pay attention to what Monika heard."

"Always do. Ciao."

She wiggled her fingers at him and was out the door.

Harry set aside the instruction booklet and opened the paper on the counter. He found Monika's column, "Monika Hears," on page 3. His eyes slid down the lines of text until he saw it.

Monika hears that Clair-Ann Taylor may still be carrying the torch for her lost love, Jeremiah Brown. Was it race mixing or religion mixing that parted the star-crossed lovers?

Well, well, well. Looks as though Monika got an earful from some-body. Unless she's moved over to creative writing.

Harry skimmed the rest of the column, but that was all Monika said about Clair-Ann.

I wonder how what Monika heard relates to what the young woman said to Ember? If it relates at all. Although, I don't see how it can't.

A customer entered and interrupted Harry's thoughts. He pushed the newspaper aside, prepared her flat white to go, and sent her down to Jack Bonhoffer to pay for the drink.

It seems a thwarted love affair, added to a less than caring and nurturing matriarch, is the source of Clair-Ann's intense anger. But is that anger enough to kill? And kill not just one, but five people? And if the answer is yes, what event triggered the release of Miss Hyde?

75

TUESDAY, 20 FEBRUARY 9:14 AM

THE SOUND OF THE SIREN CUT OFF MAGNOLIA NADINE IN MID-sentence.

Police Chief Tommy Jager stood, uttered, "What the...," and then left the Niners Coffee Klatch meeting. Following him out the door was Graham Huston.

Harry, Ember, and the remaining Niners went to the window to see what was going on.

Reverend Billy Bob Baskin said, "Something's going on over at the *Chronicle*."

Harry moved over to the door, opened it, and said, "Might as well join the fun."

Ember, Billy Bob, Caroline McCluskey, Magnolia Nadine, LouEllen Mueller, and Harry crossed East Main Street, walked across the Green, crossed West Main, and joined the gathering crowd in front of the *Chronicle* office.

"What's going on?" Ember said.

Harry, who was tall enough to see over most of the heads, said, "Not sure. There's glare on the window. Looks like there might be some kind of standoff inside the office."

A moment later, the door to the newspaper office opened and Sergeant Andrew LaPorte stepped onto the sidewalk, followed by Officer Kristine Combs, who was holding the arm of a hand-cuffed Clair-Ann Taylor.

"Show's over, folks," Sergeant LaPorte said, "you can all go on about your business."

The crowd started to disperse, but Harry pulled Em down to the next store front, waited until everyone was gone, and then entered the *Chronicle* office.

Graham was comforting a visibly shaken Monika.

"Anybody hurt?" Ember asked.

"No," Graham replied, "but that crazy woman would have diced up Monika if it weren't for some fast thinking on our girl's part."

"What did you do?" Ember asked.

"Threw my computer screen at her," Monika answered. "That gave me time to run to the press room, and I was able to hold her off until the police arrived."

"She used a broom to hold that psycho at bay," Graham added.

"Glad you weren't hurt," Harry said. "It does seem, though, you touched a nerve."

"And how," Monika said.

"An occupational hazard," Graham said. "Touching nerves, that is."

"Are you going to press charges?" Ember asked.

Monika shook her head. "I think we all know there's something bigger here than an assault charge."

"That we do," Harry said. "That we do."

76

REECE SOVERN LOOKED ACROSS THE TABLE AT CLAIR-ANN TAYLOR. "You want to tell me what on earth was going through your mind?"

"Did you see what that bitch said in the newspaper about me?"

"I read the paper, yes. Obviously, you did too. So that justifies you going after Monika Crow with a butcher knife?"

"Is she going to press charges?"

"I don't know," Reece lied.

"Then I don't have to answer any of your questions."

"No, you don't."

"Okay. I'm not saying another word."

"Your choice. Helen, will you escort Ms. Taylor to a nice, comfy cell?"

Officer Helen Beauregard touched Clair-Ann's arm. "Let's go, ma'am."

Clair-Ann stood, and Reece watch the two women leave.

Something in that snippet of gossip triggered Clair-Ann. Reece stood. *I think I'll talk to Ms. Crow and have GJ find out what that bit of gossip was all about.*

———

Having gotten the backstory from Monika for the post in her column, Ember decided to pay a visit to the Reverend L.P. Brown, pastor of Mount Zion Missionary Baptist Church.

She drove north on State Highway 28; took a right on FM 1881, drove for a mile, and then turned left on Buford Field Road. After another two miles, she saw the small church on the right.

A field of brown, tilled earth surrounded the white frame building. She turned into the driveway and parked in a spot in front of the building. Hers was the only car in the lot.

I wonder if anyone is here.

After a moment or two, Ember shrugged and got out of her car. She walked up to the door, took hold of the handle, and pulled. The door opened, and she walked into what she'd call the narthex. She wasn't sure what Baptists called it.

Straight ahead was the worship area. A center aisle divided the rows of pews. The pulpit was very prominent at the far end of the aisle.

Ember entered the sanctuary and called out, "Hello. Is anyone here?"

A minute later, a large man came out of a door to the right of what she'd call the chancel. He had a smile on his dark mahogany face. His hair was grizzled white.

He said, "Hello. I'm L.P. Brown, the pastor here at Mount Zion. How may I help you?"

"I'm Ember Cole, pastor of Saint Luke's Methodist Church in Magnolia Bluff."

Pastor Brown closed the distance, Ember held out her hand, and they shook hands.

"We don't get many visitors from Magnolia Bluff," Brown said. "Especially ministers."

"I'd like to ask you about your son and Clair-Ann Taylor."

"Uh-huh. I had a hunch when I saw a white woman that you weren't here for a friendly chat about Jesus. Did *she* send you?"

"She?"

"Yeah. Her mother, Caldwell Taylor."

"You didn't hear? Cally was brutally murdered."

"I'm sorry to hear that. Although I'm not sorry she's no longer here. She was about as mean and nasty as they come."

"She wasn't a pleasant person, that's for sure. She was my lay leader and caused me no end of grief. I understand your son doesn't live in town."

"No. He lives in Dallas. Has a good job in a bank."

"Good for him."

"We're proud of him. Told him he needed to get himself a career. Too many young black men go into sports. Just a life of sin with no future. But you want to know what happened between him and Clair-Ann."

"Yes. I've heard the gossip. I'd like to hear what actually happened."

"Why?"

"Because if I understand what happened between your son and Clair-Ann, I might be able to catch a murderer."

Brown shrugged. "It's a sad story, but if you think good will come of it..." He sat in a pew and motioned for Ember to sit.

"It's like this, Pastor Cole, that woman blackmailed me into breaking up those high school sweethearts. I hated to do it. But even more, I hated to lose my church. And maybe that's the problem."

Brown let his eyes roam the building and when they came to rest on the pulpit, he said, "I thought this was *my* church instead of the Lord Jesus Christ's church."

His eyes came to gaze into Embers. "One sin, Pastor Cole, one sin that led to another. Two broken hearted kids. I don't know about Clair-Ann, but I know my Jeremiah lost something the day he ended their romance. And I lost my boy. He doesn't talk to me anymore. Oh, he's respectful. But he's gone. His heart is closed."

"I'm very sorry to hear this story. I know about sin, but I have no children."

"The sins of the fathers."

Ember nodded. "Your story brings a personal understanding to that verse. I'm so very sorry."

"Not your fault. It was a hard lesson, and I pray to God that I learned my lesson and that He'll heal the rift between me and my boy."

"I'll pray for that, as well. So Cally Taylor blackmailed you into persuading your son to end his relationship with Clair-Ann."

"That's it in a nutshell. How is Clair-Ann?"

"She's a bitter young woman."

"That's too bad. She seemed to be such a lighthearted gal."

"I'm sorry to bring pain into your day, Pastor Brown. But this bit of information is helpful. Very helpful."

"That's good to know. There was no love lost between that woman and me, but she was God's instrument and she didn't deserve a brutal death."

"There's a lesson here for all of us. May God grant you and your family His peace."

"And also to you, Pastor Cole."

They stood, shook hands, and Ember walked back to her car.

When she was behind the wheel, she smiled. *The puzzle is nearly complete.*

77

TUESDAY, 20 FEBRUARY 2:08 PM

HARRY WAS SITTING AT HIS TABLE IN THE CORNER OF THE REALLY Good, enjoying a doughnut and a cup of Kenya AA brewed with his new Bodum vacuum siphon coffee maker.

This is indeed worth all the hype, he thought. *Might have to switch over to vacuum siphon coffee exclusively.*

He looked at his tablet and tapped the app for the spy cams observing Clair-Ann's house. Nothing was going on at present, but he noticed that a little over an hour ago Clair-Ann had returned home.

Today Monika. Tomorrow morning, another anonymous I-saw-what-you-did letter. On top of what she went through today, the next letter just might get us some results.

The door chime sounded, and Harry looked up from the tablet. Walking towards him was Telford Whitacre.

Harry stood. "Good afternoon, Telford. Have a seat. Coffee? Tea? Something to eat?"

They shook hands, and Telford sat. "A coffee and a slice of pie would be nice."

"Coming right up, my friend." Harry caught Estrelita's attention, told her Telford's order, and sat. "How are things going?"

Telford rubbed his hands together and a smile spread across

his face. "Very good. Very good. We are restocking, filling internet orders, and have even had some drop ins. Hopefully, they'll spread the word and when we officially open we'll have a good local group started."

"Hopefully. A good tobacconist is difficult to find in small town America."

"I think we'll be well positioned for the start of tourist season."

"The tourists and all the festivals will hopefully fill your coffers with lots of filthy lucre."

Telford laughed. "We like that, don't we?"

Estrelita set coffee, cream, sugar, and a slice of strawberry pie before Telford.

"Oh, my. This looks delicious. Did you make this?"

"My cook, Miguel."

Telford put a forkful of pie in his mouth and groaned his pleasure. "Heavenly," he said after he chewed and swallowed. He took a sip of coffee. "Oh, my." He took another. "Oh, this is very good. Kenya Double A, but how did you make it?"

Henry pointed. "My new Bodum vacuum siphon coffee maker."

"Oh, this is the best. So rich and flavorful."

"Only the best for my customers."

"May they fill your shop to overflowing."

They touched coffee mugs and drank coffee.

"I have presents for you and Ember," Telford said.

"What's the occasion?"

"A little thank you gift for your kindness to two strangers. You've made us feel very welcome, and Terall and I want you to know we appreciate both of you."

"Em and I both know how tough a small town can be on newcomers. So we spread forth kindness to our fellow strangers."

"Thank you."

"Are you settling in okay?"

Telford told him how things were going while he drank coffee and ate pie. When finished, he took out of his jacket pocket two small cloth bags. Harry recognized them as pipe socks.

"This one is for Ember." Telford took out of the sock a smallish pipe. "It's a Doctor Plumb Tween size number eighteen. I guess I'd call it a bent egg." He handed it to Harry.

"This is very nice. Looks brand new."

"We had a good pipe repairman in Massachusetts."

"I guess so."

"And this one's for you." He handed the other pipe sock to Harry.

"What surprise is in here?"

"You'll like it."

Harry opened the sock and took out a bright red Filto aluminum radiator pipe. "Oh, my! I've never seen an all red Filto."

"I hadn't either. And the nice thing is that one has never been smoked. A rare find for a pipe that's sixty or so years old."

"All I can say is thank you very much. These are lovely."

"I hope you get many years of enjoyment from them."

"Can't speak for Em, but I know I will."

"Good. Well, I have to get back. Stocking."

The men stood, shook hands, and Harry watched him leave.

Through the window, he saw Telford light a cigar pipe before he walked back to his shop.

Now that is what I should give Reece. Save him from having to get rid of soggy wads of tobacco. Though he won't be able to roll it from one corner of his mouth to the other. The upside is it's a lot more stylish.

Harry chuckled at the thought of Reece being stylish. *That's probably never happening.*

He looked at his new pipe, thought about the letter he had to compose for Clair-Ann, and decided he'd head upstairs to his apartment and kill two birds with one stone.

Just as he was getting up from his table, the door chime

sounded and in walked Oralene Reston. She headed directly to his table.

Uh-oh, here comes trouble.

He put a smile on his face. "Good afternoon, Oralene. How are you?"

She marched up to him and stopped arm's length away. Her voice was soft and measured. "Because you helped my mama, I'm giving you a warning. You are going to pay. You and your common-law wife. You are both going to pay for what you did to my mother."

"I did nothing to your mother. Nor did Ember. We did nothing but help your family."

"I'm not talking about my mama or my brothers and sisters. I'm talking about my mother."

"I don't understand."

"I'm a Fight now. My mother, Mrs. Gunter Fight, is adopting me. And because of what you and that woman did to her, you will pay."

"We've done nothing to Mrs. Fight. Nothing. I don't know what she's been telling you, Oralene, but we've not harmed her in any way, shape, or form."

"You've been warned. You know what I am capable of. And you also know that my hands will not be sullied. Nothing will be traceable back to me. Good day, Mr. Thurgood."

She turned and left. And Harry was left muttering, "What the hell?"

78

TUESDAY, 20 FEBRUARY 7:38 PM

HARRY AND EMBER WERE SITTING BEFORE THE FIREPLACE, ENJOYING the heat and flickering flames. He was drinking coffee and smoking Holiday pipe mixture in his new Filto aluminum radiator pipe. Ember was drinking tea and smoking Molto Dolce in the Dr. Plumb she'd gotten from the Whitacres.

"This stuff is so sweet I bet I have cavities in the morning," Ember said.

"Fewer calories than dessert."

"You're right there." She puffed on the pipe, savored the sweet smoke, then said, "I think Pastor Brown's story is pretty sad. Don't you?"

"It is. But about par for the course, considering how the nasties operate around here."

"That's true. We now know why Monika heard what she did."

Harry blew a stream of smoke towards the fire. "Yep. She guessed that was a huge issue with Clair-Ann and did she ever guess right."

"But that can't be the driver for all the murders, can it?"

"Probably not. But it was a large log that joined the growing pile."

Ember drank tea. "So we still need to find out what started the fire."

"That we do. But without a doubt, it will be something to do with religion, race, or Cally."

"And perhaps all three."

"Probably all three."

Harry drank coffee. Ember puffed on her pipe. "What are we going to do about Oralene's threat?" she asked.

"Not sure there's anything we can do. Except be vigilant."

"Surely she won't be able to convince her brothers to come after us."

"Most likely not. Tommy assured me he and Buck talked with all the boys and told them flat out they knew they were guilty and would be watching them."

"What did the boys say?"

"Nothing. Which Tommy and Buck took as a sign that the boys knew they were in trouble."

"So who will she get to do her dirty work?"

"A good question to which I have no answer."

Ember drank tea. "Well, I'm in God's hands and I will fear no evil."

Harry smiled and drank coffee.

"I know you don't believe. It would be nice if you did, but you are who you are and I know that you are a good man, Harry Thurgood. So I think God has you in His hands, too."

"And I hope he does as well."

"On a different note, I think I might get into this pipe smoking thing."

"Really?"

"Yeah. Much, much better tasting than cigarettes or weed. Plus there's no spacey high and no nicotine rush. Just this sweet taste." She laughed. "It's like smoking a doughnut."

Harry chuckled. "A fitting description for that pipe tobacco."

"Never in a million years would I have ever imagined me here with you doing this."

"You're okay with it?"

"Yes. Yes, I am. Pleasure is good. God gave wine to us to make our hearts glad. God wouldn't have done that if pleasure wasn't good." She puffed on the pipe. "Pleasure's something I denied myself since leaving Vegas. But not anymore." The last sentence she said with a smile.

"Epicurus essentially says the same thing: the happy life is the life of pleasure. Ethically responsible pleasure."

"That's interesting."

"He also believed virtue was instrumental in achieving happiness."

"So no screwing your lover on the Green."

"Uh, no."

"How about in bed?"

"That's permissible."

"Then let's do something permissible."

———

Reece Sovern was slowly chewing a bite of the cheeseburger GJ had dropped off for him. His mind, though, wasn't on the food. It was drifting back and forth between GJ's conversation with Suzy Roy and his talk with Monika Crow.

Monika had been pretty tightlipped and hadn't wanted to give him any information. She did, however, confirm that Clair-Ann and Jeremiah Brown had been an item in high school for a time, until the boy ended the relationship. Her guess was that Cally had something to do with the breakup.

Reece swallowed the bite of burger and took another.

And that break-up may be the reason for all the anger towards her mother that Clair-Ann was dumping.

He put the burger down, finished chewing, and swallowed. He leaned back in his chair, put his hands behind his head, and continued ruminating.

In fact, it goes a long way toward explaining why Clair-Ann attacked Monika. That nerve is still very raw. But that was all some time ago. If Clair-Ann did kill all those people, why now? Why not then? When the wound was fresh?

Reece sat up and picked up his cheeseburger. *Something must've ripped the scab off the wound. And that's the missing puzzle piece I have to find.*

79

WEDNESDAY, 21 FEBRUARY 8:04 AM

REECE SOVERN READ THE NOTE CLAIR-ANN HANDED HIM. LETTERS and words had been cut out of a newspaper and glued to a sheet of paper. The note read:

> You thought you were careful.
> You weren't.
> I saw you. I saw what you did.
> You're not God.
> You now need to die.

"When did you get this?" Reece asked.

They were in the living room of the Taylor home, and Clair-Ann was pacing back and forth before him.

"I told you. This morning. I found it in an hour ago. Someone is stalking me. I want protection."

"You get any more of these?"

"One. I threw it away."

"What did it say?"

"I saw what you did. You won't get away with it."

"Mind if I keep this?"

"No. Take it. I want protection. Someone is after me."

Reece handed the note to GJ, who put it into an evidence bag.

"Do you know what they're talking about?" he asked.

"What do you mean?"

"What did this person see you do?"

"I don't know. I have no idea. It's some sicko."

"Have you gotten something like this before?" GJ asked.

"No. Why would I? You think I'm guilty, don't you?"

"Guilty of what?" Reece asked.

"Those murders. I lose my cool and now you think this sicko is saying I killed those people."

"Did you?" GJ asked.

"No! I called you for help because some nut job is stalking me. Threatening to kill me. And now you think I did it. Well, I didn't. Just go. Get the hell out of my house."

Reece stood.

Clair-Ann stopped pacing and pointed towards the door. "Get out of here. Now."

"Or what?" GJ said. "You'll attack us with a knife?"

Clair-Ann lunged for GJ, but the investigator was faster. She had Clair-Ann in a half nelson before anyone could blink.

"Do we arrest her, Sarge?"

"Let me go, you bitch. Let me go. I'll sue."

Reece nodded. "Let her go. We're leaving, Clair-Ann. But any more shenanigans like that and it's a cell for you. Again. Come on, GJ."

The police investigator released her hold and Clair-Ann ran behind the sofa.

"Get out. Now."

Reece nodded his head towards the living room doorway and the two left.

Once on the street, GJ asked, "What do you make of that?"

"I'm not one for plays. But I do remember high school English class with Mrs. Osborn. And Clair-Ann would make a great Lady Macbeth."

"Don't follow."

"The scene where she says, 'Out damn spot, out.' Or something to that effect."

"Don't get it."

"Look it up. In the meantime, I'm going to ask Tommy to have Helen Beauregard keep an eye on Ms. Taylor."

Reece headed for his car, GJ walking next to him.

"I think I'm going to beat Thurgood on this one," he said. "And will that ever feel good."

80

WEDNESDAY, 21 FEBRUARY 8:21 AM

VIA THE APP LINKED TO THE SPY CAMS, HARRY WATCHED REESE AND GJ leave the Taylor home.

I hope that was related to the note Clair-Ann most likely found this morning. Because if it was, then things are heating up.

Harry took a bite of his doughnut, being careful not to get the powdered sugar on his burgundy ascot with the navy blue paisley pattern.

Do I drop off another tonight, or wait a day or two?

The bite of doughnut swallowed, he sipped the hot Yemen Mocha Mattari that was in his coffee mug.

Wish I knew what she said to Reece. I could just ask, but then he'd want to know how I knew he'd talk to her.

He took another bite of his doughnut. *Best to figure out a circuitous route so he gets lost in the details.*

The spy cam showed Clair-Ann running to the garage. Coffee mug almost to his lips, he slowly lowered it to the table. *Wonder what's going on there?*

The door chime rang, and Harry saw Brandon and Joyce entering the shop. He closed the cover on his tablet.

"Hey, you two," Harry said. "You're early." He stood and walked over to them.

"I have a showing at ten," Joyce said.

"So we decided to get coffee now," Brandon said. "I want to avoid your nine o'clock regulars."

"If you haven't found any bodies," Harry said, "I don't think Huston or Jager will be interested."

"I suppose you're right," Brandon said.

The door chime rang and in walked Reece Sovern.

Harry watched Sovern and Brandon both do double takes. "No fisticuffs, you two."

Sovern paused, took in a deep breath, and exhaled. "Turner. Joyce." And without waiting for them to reply, turned to Harry and said, "Do you have a minute?"

"I'm at your disposal." To Brandon and Joyce, Harry said, "Catch you two later."

He then motioned for Sovern to follow him back to his table in the corner.

The two men sat, and Harry asked the sergeant investigator what was on mind.

"I'm a simple man, Thurgood, so indulge me. The Reverend made some comment about Clair-Ann being like a character in some play. Electric, or something like that."

Harry smiled. "Elektra. Yes, she did."

"Would you explain that to me again?"

"Sure. The ancient Greek tragedy writer, Aeschylus, wrote a trilogy based on the story of Agamemnon's return from the Trojan War, his murder by his wife Clytemnestra, and then Clytemnestra's murder by her son, Orestes, and then Orestes being brought to justice."

"Okay. So how does this Elektra person figure in all of this?"

"In some versions of the myth, she plots with her brother to kill their mother. In others, she joins him and together they kill their mother."

Sovern thought a moment, then said, "So the Reverend was saying Clair-Ann is like this Elektra because she killed her mother for not taking care of her father."

"You got it."

Harry watched the emerald green corona slowly roll to the other side of the investigator's mouth.

"Seems farfetched to me," he said at last. "Cally didn't kill her husband."

Harry shrugged. "Call it a symbolic murder of the husband. She did everything she could to destroy him."

"I suppose. Still…"

"Look. People kill for all sorts of reasons. Rebecca killed, what, six, eight people all to avenge her boyfriend?"

Sovern slowly nodded.

"Then there's Merrick's murder because of jealousy. What about Terresa Brown? And—"

Sovern held up his hand. "Okay. I get your point. Even so, four people *and* the mother?"

"There's a whole lot of the iceberg no one ever sees."

The sergeant investigator slowly nodded. "What Monika dug up."

"Yep. And Emmy got it straight from Pastor Brown that Cally was behind that one."

"The breaking up of Clair-Ann and the preacher's kid?"

Harry nodded.

"Jesus." The cigar made its journey to the other side of Sovern's mouth. "Okay. I'm following. But what lit the fuse?"

"Don't know. *You* have no idea?"

"Not at the moment. Although someone apparently knows because Clair-Ann's started getting threatening notes."

"She has?"

Sovern nodded. "Asked for protection. I mentioned it to Jager, and he agreed to send Helen Beauregard to keep an eye on things. And don't say anything. We're keeping this quiet."

"I won't say anything, but half the town's probably wondering what Helen's car is doing parked outside the Taylor place."

"You're probably right. Let's keep them guessing, okay?"

"Mum's the word, Reece."

Sovern stood. He held out his hand. Harry stood and grasped it. "Thanks for your insight. I appreciate you talking to me."

"Anytime, Sarge."

Sovern smiled, turned, and left.

Wonders never cease. Harry said to himself. *He just might solve this case.*

81

WEDNESDAY, 21 FEBRUARY 9:02 AM

THE NINERS WERE SITTING AROUND THE TABLES POURING COFFEE into mugs and putting pastries on plates.

Graham Huston said, "So what's new, Tommy?"

The police chief chuckled. "You mean what can I tell you that will hopefully sell newspapers."

"Need to keep the lights on, pay the ink supplier, and cover a few paychecks."

Chief Jager took a huge bite out of a cheese danish, thought a moment while he chewed, and said, "Let's see... Some college student, texting on her phone, ran a stop sign, and plowed into Hazel Anderssen's car. But you probably already knew that."

Huston nodded.

"Did Hazel get hurt?" Caroline McCluskey asked.

"Nope," Jager answered. "The student's Toyota was totaled. But Hazel's old Chrysler Imperial just had a few scratches."

"They don't make cars like they used to," Reverend Billy Bob Baskin said.

"That's good and bad," Harry said.

"Does anyone know why Helen Beauregard's car is parked across the street from the Taylor house?" Magnolia Nadine Roane asked.

Harry just about spewed his coffee.

Caroline laughed. "Harry knows."

"Did Sovern tell you?" Jager asked.

"He was in about an hour ago to ask me a question," Harry said.

Jager nodded. "He told you."

"I told him I wouldn't say a word, but that I wouldn't have to as half the town would be wondering why her car was parked there."

"Okay, so why is it there?" Magnolia Nadine asked.

"Just a convenient place to have a coffee and a doughnut," Jager said.

Billy Bob shook his head. "So you're not going to tell us."

"Tell you what?" Jager said around a mouthful of cream cheese Czech kolache.

Harry chuckled. "Beware. Little brother is watching us."

Caroline laughed. "Good one, Harry."

"You've been awfully quiet, Mrs. Thurgood," Huston said.

"Just enjoying the coffee, pastries, and conversation. Might use it in a sermon. Never know."

"Uh-oh. I'm in trouble now," Huston said.

"What's the matter, Graham," Harry began, "afraid of a little competition?"

"No offense, Ember, but your sermons are probably about as effective as the paper," Huston said.

With a smile touching her lips, Ember replied, "Maybe more. After all, we're moving back to the aural stage. Reading is becoming a lost art."

"You have a point there," Huston conceded.

"I guess, since you won't tell us anything, Tommy, I am going to have to put out a few feelers to find out what's going on," Magnolia Nadine said.

Jager stood. "You do that, Nadine. I gotta run. You folks have a great day."

"Now that Jager is gone, Harry," Huston said, "care to tell us what's going on?"

"All I know is that Sovern asked me about a comment Emmy made concerning Claire-Ann—"

"Which is?" Magnolia Nadine asked.

"That Claire-Ann was like Elektra in the Greek myth."

"Oh, my," Caroline said.

Harry continued, "And that she was getting threatening notes and wanted protection. But I didn't tell you any of this."

Caroline turned to Ember. "So you think Clair-Ann is behind all of these murders?"

"Yes. She fits the Elektra profile to a T."

82

WEDNESDAY, 21 FEBRUARY 9:18 AM

THE NINERS WERE SILENT, ALTHOUGH GRAHAM HAD A MONA LISA smile on his face.

"Do you have proof?" Caroline asked.

Ember shook her head. "No, we don't."

"Have you told this to Tommy?" Billy Bob asked.

"Sovern," Harry answered.

"So why isn't she in jail?" Magnolia Nadine asked.

"No proof," Ember repeated. "It's just a theory at this point."

"But one that makes the most sense," Harry added.

Caroline caught the look on Huston's face. "So you're in on this too, aren't you?"

"You'll read about it in the paper," Graham replied.

"You three are incorrigible," Caroline said with a smile.

"Hopefully, Reece gets some evidence soon. I don't like the thought that a murderess is on the loose," Magnolia Nadine said.

"It's just a theory," Harry said. "But Reece is working it."

Caroline stood. "I have to run. Have a good day."

Billy Bob and Magnolia Nadine also excused themselves, leaving Graham sitting with Harry and Ember.

"What do you think, Harry, will Reece get his woman?" Graham asked.

"I think he's on the trail. I'm cautiously optimistic."

Graham stood. "Thank goodness he has a few friends who are willing to help."

Harry stood. "It's like the song: I can get by with a little help from my friends."

"The Beatles. See you all later."

Graham left, and Harry, Ember, and Estrelita put the tables and chairs back in their original spots.

When they were done, Harry and Ember moved to Harry's table in the corner.

"So what's next?" Ember asked.

"I think we drop one more note in the mail slot."

"How are you going to do that with Helen there?"

"She can't be there twenty-four seven. If Reece gets someone to spell her, then I guess I get creative."

Ember touched his arm. "Be careful. It won't look good if the minister's husband gets arrested."

"Don't worry, my love. Like the other song says, we can work it out."

83

WEDNESDAY, 21 FEBRUARY 1:09 PM

GEORGIA JEAN RIGGINS WALKED INTO DEAN'S TACTICAL AND SELF-Defense.

She'd checked the Marble Falls business's background to make sure it was legit. Dean Angostino opened the business ten years ago.

He was a Los Angeles native, who'd relocated to Texas, and had not so much as a speeding ticket since becoming a Texas resident.

The layout of the shop was simple. To her right, a wall with pictures of people shooting. To her left was a long glass case that also served as a counter.

Displayed on the wall behind the counter were a variety of firearms, edged weapons, and blunt-force tactical weapons. At the far end of the shop was a door.

"How may I help you?" a man asked.

GJ eyed the somewhat overweight employee. *Probably in his fifties and I'd have him on the floor in ten seconds flat, and his gun in my hand.*

She took her badge out of her suit coat pocket and showed it to him. "I'm Investigator Riggins of the Magnolia Bluff PD and I'm looking for Dean Angostino."

"He's teaching a class in back. Should be done...," he looked at his watch. "Should be done in about ten minutes."

GJ nodded.

"Take a look. We offer a discount to law enforcement."

GJ walked along the glass case. Her eyes took in the revolvers, the pistols, and the tactical batons. She stopped when she reached the knives.

"You sell many of these?" she asked.

"Yes. We sell quite a few knives."

"To women?"

"Not so much. Mostly young men."

GJ took a picture out of her pocket. "Ever see this woman?"

The man picked up the picture, studied it for a few moments, and then set it back down. "I think she was here for self-defense lessons."

GJ picked up the picture and returned it to her pocket. "She buy any knives?"

"Not that I recall."

The door at the back of the shop opened, and three women and two men filed out.

"Class is over. Let me text Dean."

The man typed on his phone and a minute later a tall, muscular man emerged from the back. He had nearly black hair and wore a white shirt and black slacks.

He walked up to GJ. "I'm Dean Angostino."

"I'm Investigator Riggins. Do you have a minute?"

"For the police? Always. Follow me. My office is in the back."

GJ followed the business owner to his office. He sat behind his desk and indicated with his hand a chair she could sit in. GJ stood by the chair, but did not sit.

"How may I help you?"

She pulled the picture of Clair-Ann Taylor from her pocket and put it on his desk. "Ever see this woman before?"

"I gave her private self-defense lessons maybe a year ago? Good student."

"What kind of self-defense lessons?"

"She wasn't interested in firearms. And she didn't want any long-term martial arts training, either. So I taught her bartitsu. She was a fast learner. A natural at it."

"You do any knife work with her?"

"Yes, I did."

"Was she good?"

"A natural. Best knife fighter I've seen since I left LA."

84

WEDNESDAY, 21 FEBRUARY 4:07 PM

REECE SOVERN WAS ALL SMILES. HE TOOK THE INFORMATION GJ HAD uncovered about Clair-Ann to Assistant District Attorney Chuck Dylan, and the arrogant SOB liked it.

"Good work, Sovern," he'd said. "I'll take this to Judge Jones. We should be able to get an arrest warrant."

Reece removed the cellophane from an emerald green perfecto, stuck the stogie in his mouth, and leaned back in his chair. His fingers were laced together over his stomach.

This is a good day. All the pieces of the puzzle are falling together, and this case will soon be history. It looks like Thurgood was right. When this is a wrap, I'll have to thank him. Might even buy some of his expensive coffee to celebrate.

Reece let out a chuckle. *This will certainly show that big city show off, Turner, that we small town cops aren't ignoramuses. Can't stand that guy. I'll take arrogant Thurgood over that pompous New York City ass of a cop any day of the week.* The cigar rolled to the other corner of his mouth. *Yep. Today's a very good day.*

Harry Thurgood opened the app for his spy cameras. He played back the earlier video and watched Clair-Ann leave by the back door. Then, an hour later, she returned and lugged into the house a couple of large boxes and five bright red gasoline cans.

What the heck is she doing?

He looked at the timestamps. She was gone from a quarter after eleven to a quarter after twelve.

Clair-Ann is building up to something, and I have a feeling it's not a good something.

———

Officer Helen Beauregard watched the curtain over the living room window move ever so slightly.

She's watching me again. Helen smiled. *And I'm watching her.*

Having borrowed her nephew's drone, Helen could watch the rear of the house, as well as the front.

She'd caught Clair-Ann leaving in the morning. Unfortunately, she didn't see her return because the drone needed recharging.

However, I know she's back. That curtain moves a dozen times a day.

She watched it move back to its normal position.

Sure hope Reece decides what to do on this case soon. This is just mind numbingly boring.

Helen chuckled. *I think I'll take a walk. I need to stretch my legs. Besides, it will wig out Clair-Ann, not knowing what I'm doing.*

She opened the car door and got out.

85

THURSDAY, 22 FEBRUARY 2:47 AM

HARRY THURGOOD, DRESSED COMPLETELY IN BLACK, INCLUDING THE balaclava to hide his face, approached the Taylor home. The clouds, moon, and stars were playing hide and seek with each other.

A block away from his destination, he stopped. A black patrol car was parked across the street from the Taylor home. He thought a moment and decided to cut through the yard of the house to his left and take the alley the rest of the way.

Staying in the shadows provided by the house and the enormous live oak, he crept through the yard and came out into the alley. All was quiet. Not a creature was stirring.

I need a diversion to get whoever's in the cop car to leave long enough so I can slip my note through the mail slot.

He walked down the alley, shining his pencil flashlight on the pavement and along the edges of the yards and garages. Four houses past the Taylor place, panning the thin beam of light along the edge of someone's yard, he found a flower bed with brick edging.

Harry put his flashlight away. *This is exactly what I need.*

He wrenched a brick free from the soil and hefted it in his hand. *This baby will create a little excitement.*

Creeping through the yard towards the street, he stayed in the shadows so his black attire would blend in.

Reaching the front of the house, he surveyed the residences across the street, and found what he was looking for: a house with a large picture window and a small security sign in the front flower bed.

Clutching the brick, he took a deep breath, dashed across the street as fast as he could, stopped for just a moment, hurled the brick through the picture window, and dashed back across the street into the shadows of the house that had provided the brick.

He paused, peeked around the corner, and saw a person leave the cop car.

Good. Whoever it is, they weren't sleeping on the job.

He trotted down the alley to the Taylor home, crept through the backyard until he reached the front porch. He watched the officer walk down to the house he'd just vandalized. When the cop was in front of the house, he climbed over the railing onto the porch, slipped the note through the mail slot, and then made his way back to the alley.

Heading home, he said, "This one ought to do it."

The words were blunt and straightforward: *Turn yourself in, because I'm coming for you.*

————

Helen Beauregard was suddenly awake. *What the hell?*

She watched the figure, outlined in the light of the partially obscured moon, dash across the street and throw something at one of the houses.

As the figure ran back across the street and vanished into the night, she got out of her car and hurried towards the porch light that had just came on.

I wonder what that was all about. Kids playing pranks?

What she found when she arrived at the home was a shattered picture window and a very puzzled and angry Florence Neidermeier on the other side of the window looking at her.

She began taking Mrs. Neidermeier's statement when it suddenly dawned on her. *Oh, my God. Clair-Ann. Maybe that was her...*

"I'll be right back," she told the old woman, and ran down to the Taylor home.

All was dark inside the house. Helen mounted the porch steps and rang the doorbell. After the second push on the button, the porch light went on, the door opened a crack, and Clair-Ann's voice said, "What do you want?"

"Clair-Ann, this is Officer Beauregard. There was an incident at Mrs. Neidermeier's home. I want to make sure you're all right."

"What do you people care?" And the door slammed shut.

"Ungrateful bitch," Helen muttered, descended the porch stairs, and was halfway to the sidewalk when she heard Clair-Ann's voice.

"He was here. My stalker was here."

Helen turned and started back up to the house. "What makes you think your stalker was here?"

"I got a note. Come here and take a look."

When Helen reached the door, she said, "Let's see."

"Come in. It's too cold out there."

Helen stepped into the house, past Clair-Ann, who'd stepped aside to let the officer in. As Helen started to turn to talk to her, she caught movement in her peripheral vision, felt intense pain a moment later, and then the lights went out.

86

THURSDAY, 22 FEBRUARY 3:32 AM

MBPD Officer Logan Ytzen stopped his patrol car next to Officer Helen Beauregard's vehicle. He got out and panned his flashlight beam around his fellow officer's car. When he saw nothing out of the ordinary, he opened the driver's door and shined the flashlight beam inside the car. It was empty.

Ytzen got back into his vehicle and drove on down to the home of Florence Neidermeier.

As he approached the front door, the old woman came out of her house. "It's about time you got here. That young woman left off talking to me as though a swarm of hornets were chasing her. Said she'd be back. But didn't come back at all. And me with my broken picture window."

"Do you know where she went?"

"I saw her run down to the Taylors."

"Thanks for calling to let us know."

"Is there something going on?"

"What do you mean?"

"Is there a reason why that young woman's been parked across from the Taylors's home?"

"Just routine business. Now, if you'll excuse me, I want to make sure everything is all right with Clair-Ann and her father."

"What about my window?"

"You better call your insurance company."

Ytzen got in his car and backed down the street, stopping in front of Helen's car. He got out, walked up to the Taylor's front door, and rang the doorbell.

When there was no answer, he rang a second time, and when there was no response, he pounded on the door.

After a minute, he keyed his radio transmitter. "Daisy, this is Logan. We may have a situation at the Taylor home. There was no response to the doorbell or my pounding on the door. And I don't see Helen anywhere."

"Okay, Logan. I'll let Sergeant LaPorte know."

"Thanks, Daisy."

Logan walked back to his car, turned around and, leaning against it, let his eyes roam the exterior of the Taylor place.

This is weird. No response to the doorbell or my pounding. And no Helen. Something's not right.

87

REECE SOVERN SLID HIS GLASSES BACK UP HIS NOSE SO THAT THEY were once again sitting on the bridge. The emerald green corona rolled over to the other side of his mouth.

In his pocket was a warrant for the arrest of Clair-Ann Taylor. Assistant DA Dillon had finally tracked down Judge Jones as he was unlocking the door to the Pickle Dilly Bait and Tackle shop.

Reece could just imagine Jones's response to being forced to work at such an ungodly hour of the morning. But sign the warrant he did.

Now the entire MBPD and half the sheriff's department had the Taylor home surrounded, waiting for the Rangers to send more backup and the sniper squad.

Clair-Ann had answered Reece's knocking at her door with a shotgun pointed at his face. He'd backed away, and she'd closed the door.

He'd called in and in no time, the house was surrounded.

Chief Jager and Sheriff Blanton joined him, and the three of them stared at the house.

"Nothin' good's gonna come from all this," Blanton said.

Jager nodded. "Nope." He turned to Reece. "Did you get her cell number?"

"GJ got it from her friend, Suzy Roy. The landline number she got from the internet."

Jager shook his head. "Huh. Nothing's private anymore."

"Ain't that the truth," Reece agreed.

"You just figure that out?" Blanton said.

"Nope. Just sayin'," Jager answered. To Reece, he said, "Did she pick up when you called?"

"No. I left a message on both phones with my number. Hopefully she'll call."

Jager nodded. "Hopefully. You think she has Helen?"

Blanton said, "Yup."

Reece said, "Probably. Helen hasn't shown up anywhere, and that isn't like her."

"No, it's not," Jager agreed.

Reece's phone rang. He looked at Jager and took the phone out of his pocket.

"Sovern."

After a moment, he nodded to Jager and put the phone on speaker.

"Clair-Ann, no one is going anywhere. Your house is surrounded, and I have a warrant for your arrest. I'm asking you to give yourself up. It's best for you if you do."

"I'm not giving myself up. I have to take care of my father. He needs me. So you all need to go away. If you don't, I'm going to kill Helen. I'm going to gut her like a trussed up pig."

"I don't think you want to do that. Even if we let you leave, the Rangers are coming. And their snipers can take out the eye of a blue bottle at a thousand yards. You won't be around to take care of your father."

"I'll kill her. Let me go. So I can take care of my father."

"Clair-Ann, if you kill Helen and the Rangers kill you, who will take care of your father?"

There was silence. Reece looked at Jager, who shrugged.

"Are you there? If you are, talk to me."

"What's there to talk about? You all think I'm guilty."

"That's for the court to decide. The best thing you can do for yourself and your father right now is to release Helen and turn yourself in."

Silence. Reece checked his phone and saw that she hadn't disconnected.

Finally, she spoke. "It's a trick. You have one hour to let me and my father go, or your precious officer dies."

"She's gone," Reece said.

"So, what do you think? Do we let them go?" Jager asked.

"Won't get far if you do," Blanton said.

Reece thought for a moment. "I'm going to call the Reverend. Maybe she can talk some sense into her."

"You mean Ember?"

Reece nodded and told his phone to call Reverend Cole.

88

THURSDAY, 22 FEBRUARY 6:41 AM

"Sovern wants you to do what?" Harry said.

"Talk to Clair-Ann. Try to get her to turn herself in," Ember replied.

"I don't like it, Em. The woman is a psychopath. What if she holds you hostage?"

"Harry, love, you remember when you quipped 'He has the whole world in his hands'?"

"Vaguely."

"Well, He does. I believe Jesus will protect me. And if it's my time to go, it's my time to go. If not, I won't."

"That isn't very comforting, Rev."

"Well, Mister, it will have to do. Clair-Ann and Mr. Taylor are my parishioners. And this is their time of need. I have to do this."

"Time of need, my foot. She's a killer. And your name is not Daniel."

"Ha, ha. She's sick, Harry. Mentally and spiritually sick. I need to minister to her. I am her spiritual doctor. Maybe even her mental doctor."

"I'd put my foot down and tell you you can't go—"

"But you won't, because you know I'm right. Now, let's go, Mister. We have work to do."

"We?"

"You're the minister's husband. You can pray for me."

"I don't believe in prayer."

"You better start. Get your hat and coat."

———

"Thanks for coming, Reverend," Sovern said.

"Clair-Ann and Mr. Taylor are my parishioners. Of course, I'd come."

"I think you have a lot of nerve, Sovern," Harry said, "putting a civilian's life on the line." He felt Ember's hand squeezing his arm and turned to look at her. "Well, he does."

"It's all right, Harry. I want to help."

Harry looked at Sovern. *At least he's smart enough to stay out of our disagreement.*

"What do you want me to do?" Ember asked.

Sovern looked at Harry, cleared his throat, and turned to Ember.

"We want you to talk to her and convince her to turn herself in."

"I will talk to her. Hopefully, she'll see that it's best to turn herself in. I can't convince her. She'll have to convince herself."

"Fair enough. We'd like you to wear a wire—"

"No. I won't do that."

"We need to monitor the situation, in case we need to extract you. And record her confession."

"If the situation gets to that point, I'll probably be dead before you reach the door. However, I doubt things will get to that point. Besides, I am Clair-Ann's pastor, and this is a pastoral call. I'm not a spy."

"But—"

Ember shook her head. "No. No wire. And that's final. Let me do my job. The rest is in God's hands."

"Well, Sovern, looks like you and I will be praying from the sidelines." Harry saw the what-the-hell-are-you-talking-about look on the investigator's face. "It's like we're cheerleaders."

Ember rolled her eyes. "Call her and let her know I'm coming."

Sovern told his phone to call Clair-Ann. When she didn't answer, he left a message.

"Start praying, boys," Ember said, and set off for the Taylors's front door.

Harry watched her for a moment and then leaned over and whispered in Sovern's ear, "If anything happens to her, you're dead."

"Are you threatening an officer of the law, Thurgood?"

"You take it however you want, Sovern."

Harry turned his attention back to the Taylors's home and saw Ember pressing the doorbell button.

89

THURSDAY, 22 FEBRUARY 7:27 AM

EMBER SAT ON THE SOFA ACROSS FROM CLAIR-ANN, WHO WAS sitting on a large overstuffed chair.

"This is a nice room," Ember said. "I don't believe I've been in this room before."

"This is the living room. Mother never used it. She didn't like it. We avoided the room, because you didn't want to get her upset."

"Was she violent?"

"Yes, but not often. She didn't need to be. At least usually. She could demean and belittle you quite effectively with a look or some cutting remark."

"Where's your father?"

"He's sleeping. I gave him an extra sleeping pill."

"And Helen?"

"She's tied up. I put her in the pantry. I haven't hurt her, other than what I needed to do to subdue her."

"Why?"

"The stalker. She was outside watching me, and then I got another note. She either planted it, or is in on it."

"She was here to protect you."

"She was? Why didn't they tell me?"

"I don't know why."

"They should've told me."

"Yes, they should have. What did the note say?"

Clair-Ann closed her eyes for a moment and then said, "Turn yourself in now. Because I'm coming for you." She opened her eyes. "I thought Helen was in on it and was going to hurt me."

I don't like lying to her, Ember told herself. *But if I tell her the truth...*

She prayed a silent prayer before saying, "Why should you turn yourself in? What did you do?"

"I thought I could hide it, but God must've seen me. I did what He should have done years ago."

"And what was that?"

"I got rid of a very bad person. A terrible person. I saw to it that justice was done, because I couldn't trust God to be just."

"So you killed your mother?"

"I brought her to justice. She has paid the price for her arrogance, her uncaring, her terrible meanness, and the crushing of a truly great man. I made the world a better place and saved my father. Something God was dragging His feet on doing."

"Perhaps your mother, through her meanness, arrogance, and uncaring, was actually doing the work of God."

"Do you honestly believe that?"

"Yes, I do."

"How can God use such a despicable person? Isn't He all good? Isn't He love?"

"He is. But like us, He isn't one thing."

"What do you mean?"

"God is love, but He is not only love. God is just, but He is also mercy. You have many facets to your personality. You are a multi-faceted being. You aren't simply one quality. It's the same with God. And because He is all knowing, He knows what we do not. His ways, therefore, are not our ways because we are limited, and He is not."

"So what does that have to do with the bitch who was my mother?"

"In the Book of Job, God uses Satan to accomplish good. The good being the perfection of His devoted worshipper Job. Could it be that your mother was God's instrument to perfect your faith, that of your father's, and mine?"

Clair-Ann was silent and Ember could tell the young woman was contemplating what she'd said. After a time, Clair-Ann spoke.

"I don't see why God would use her. She was evil."

"So is Satan, yet God uses him continually to accomplish good. All the prophets in the Bible were imperfect, some, like Jonah, very much so, yet God used them all to accomplish His purposes. That's why it is always best to let go. To stop trying to control everything. Let God do that. Our job is to love Him and love our neighbors as ourselves."

"So you're telling me I was wrong?"

"No. Because maybe you were God's instrument. I don't know. But what is done is done. At least from our perspective. All actions have consequences. But much of the time we don't understand the full scope of those consequences, and most of the time never see their full effect."

"Well, I don't think I was wrong. She was evil. She deserved to die a horrible death. She should've suffered more."

"What about the others? Why them?"

"They were bad people. They deserved to die."

"You killed them to cover up the murder of your mother and to confuse the police. Didn't you?"

"They were bad."

"How were DeWayne and Lila bad?"

"They were mixing religion and race."

"That's bad?"

"That's why Jeremiah broke up with me. He said we couldn't be together because he was black and I'm white. He was Baptist and I'm Methodist. He said mixing wasn't what God wanted."

"And you believed him?"

"He was a preacher's kid."

"So why Zelmo?"

"Because he was screwing all those white girls."

"Did you want to date him?"

Clair-Ann jumped up out of her chair. "Who told you that?"

"No one. But I think it's fairly obvious."

Clair-Ann started pacing. "Yes, I wanted to date him. But he said no. And I couldn't understand why not and he wouldn't say. After all, he only liked white girls and I'm white.

"Then Vonnie, she's a distant Taylor, and I was at her place getting information for Dad, told me that Zelmo was screwing my mother and how that was a despicable thing for my mother to do. It kind of slipped out, and she tried to cover it up when she realized I didn't know.

"When I confronted Mother, she said I was crazy. But Zelmo admitted he'd been screwing her for months and was giving up 'girls' for 'real women'."

Clair-Ann stopped before Ember and screamed, "So I killed them all! I killed all the hypocrites."

Her chest was heaving, and she was purple with rage.

"Clair-Ann, please sit."

Ember thought the young woman might strike her, but then she got hold of herself and sat.

"I killed them and I'm glad I did. I would've killed Jeremiah, too, but he doesn't live here."

"I thought you loved him."

"I did. But if he thought we were sinning, he shouldn't have asked me out. He set me up and broke my heart. What kind of Christian does that?"

Should I tell her the truth? Will it make any difference? I don't know.

Ember took a deep breath and exhaled. "Clair-Ann, from our perspective, I think we both agree that your mother was not a nice person."

"No, she wasn't. She told me I was a disgrace dating Jeremiah. That I was disgracing the Taylor name. And then I find out she's just a goddamn hypocrite. She was disgracing Dad, her husband. It would kill him if he found out she'd cheated on him."

"I had a talk with Reverend Brown."

"Jeremiah's father?"

"Yes. Your mother blackmailed him into convincing Jeremiah to break it off with you."

"She did?"

"Yes. Jeremiah loved you and wanted to be with you. It was your mother who ended your relationship."

Ember watched Clair-Ann's face turn red and then she let out a primal scream of rage. "That witch. That no good, disgusting witch. Oh, God. Oh, God."

Clair-Ann dissolved into tears and gut-wrenching sobs. Ember let her cry until she was empty. Then the young woman said, "God, I wish I would have made her suffer more. I wish that more than anything. She died too quickly."

"The question now is, what are you going to do? Your home is surrounded. The Rangers will be here soon, if they aren't here already. If you walk out of this house, a sniper will kill you. This is the end. You do have a say in how it will end. So, what are you going to do?"

"I can't leave my father. I promised him I'd always be with him."

"What if I promise to check on him every day? Would that help?"

"You'd do that?"

"Yes."

Ember watched the young woman's face. It looked as though she was thinking, and Ember hoped she'd decide to turn herself in.

"I'll need some time to explain to Dad, because I promised to never leave him. Wait here. I need to give you something."

Clair-Ann left the room and returned some minutes later carrying an old-fashioned briefcase. "This is for you. Now wait by the front door while I get Helen."

Ember walked out of the living room to the front door. In a few moments, Clair-Ann returned with Helen Beauregard, who had her hands tied behind her back and a gag in her mouth. Clair-Ann was carrying a short-barreled shotgun.

"Reverend, open the door and let Helen go first, then you follow."

Ember followed the instructions and in a few moments they were at the police line and paramedics were looking after Helen.

"Well, what did she say?" Reece asked.

"Are you okay, Em?" Harry asked.

"I'm fine. She said—"

An enormous blast sent flames skyward and littered the lawn and street with glass, fragments of bricks, boards, and burning shingles.

90

THURSDAY, 22 FEBRUARY 3:10 PM

HARRY CLOSED THE REALLY GOOD EARLY SO THAT ALL THE principal people on the case could listen to Ember's recap of her visit with the now late Clair-Ann Taylor.

Estrelita had just finished setting carafes of coffee and trays of sandwiches and pastries on the table.

Sitting around the table were Graham Huston, Monika Crow, Reece Sovern, Tommy Jager, Chuck Dillon, and Harry and Ember.

Harry began the meeting. "I thought it would be helpful to get you all together so Em could tell you what Clair-Ann told her."

Pointing to Graham and Monika, Dillon asked, "What are they doing here?"

"They played a key role in this case and they are the press," Harry answered.

"I don't like it," Dillon said.

Harry shrugged. "You can leave."

"I'm the assistant district attorney. I should be here."

"And I'm the coffee shop owner who invited you here. So make up your mind: are you staying or leaving?"

Dillon shot Harry a nasty look, helped himself to a doughnut and coffee, and said, "Let's get this show on the road."

"Very good," Harry said. "While the police were investigating the murders, Graham, Monika, Em, and I were doing our own spade work."

"Why?" Dillon said.

"Because the official investigators were barking up the wrong tree," Graham said.

"As usual," Monika added.

"Let's be kind," Ember said. "We're all on the same side. We all want the same thing for our town."

Sovern cleared his throat. "Harry provided some valuable insight that helped the investigation."

Dillon glowered at the investigator, but didn't say anything.

Harry continued. "The circumstances kept pointing to Clair-Ann; however, we didn't have any facts to back up our suspicions. And I said as much to Reece."

"And I appreciated your insights. They were very helpful," Sovern said.

"So what Graham, Monika, Em, and I decided to do was to see if we could get Clair-Ann to turn herself in."

"How?" Dillon asked.

"At this point, our methods don't matter," Harry replied. "Suffice it to say, they did bring things to a head. Okay, Em, your turn."

Ember told the group about her talk with Clair-Ann, leading up to the release of Officer Helen Beauregard and the subsequent explosion.

"And that's it?" Dillon demanded.

"It is," Ember said.

Dillon turned to Jager. "You should have put a wire on her."

"We tried," Sovern said, "but she refused."

"You should've arrested her for failure to assist a police investigation.

Jager snorted. "Lauderbach would have had her out in

twenty minutes and then she wouldn't have helped us at all. Quit being a dick, Chuck."

Dillon glowered at Jager, but said nothing.

Sovern asked, "What was in the briefcase, Reverend?"

"I don't know. Clair-Ann gave it to me and that was that."

"It might be evidence," Dillon said. "I need to examine it."

Ember smiled. "The operative word here, Mr. Dillon, is might. The briefcase is mine. You can get a warrant to examine it."

Dillon's face turned red. "You two are continually obstructing the police and the DA's office. So let me make this clear: the next time you stick your nose into one of my cases, or any of our cases, I'm going to throw the book at you. You'll be in jail forever."

He stood, looked at Graham Huston, and said, "And that goes for you," and, turning to Monika, "you also."

The Assistant District Attorney stormed out of the shop.

With a smile on his face, Harry said, "Looks like Lauderbach might be very busy in the future."

Jager laughed. "He will be if you four keep playing detective."

Sovern cleared his throat, and the green corona moved to the other side of his mouth. "Y'all are helpful at times. But it would be best if you quit being cowboys."

"I have a newspaper to run," Graham said, "and since when has investigative reporting become a criminal activity? I just might hire Harry and Ember to be reporters."

"No need," Harry said. "I got word today that I'll be on the MBPD's Citizen Advisory Board."

Jager and Sovern together said, "You're kidding."

"Nope. So I guess I can continue to be a bug in your soup. Only officially."

"Good grief," Sovern said.

"I don't know how you do it, Thurgood," Jager said. "You make the best coffee in town, while being a royal pain in the ass.

Yet, you're still a nice guy." He stood. "Well, I'd best get going. You, too, Sarge. We have paperwork to do."

Harry stood. "Before you go, I have a present for you, Reece."

Sovern stood. "A present? For me? Why?"

"Because you're a good guy. You just need a little style. Especially now that you're a sergeant."

Harry reached into his pocket, took out a small rectangular box, and handed it to Sovern. "Open it."

The investigator took the box, turned it over, and looked at Jager, then back to Harry.

"Open it," Ember said. "Harry and I think you'll like it."

Sovern opened the box and took out something that looked like a perfecto cigar. "What is it?"

"It's a Vauen Zeppelin. Also called a cigar pipe, or a torpedo pipe, or a briar cigar. Go ahead, put it in your mouth. I put a soft bit on it, because the stem is harder than the cigars you're used to."

Sovern took the cigar out of his mouth and put it in his jacket pocket. He looked at the Zeppelin, turned it over in his hand, and finally put it in his mouth. After a moment, he hooked his thumbs in his belt, leaned back a bit, and angled the pipe upwards.

Ember quickly took a picture with her phone. "Now that's styling," she said.

And everyone laughed.

91

THURSDAY, 28 FEBRUARY 2:41 PM

HARRY AND EMBER WERE SITTING AT HARRY'S TABLE IN THE BACK corner of the coffee shop, eating lunch. The shop was empty, the last lunch patron having left a while ago.

Ember popped a chip into her mouth and Harry took a bite of his BLT at the same time the chime rang over the door.

"Well, look who's here," Harry said.

Ember turned a quarter turn and waved. "Hi, Reece."

Harry stood. "Want coffee?"

"Uh, sure. Might as well."

Harry motioned to Estrelita and pulled out a chair for the Sergeant Investigator. Both men sat.

"So, what's the occasion?" Ember asked.

"Finally got the ME's report this morning," Sovern said.

Estrelita set before him a mug of steaming black coffee and left.

Reece took a sip. "Thank you. This hits the spot."

"Want anything to eat?" Harry asked.

"No, I'm good. Thanks."

"Does the report confirm the ID of the bodies?" Harry asked.

"Yes, it does. Owen Taylor and Sinclair Ann Taylor."

"As if it could be anyone else."

Sovern drank coffee, then said, "Right. But we have to cross Ts and dot Is."

Harry nodded. "I suppose you do."

"So now what?" Ember asked.

Sovern set the mug down. "The case is closed, based on your statement. Clair-Ann admitted to the murders. Nothing more to pursue." He drank coffee, then cleared his throat. "May I ask what was in the briefcase? I know you must've been keeping it hush-hush for a reason."

"It contained Mr. Taylor's book, as much as he'd completed, and his research notes. Clair-Ann included a handwritten note asking that I give it to Burnet College, which I did."

"Which tells me she planned on killing her father and committing suicide," Sovern said.

Ember nodded. "I suppose it does. But the outcome is the same, isn't it?"

A frown descended on Sovern's face.

"Cally Taylor's actions created a family tragedy. She destroyed her marriage, her husband, her daughter, and through her daughter, herself. Clair-Ann was just part of the tragedy created by Cally. And in tragedies, everyone dies."

"That's a cheery thought," Sovern said. He finished his coffee and stood. "I just wanted to let you know what the ME said." He turned to leave, stopped, and turned back. "Oh, Hetta likes the gadget you gave me. To be honest, not that I'm not appreciative, but I do miss the taste of a real cigar."

"That's easily solved," Harry said.

"It is?"

"Yep. Just cut off a piece of cigar, stick it in the Zeppelin, and then draw on the pipe. You'll get the taste of the cigar."

"Huh. That's simple. Thanks. Gotta keep the Missus happy."

They watched Sovern leave.

"Well, that's that," Harry said. "Case closed and we're still walking the streets."

When Ember didn't respond, he asked what was the matter.

"I was thinking of Clair-Ann and all the other Elektra figures. They get the blame, but in actuality, they are the victims. Clair-Ann was trying to right a wrong."

"Not in a good way, though."

"No, not in a good way. But for her entire life she was crushed by her mother. Finally, she reached the breaking point. She gets the blame for what her mother did. That isn't fair, is it?"

"No, it isn't."

"Who mourns them, Harry? Who mourns the real victims? Who mourns for Elektra?"

EPILOGUE

MONIKA CROW HEARS A LOT OF THINGS. NOT ALL MAKE IT INTO HER column, "Monika Hears". But there are plenty of juicy tidbits that do.

In the past couple of months, these are a few of the tidbits Monika has heard.

Landon Pace and Joetta Reston tied the knot common law-style. Two days later, the new Mrs. Pace gave birth to a healthy baby boy: Josiah Landon Pace.

Tipper Duvall was elected the new lay leader of Saint Luke's Methodist Church. Reverend Cole said she was very excited to have Mrs. Duvall in the position.

Harry Thurgood changed the name of his shop to the Really Good Wood-Fired Coffee and Ice Cream Emporium. He doesn't serve ice cream, though. It's frozen custard. And everyone still refers to the shop as the Really Good.

Florence Neidermeier was heard to say she received an

anonymous check for five thousand dollars with an apology note for her broken window. She's planning on taking a cruise with the money.

Gunter and Mary Lou Fight announced the adoption of Oralene Reston by holding a formal dinner at the Fight home. The new Miss Fight sang and played the piano for the guests.

The Reverend Ember Cole is expecting. Word has it that the twins will be born in December.

Magnolia Bluff, Texas. A quiet and friendly little town. A good place to raise a family. A place where neighbor greets neighbor. A place where murder waits in the wings.

AFTERWORD

I hope you enjoyed *Who Mourns Elektra?*.

If you did, please leave a review where you bought the book and on your favorite social media sites. Your review is like word of mouth advertising. And it is pure gold.

Become one of my VIP Readers!

You'll get a free copy of *Vampire House and Other Early Cases of Justinia Wright, P.I.* (it's an introduction into the exciting world of Private Detective Tina Wright and her brother Harry), a monthly email announcing other goodies from my pen, as well as curated content. And you'll be the first to know about the next release in the Magnolia Bluff Crime Chronicles!

Sign up today for your free book at BookFunnel! Just scan the QR code!

ABOUT MAGNOLIA BLUFF

"A multi-author crime novel series, you say? What is that?"

That's the question I got when I proposed the idea to my fellow Underground Authors back in 2021.

We'd just collaborated on a short story anthology, and I was interested in taking the idea of collaboration to the next level.

A multi-author series is what happens when a group of authors decides to write a series of novels. In the case of the Magnolia Bluff Crime Chronicles, the Underground Authors decided to create a fictional town that would be the common denominator for each of the books in the series.

Each author would have his or her characters, perhaps use some of the characters the other authors created, but all of the action would take place in the beautiful little Texas Hill Country town of Magnolia Bluff.

We now have a dozen authors showing us a dozen different sides of the town.

There's humor, dark dilemmas, suspense, romance, thrills and spills — all told through a dozen voices giving us a whole lot of good storytelling. The kind that will keep you up past your bedtime, or make you miss your bus stop.

Stay tuned. There's lots happening in Magnolia Bluff. And you don't want to miss any of it.

Magnolia Bluff. A small town. A quiet town. A town with murder waiting in the wings.

COMING NEXT TO MAGNOLIA BLUFF

Up next in the Magnolia Bluff Crime Chronicles lineup is Linda Pirtle's *Girlfriend Retreat… Cheaper Than Therapy.*

What can go wrong when a group of friends meet up in Magnolia Bluff for their annual get together? A lot, actually. Murder and mayhem for starters.

Here's a preview of *Girlfriend Retreat… Cheaper Than Therapy* coming out in March 2024. Enjoy!

MEMORANDUM

To: Anita, Barbara, Betty, Caroline, Cheryl, Jana, Jane, Janie, Judie, Margaret, Mary Ann, Merita, Sandra, Sharon, Sylvia, Betty
From: Planning Committee
Re: Retreat

Greetings,

It's almost time for our annual gathering, and I'm sure that each of you is looking forward to it as much as I and the members of the planning committee. At last year's meeting, we all decided to do something totally different for this year. So, the committee has planned a weekend which we know you will enjoy.

The festivities will begin at 4:00 p.m. on Thursday evening at the infamous Texas Hill Country Circle R Ranch located near Magnolia Bluff. The cost will be $89 per person per night. Please call the ranch at 830-881-9000 to make your reservation. Ask for the McCluskey discounted rate. If you are driving, I have enclosed directions. If some of you plan to fly and can arrive at the Austin airport by 2:00 p.m., let Caroline know. She will arrange a shuttle to pick you up.

Magnolia Bluff is a small, relaxing, and picturesque community nestled next to the Burnet Reservoir. We have planned a couple of tours for your enjoyment. Bring a swimsuit, jeans, boots, hat, and plenty of sunscreen. Since the temperature drops at night, you might need a lightweight jacket also. Be prepared for a weekend like none other you've ever experienced!

Mary Ann

Chapter 1

Monday, 8:30 a.m.
Harry Thurgood's Really Good Wood Fired Coffee Shop

Caroline McCluskey smiled as she entered the Really Good and waved at her friends, who occupied the round table next to the large plate glass window which offered a bird's eye view of Main Street as well as the town's Green. From their vantage point, the busybodies of MB – the moniker which Carolyn kept to herself – could solve the world's problems and / or recount the flaws of their neighbors.

Harry Thurgood met the town's librarian at the counter. "One mocha latte and one bear claw coming right up for Ms. McCluskey, the only Magnolia Bluff customer I have this morning with anything exciting to report." Harry turned to his cook Miguel who had already popped Caroline's usual sweet roll into the microwave. "Go," Harry said. "I'll bring your order to you."

Caroline laughed. "My, don't I feel important."

"You are always special," said Billy Bob Baskin, standing to pull a chair out for her.

"Oh, you say that only because you want Caroline to include you in her next cozy mystery," teased Magnolia Nadine, lifetime president of the Junior Service League and director of the Magnolia Bluff Women's Building.

"I beg your pardon," Baskin said, feigning disdain. "She promised that she would do just that, so I don't have to sweet talk her."

"Hey, you two, give Caroline a chance to at least say hello to us," chided Tommy Jager, an Adonis look alike and Police Chief of Magnolia Bluff.

"Yeah," said Daphne, owner of the Head Case Salon. "You can guess who's my first client today if I were to report how really grumpy she becomes when I'm late. One of these days, I'm going to. . ." Daphne stopped. The sound of a cane's dull thump, thump, thump caused Daphne to pause. "Oh, good grief, there she is now."

"Pretend you don't see her," Rob Carter said. Rob was the newest member of the group.

"Too late," Baskin said, standing and speaking rapidly. "Gotta go. Have a meeting with the fellowship committee in ten minutes."

"Good Book tells us it's a sin to lie, says the chairwoman of that committee," Caroline teased. "I'll drop by the church later. We'll have a short meeting to ensure you're not fibbing."

Baskin nodded and made his way to the door.

Mary Lou Fight, the most feared and most powerful woman in town, sashayed over to their table and addressed Daphne. "Ms. Leigh, I thought I'd find you here." Ignoring the fact that she might have interrupted an ongoing conversation, she wrinkled up her nose and frowned. "I need to postpone my appointment until Friday afternoon. Can you arrange your schedule to accommodate me?"

Daphne sighed and responded sweetly. "Mary Lou, darling, you just come on in anytime tomorrow that suits you. I'll be sure and work you into my schedule." Her smile vanished as soon as Mary Lou harrumphed a stoic thank you and waltzed out the door.

Rob Carter shook his head. "What is it with that woman?" As reporter and photographer for the local newspaper, the *Chronicle*, Rob had earned a seat at the table for his coverage of the resurrection of Crystalline Flats, a town that had been buried when the Corps of Engineers flooded it to form the Burnet Reservoir.

"That story would take all day," said Harry. He placed Caroline's order in front of her and settled into Baskin's empty seat.

"And, we don't have time," said Graham Huston, editor of the *Chronicle*. He motioned to Caroline who was chewing her first bite. "Talk. What can we do that will guarantee your high school classmates the time of their lives this weekend?"

Caroline swallowed a sip of coffee. Before she could answer, her cell phone rang.

"Don't answer it," ordered Magnolia Nadine. "We want to hear more about your friends."

"Have to. Might be one of the girls," Caroline said, rummaging in her purse in pursuit of the instrument of interruption. She found it and saw her friend smiling at her. "Hello, Mary Ann. So glad we have technology that allows us to Face-Time with each other."

"Before I begin," Mary Ann said, "Let me say that Sharon, Barbara, and Janie are joining us. They are as excited as can be."

A chorus of "hellos" and friendly smiles greeted Caroline. "Great," Caroline said. "Do you mind if I put you on speaker? I'm at the Really Good with my early morning friends who also look forward to meeting each of you. They've helped me plan some special events you four won't know about until you arrive."

"That's just like you, Caroline, to plan surprises for us," said Janie. "Can't wait. I know we're going to have the time of our lives."

"Okay, Mary Ann, bring me up to date." Caroline said. "But hold on a minute. I want to write down the names of everyone who plans to attend." Caroline retrieved a small notebook and a pen from her purse.

* * * * *

A stranger sitting at the next table chuckled internally. *You think?* The person opened what appeared to be a daily planner, flipped to a blank page, and waited for more information. *I've waited a long time to get even with you, Miss Super Sleuth.*

Chapter 2

A Fire truck, siren blocking the sound of Chief Jager's two-way radio, roared down Main Street.

Chief Jager stood and said, "Excuse me." He ran outside and quickly drove away in his black, unmarked police SUV. Rob Carter grabbed his camera bag and followed.

Thurgood grinned. "Well, Huston, I see you've trained that novice reporter well. He jumped at the chance to beat you for the story."

Huston nodded. "There's something you and I need to discuss privately when" – he motioned to Caroline – "she leaves."

"Got it," Thurgood said and returned to the counter to greet his next customer.

"Repeat what you just said, Mary Ann," Caroline said. "A fire truck and an ambulance just flew by, and I couldn't hear you."

"No wonder," said Daphne. "For a moment there, I thought the commotion was close to my street."

"It's either a wreck or a fire. Something's probably happened out at the reservoir. We have a lot of tourists in town this weekend," Caroline explained.

"Other than our visit and whatever that emergency was, is there anything else exciting besides a gathering of goddesses going on in Magnolia Bluff?" asked Sharon.

Daphne stood and mouthed a "goodbye" to Magnolia Nadine and Caroline.

"One of our wineries is sponsoring a beauty pageant for Miss Wine Queen of Burnet County," Caroline said.

"Ugh. Don't think I'd want that crown," Barbara said.

"Well, I can see you wearing a lopsided tiara after you've sampled all of the wine," said Sharon.

"That's true," said Barbara, laughing. "Frankly, I'd have to be drunk just to compete in that pageant."

"Let's stay focused," said Mary Ann.

"Yes, let's," said Janie. "I hope you've received all positive RSVPs."

"Mostly," said Mary Ann. "Everyone plans to attend except for Betty and Sylvia. Both of them are going to be on some obscure island to help with the rebuilding of a Baptist church that was destroyed by a fire."

"Oh yeah," said Sharon. "I remember hearing about it on the news. According to the reporter, the fire was deliberate. And several people died."

"Let's keep those two in our prayers," said Caroline. "Ask the Lord to keep them safe."

"Hold on," said Janie. "Mary Ann, didn't you get regrets from two more classmates?"

"Yes, I was getting to them."

Magnolia Nadine's phone rang. She answered the call, her face went white, and her right hand began to shake, making it difficult to keep the phone to her ear.

Caroline feared Magnolia Nadine was on the verge of fainting. Without speaking a word, Magnolia Nadine grabbed her Louis Vuitton and ran out the door. *I'll speed up this call and check on her ASAP,* Caroline thought.

"Can you repeat that?" Caroline asked. "I need an accurate count so that if necessary, some of the rooms that are on hold at the ranch can be released."

"Sure. Nurse Jane has been called by Tyler ISD to fill in for one of their school nurses who's on maternity leave. She'll be working for the rest of the semester. Sandra called, and her arthritis has flared up, so driving that far is out of the question."

"That's not what she told me," said Sharon, "when she called me last week."

"Care to share?" asked Caroline.

"Well, she said she suspected Caroline would want us to go riding, and Sandra is afraid of horses. Besides, she also said that she didn't want to be the only one without boots, and if she bought a pair, it would be a waste of money because she'd never put them on again."

"Oh, for crying out loud," said Barbara. Then she laughed. "She could call Anita. I bet our famous designer has a couple of spares she could lend to Sandra. I'll call Sandra and suggest that she do so."

Mary Ann laughed. "Speaking of our fashionistas, Jana said she had bought a new pair of Lucchese boots with pink tulips on the sides."

"Why does that not surprise me?" Caroline said and chuckled. "No telling how much she paid for them."

"Almost fifteen hundred dollars," said Janie. "I saw them on the internet. They're beautiful but way out of my price range."

"Okay," said Caroline. "So that leaves Cheryl, Margaret, and Merita who, I hope, are coming."

"They'll be there. Haven't heard from Judie yet," said Mary Ann, "but I do recall that she and her fiancé were planning a trip to Germany for the first two weeks in March. Now that I think about it, their trip may conflict with ours."

"Well, we'll have a good time. Looking forward to seeing all of you." Caroline closed her notebook. "Oh, by the way, will anyone need the shuttle from the airport to the ranch?"

"No," said Sharon. "Mary Ann, Margaret, and Merita are riding together. Janie and Barbara are meeting at my house and we'll ride down together."

"Wonderful," said Caroline whose cell phone rang. "Oh, guess I need to hang up now. Magnolia Nadine's calling. See you girls Thursday." She briefly heard a chorus of goodbyes before she answered her next call. "Hello, Magnolia."

Magnolia Nadine was crying. "Come quick, Caroline. Meet me at the hospital." The call ended.

Caroline left enough money on the table to cover her meal and rushed to her vehicle. *Oh, Dear Lord, I don't know what's happened. Please keep Magnolia Nadine safe.*

ABOUT THE UNDERGROUND AUTHORS

One afternoon back in June of 2020 I got an email from Caleb Pirtle III inviting me to join an author co-op he was organizing. The purpose of the group would be to promote each other's books. Writing, after all, is easy. Marketing, on the other hand, is difficult. But many hands make light work, and that's what we were hoping for.

In addition to promoting each other's books, and keeping each other up to date on what's happening on the business side of writing, we collaborated on a short story anthology, and are now writing a crime fiction series set in the lovely little Texas Hill Country town of Magnolia Bluff.

The current members are Linda Pirtle, Cindy Davis, James Callan, Breakfield & Burkey, Kelly Marshall, Richard Schwindt, Jinx Schwartz, Joe Congel, Kay McNiven, Rob and Joan Carter, April Coker, and myself.

All are fine writers and I'm proud to be associated with them.

CW Hawes

ALSO BY CW HAWES

CW Hawes is a multi-genre author working in the mystery, paranormal, horror, post-apocalyptic, and alternative history genres.

Justinia Wright Private Investigator Mysteries

Sister and brother duo, Tina and Harry Wright, are private investigators in Minneapolis, Minnesota. They live larger than life lifestyles while fighting crime. Especially murder.

The series is contemporary, yet the style harkens back to those mysteries written in a gentler era. The books are not thrillers. They follow the tried and true whodunit formula. The pacing is slower to start and gradually builds to an exciting climax. There are quirky and fun characters, plenty of humor, and loads of sibling rivalry.

If you like puzzles, if you like a romp through good food and wine, if you like to vicariously chase down bad guys — these books are for you.

Pierce Mostyn Paranormal Investigations

If high action and adventure in the world of the Cthulhu Mythos is your thing, meet Special Agent Pierce Mostyn and the world of the Office of Unidentified Phenomena. There be monsters here!

Here is what one reviewer wrote of *The Medusa Ritual*:

A Thrilling Read!

Bam! Brarwsh! Boom! Those are the images I feel when Mostyn and his team are fighting the bad guys.

Mostyn and his crew are looking for a book that is ancient and evil. It has brought Medusa back to life and has inspired Medusa to get back to turning people into stone.

They are stymied by a man wearing a mask. And he and his henchmen are not giving up their freedom.

A lot of rambunctious action is going into the war. Will Pierce Mostyn win this battle?

If you like monsters and plenty of action, Pierce Mostyn is for you!

The Rocheport Saga

The world as we know it is gone. An unknown plague wiped out most of humanity overnight. The survivors are now faced with the challenge of what to do next.

Bill Arthur knows what needs to be done. The world must be built again. Only this time better. Eliminate the mistakes made the first time around. And that is what he sets out to do.

Bill, with a small group of friends, settles in Rocheport, Missouri and begins to rebuild. The only problem is not everyone agrees with how he wants to recreate a new world.

The small community is beleaguered with problems. Bill wants to quit, but knows he can't. But will he be able to build his dream? Or will he have to settle for second best?

The Rocheport Saga has been called the thinking person's post-apocalyptic series.

Dig in and see if Bill can pull off his dream.

Other Works

Being a multi-genre author, CW has other books and stories to satisfy your reading itch.

You can find all of his work on the My Books page of his website. Just click, tap, or scan the QR code!

ABOUT CW HAWES

CW Hawes is a multi-genre author because he is a multi-genre reader. He's penned The Justinia Wright Private Investigator Mysteries, The Rocheport Saga: A Post-Apocalyptic Steam Powered Future, the Pierce Mostyn Paranormal Investigations series, and assorted alternative history and horror offerings.

Born and raised in the Cleveland, Ohio area, CW spent 49 years in the Land of 10,000 Lakes (aka Minnesota), and now proudly hails from the Lone Star State (aka Texas).

He hasn't met a pizza he doesn't like (okay, he detests pineapple), is something of a tea snob, and rocks out to Handel and Vaughan Williams.

You can reach him at his Website, just tap, click, or scan the QR code!

X/Twitter, just tap, click, or scan the QR code!

Facebook, just tap, click, or scan the QR code!

www.ingramcontent.com/pod-product-compliance
Lightning Source LLC
Chambersburg PA
CBHW072322280626
47159CB00027B/261